Kit folded his arms across his chest and refused to feel guilty. "Where the devil have you been?"

Emily stood and laid a restraining hand on his arm. "Is this the best place for this discussion, Kit?"

He nodded decisively. Miranda might still hold a certain power over his body, but he wanted everyone to know that it was not *he* who had driven her away. He had chosen his wife poorly ten years ago, and he would not be that unguarded, reckless man ever again. He'd paid a high price for her abandonment. Some whispered he'd murdered her for her dowry, though he'd never been outright accused of any crime.

He stared Miranda down. He would not say another word until she answered him.

"Where I was wanted." Miranda's eyebrow quirked upward innocently, and when she glanced at his companion, her smile was full of pity. "I am sure you are overjoyed to be witness to our happy reunion after so many years apart. I regret spoiling your first season out of mourning with my return, Lady Brighthurst, but you still cannot have him."

HEATHER BOYD

KEEPSAKE

Distinguished Rogues

5

Dedication

—— ♦ ——

For M&M&M

Michelle—for her continued support and generosity
Molly—for her smiles despite my preoccupation with work
Melissa—for being the strongest person I virtually know

Much love to all.

Prologue

On the Eve of a Wedding, 1803

"Are you comfortable?" the Marquess of Taverham whispered into the silence of the blue guest bedchamber at Twilit Hill, his country estate. The room had been assigned to Miranda since the night of her arrival and it was soon to be hers forever.

"Yes. Very," Miranda Birkenstock assured her betrothed. She drew in a deep breath, temporarily at peace with the night and her own desires.

If all they had were these nighttime hours, Miranda would be blissfully overjoyed to be Taverham's wife and a marchioness, but the difficulties of the days threatened to smother her happiness.

She had never imagined she'd be accepted easily into his life—her family's fortune came from trade and she didn't possess the same distinguished pedigree other well-born debutants could claim. Her friends were concerned she was rushing into the marriage without proper consideration and on the eve of her wedding she feared they might be right. Yet her father was beside himself at the valuable connections the marriage would bring to him and it was far too late to reconsider.

She couldn't blame her friends for worrying. She was headed for a very different life than most of them. Miranda had just passed her seventeenth birthday. Taverham would be nineteen years in a few months time. She was aware that Taverham's guardians didn't exactly approve of his plans to marry her. They were both so very young.

She had tried very hard to make friends among Taverham's acquaintances and family, and she'd thought some had accepted her. And some definitely had not. Those closest to Taverham made little effort to hide their dismay over tomorrow's wedding. His stern and unsmiling mother was the worst at hiding her disapproval.

Taverham tugged her into his arms and settled her there with a steady hand to her lower back, pressing her close against his long limbs, which always burned with fiery warmth.

She hugged close to her betrothed—eager for the reassurance that always came with being near him.

Today's lecture from his mother had been on the uncomfortable topic of delivering an heir as soon as possible and the great obligation she had in ensuring the child thrived. Miranda was not to run about. She was not to exert herself. She was not to impose on her husband's time unless it was for the purposes of getting his heir and a spare.

The frank and blunt discussion of what was expected of her had turned her ears pink with embarrassment. Miranda might have only seen seventeen years of life, but delivering a healthy child was of course imperative, and not just for her husband's sake. She also longed for a child—to love, to nurture—and nothing would influence her wish to be a devoted and involved mother.

She would stand up to the marchioness, and everyone, and be seen as her husband's equal in this marriage. She couldn't let anyone shake her confidence in herself. Taverham had chosen her to be his marchioness, the mother of his children, a partner in his life.

Miranda had a difficult road ahead but she was ready.

She would bring her future husband around to her way of thinking about the manner in which they would raise their children and together they would repair his estate.

She would persevere through the difficulties because she loved him.

"Mama and Emily have worked wonders with the staff to have the house ready for the wedding don't you think," he asked in a whisper. "Tomorrow will be perfect, despite the rush. I promise you there is nothing you need do."

"I'm sure everything will work itself out," she murmured, hiding her resentment.

Emily, Lady Brighthurst, seemed to hold great sway over her husband's decisions and although she had tried very hard to become friends the lady had not exactly welcomed her with open arms.

They saw the world very differently, valued people and things too. Miranda saw no point to having ice sculptures adorn her wedding breakfast tables and had said as much, but been overruled. Lady Brighthurst had claimed them essential for such an occasion and Miranda's future mother-in-law had supported Emily's frivolous wishes, not Miranda's far simpler suggestions.

Despite her hopes of managing her own home, it had become very clear that Kit's mother ruled this house and wasn't about to relinquish her control to any new wife, though what Emily wanted always seemed to come to pass. Emily had somehow won the marchioness' approval. Miranda would learn that secret and soon.

Taverham kissed her brow, slid from beneath her gently, and left the bed. Miranda lay in a puddle of untidy sheets an uncertain moment and then rolled over to watch him dress. He paused beside the bed, facing the fire. The light thrown by the pitiful flame made him appear much older than his years.

He nodded to himself and collected his clothes.

"Are you going?"

"Tomorrow is an important day and you shouldn't lose any more sleep because of me."

"I don't mind." Miranda smiled wickedly. She raised one knee, slowly rocking it to and fro. She had learned a little of teasing these past weeks and had a fair idea of what her future husband liked to see when he came to her bed.

Taverham's gaze shifted to her activity. He licked his lips. "Are you not weary?"

"No. I never feel tired when I'm with you." Making love to Taverham was not a chore in any sense of the word. He was adventurous but liked to have his own way. In fact, these secret meetings had made her feel irresistible. If she could have him like this forever the other problems she faced would fade to nothing in time.

He shook his head, a rueful smile passing over his lips. "You make me forget my purpose. What will I do with you once we are wed?"

Miranda would turn herself inside out to please him. She raised herself to a provocative sitting position, brazenly revealing her breasts to him. She slowly stroked the nipple of one. His gaze narrowed to what she was doing.

"I have an idea of what we could do together," she whispered.

As hoped, his gaze flickered over her skin and she warmed from head to toe at his heated expression. His clothing dropped to the floor. "So do I, but..."

She smiled at the desire in his eyes. Keeping him close would only strengthen the bonds between them. "You do still want an heir while you are a young man, don't you?"

His gaze drifted low to rest on her stomach. His brow creased into a frown. "I had hoped we'd done enough toward that already."

A pang of fear filled her at the cold practicality of his words. If he thought her with child would he discontinue his visits to her bed? She didn't want to lose his attention, so Miranda forced her fear down and feigned nonchalance. "Perhaps we have. But it is far too soon to be certain."

His graze flew to hers and he stared.

Miranda grew uncomfortable at the anticipation lighting his eyes. She shrugged. "I am a little late, but that may be merely the stress surrounding the wedding." And dealing with his mother and friends. They both knew he was marrying her for her dowry and an heir; everyone knew he had an estate to save from ruin after all. He'd been completely open about his priorities. Marriage, estate, heir, in that order. In comparison, Miranda's hopes were very small—a home and someone to love her.

"You're with child," he said, nodding decisively, but not a smile crossed his lips. "Once our guests have departed, I'll inform Mama about your condition. She will decide what must be done. You need not worry about anything again, I swear."

Despair filled her as he turned away. She had to stop him telling his mother until she'd time to take up the reins as mistress of this house. Their unborn children, their sons particularly, had already had their lives planned out to the smallest detail. Miranda could only dread the future in store for them. Wet nurses, nannies, private and expensive tutors, and finally Eton or Cambridge would be their future.

Not with Miranda. Not with their mama. Her place was never mentioned, her suggestions brushed aside in favor of years of family tradition.

That had to change.

Miranda flew from the bed and grasped his arm before he could slip from her room. "Please. I'm uncertain. It's early days yet. Don't tell her so soon. Can it not be our secret as these meetings each night have been?"

He raked his hands through his hair and then he glanced down the length of her naked body. He groaned. "Thank God we wed tomorrow; I'll be glad to be done with all this sneaking about."

She set her hands to his shoulders and held onto him. She'd lost her heart to him the night they'd met and she'd hoped his feeling would one day mirror hers. He'd never said he loved her. Not even when he'd proposed. "I am too. After all we have done together, and I suspect there is more pleasure to be had still, I am very eager to share your bed as often as you want."

His eyes widened and he pulled her against him. "Temptress."

He kissed her hard, demanding entry to her mouth with his tongue. His hands gripped her hips with definite eagerness, and Miranda liked that about him. His arousal soon pressed against her belly, hot and full. Miranda smiled against his lips. She'd claim this small victory. The first of many, she hoped.

Still kissing her, he herded her across the room toward the bed and Miranda didn't mind his bossiness. When he released her, Miranda eased onto the mattress slowly, relishing Taverham's slow prowl toward her as he crawled on hands and knees. She lay back as his head dipped and his lips skimmed her still-flat stomach. His kiss was reverent, almost shy, when he'd never been that way before.

His kisses grew firmer as he moved lower. When he nudged her legs apart roughly and kissed her at the apex of her thighs, she covered her mouth to stifle her moan. Taverham's kisses were sweet and addictive.

Delightful tremors began and ended on the tip of Taverham's tongue, and Miranda struggled to push her worries aside. If he wanted her like this, surely they had a chance to build a satisfying life together. Beginning tomorrow, she would convince him to expect her company everywhere he went. Their wedding night would be special, the most erotic she could imagine and arrange.

Taverham quickly brought her body to the threshold of release. She squirmed to delay the moment, but as usual, he would not allow her to hold back. She sobbed as her body shook and she pressed her mound against his face shamelessly. Before the tremors had subsided, Taverham was above her, entering her with one slow, sure thrust.

Once her body grew accustomed to his return, Taverham began to move. He was quick with his thrusts, urgent in his passions. He held himself above her, both hands firmly pressed to the mattress beside her head, his eyes closed.

Miranda stroked his chest firmly as his skin grew slick with his exertions and even hotter than before. She wrapped her legs about his waist tightly and dug her fingers into his sides the way he liked best.

His thrusts grew frenzied, and when he growled out a muffled shout of release, his eyes scrunched even more tightly shut. After a moment, he collapsed upon her, exhaustion claiming his strength. "I..."

As always after their joining, Miranda held him tight and waited for him to continue his words. Yet all that greeted her was more silence. Words of love and tenderness burned on her tongue, and she longed to unburden herself of them.

He started to lift his weight from her until Miranda's fingers slipped from his skin. "I want you to be with child now," he said in a tone that brooked no argument as he sat up. As if such a matter could be ordered as he would a carriage.

"I want that too. We will have a family. As large as we want it."

"An heir first, then the rest will come later, once the estate is running smoothly again." Then he rolled from the bed and threw on a shirt, turning his back to her. His movements were brisk as he made himself respectable once more. She would not be able to lure him back to her bed again. "Rest," he whispered. "Tomorrow we wed and the future can begin."

He strode to the door without looking back.

Miranda stared after him in surprise at his haste to go. "Good night, Taverham."

He paused with one hand on the door latch. "I won't see you until the ceremony. Mama will visit you first thing in the morning to see all is well, the vicar will arrive at ten, the wedding breakfast will be served promptly at twelve, and the supper for our guests will commence at eight. I expect their amusements to last long into the night."

Since there was nothing that required her attention, she agreed with him. "I'll be ready on time."

"Good." He nodded, his expression distracted. "Immediately after we wed, I must leave you to attend to a private matter. Nothing to concern you."

Miranda sat up in surprise. "But it's our wedding day?"

"It's just one evening." He frowned. "Since Emily's marriage it's not been easy to be private with her. I'll have to set a schedule so her needs are not forgotten in the rush to repair Twilit Hill. I've no idea how long it will take tomorrow. Her husband may prove adverse to any permanent arrangement, but I'll have my way in the end."

He rubbed his eyes. "You may retire whenever you choose tomorrow night if I have not returned in time to escort you to your bedchamber. The day after, I will be engaged with my guardians over estate issues that require the most urgent attention from an early hour. In the unlikely event you need me, Branxton can arrange to have a message delivered."

He slipped out the door without further explanation.

Miranda's throat tightened, and she swallowed her hurt and shock at being so thoroughly dismissed from his life. That was *her* dowry he was planning to spend. The fortune she'd thought she'd be giving to a man she *hoped* might love her in return.

He expected to spend their wedding night with Emily.

She set her hands to her hips as anger filled her. Emily could have waited. Emily had a life of her own and a husband of her own too. She should not be forcing herself on Taverham on *their* big day.

What had Taverham said? *Emily's needs must not be overlooked.*

What needs could Emily have that her own husband couldn't satisfy?

———— ◆ ————

After the Wedding

Miranda stepped into the quiet garden and whispered, "Lady Taverham."

She was a marchioness now and married. She could barely contain her happiness and danced a few steps across the terrace to express the thrill gripping her.

A male voice chuckled to her right, startling her.

She spun in that direction. "Who is there? Taverham?"

"An old fool." Lord Applebee, one of her husband's guardians, emerged from the shadows. "Your husband should not leave you to dance alone."

She smiled despite her disappointment that she'd been unable to convince Taverham that his conversation with Emily should wait until tomorrow. "Lord Applebee, forgive me. I didn't see you there, and you certainly are not a fool. You see more clearly than anyone."

He smiled kindly. "You shouldn't be out here."

Miranda glanced over her shoulder to the crowded room she'd just escaped. "I just wanted a moment to myself. I feel like I've been smiling for hours."

To prove her point, she brushed her fingers across her jaw because the strain of smiling at everyone *had* made her face ache. Her smiles now were for herself alone. She was a married woman and excited about her new life.

"Then take in the air and return inside quickly." He shifted to stand between her and the gardens she'd hoped to escape to. "A new bride should lap up every bit of attention she can on her special day. And you deserve it all and more."

"You're too kind, my lord."

Applebee smiled and bowed. As he did, she saw the shape of two figures stumbling toward the rose garden.

Miranda chuckled softly. "Well, it seems I'm not the only one to have had the same idea of escaping the ballroom."

She wished her husband was done with Emily and would want to sneak away with her tonight. But he'd disappeared as he'd told her he would several hours ago.

Applebee glanced over his shoulder, then caught her arm. "Time to dance. Will you do this crusty old bachelor the honor of the next set, my lady?"

Although her husband's guardian wasn't the partner she wanted, she nodded quickly, eager to stay on his good side. "I'd love to dance with you."

Applebee propelled her toward the open French doors forcefully, and Miranda stumbled. As they reached the threshold, Lords Sorenson and Watts appeared, her father and Lord Louth trailing after in deep conversation.

Of all of Taverham's friends, Lord Louth had been the first to offer her real friendship. He was a nice man, one of quiet wit and boundless faith that she would be an exceptional marchioness. She smiled at him in relief. She had no need to guard her words around Lord Louth.

"Now, my dear, do not be distressed," Sorenson said soothingly, catching up her hands and squeezing them gently.

"She's not," Applebee replied, his head tilting at an odd angle.

"Oh, I thought..." Watts glanced into the garden beyond them and Miranda followed the direction of his gaze. She spied the pair in the rose garden again and noticed that they didn't seem the least bit concerned about propriety. She frowned at that, trying to picture which of the wedding guests would behave in such a bold manner at a wedding.

She took a pace in that direction, but Applebee tugged her back. "Come dance with me."

Something was wrong. A discomforting sensation filled her. She shook off Lord Applebee's grip. "Why shouldn't I know who they are? This is my home now."

No one replied to that, but Lord Louth's expression became curious too.

She cut across the lawn, aware of their whispered pleas to wait. To stop. To not approach the rose garden. Their steps were soft behind her and when she paused, they did too.

At this distance she could not see the pair clearly, but she could hear their words… and their gasps and moans of ecstasy.

She would recognize her husband's deep, rumbling voice anywhere.

A few more steps and she could see him better, clutching the breast of a woman, the pair of them deep in the throes of a passionate tryst in her garden.

She forced air into her lungs as he chuckled softly and urged the woman to go with him.

"I don't believe it," Lord Louth whispered from where he'd paused at her side. "That bastard."

As Louth made to move toward the pair, Lord Watts restrained him. "It's none of your business, lad."

She reached for Louth too, but only to keep him from blocking her view.

The woman stood, and *it was Emily*. Miranda stifled a gasp as Emily curled her arms around Taverham's broad shoulders. They kissed urgently and then Taverham swept her up into his arms and carried her away into the darkness.

"Well," Miranda's father said as he studied Miranda in disappointment. "He's taken a mistress a bit faster than I was led to believe he would, but he kept his side of our bargain and made you his marchioness. Can't help where a man's passion leads him if he doesn't find it with his wife."

He turned away and left Miranda standing in shock among near strangers. *Her father had expected this betrayal?*

Miranda certainly had not. She brushed away the tears that slipped over her cheeks, hoping for one last glimpse that proved her husband had not just run off with Emily on their wedding night.

The hope that had filled her since Taverham had proposed began to burn, the trust and love she'd felt for him curling into ash within her heart.

They were only just made husband and wife!

Lord Applebee moved to stand before her. "Surely you suspected?"

Miranda shook her head, darting a glance at those standing around her and saw a wealth of sympathy. She covered her face, too humiliated to let anyone see how deep his betrayal went, hiding the depth of her hurt.

"Ah," Watts said as he patted her shoulder awkwardly. "We should have prepared you better. We tried to reason with him but he's never going to give her up. Couldn't marry her in the first place because she'd not the funds to repair Twilit Hill, and now he has won you…"

Miranda glanced swiftly at Lord Louth and saw her own astonishment reflected in his face. He hadn't known either. At least here was one man who had never deceived her.

When their eyes met, his expression was one of fury on her behalf. "I'll call him out."

"You'll do no such thing." There were other ways to make him pay. Miranda caught his clenched fist. She couldn't allow her one friend to risk his life or reputation just for her. He was a good man and Taverham a scoundrel. "I won't have it."

The young man glanced away, and she winced as his jaw firmed into a belligerent line. "He deserves…"

She grew aware of a sharp pain in her chest and she backed away from Taverham's guardians and Lord Louth. "Taverham deserves nothing else."

Miranda had to get away. She might have been beguiled into a marriage she couldn't now escape, but she would not expose her innocent child to such a father. She wouldn't stay at Twilit Hill another moment longer.

Applebee watched her with a keen eye. "Now, Miranda. Don't do anything rash that you'll regret tomorrow."

"What is there to regret?" *Everything.* Fighting back tears, she managed to choke out, "Do excuse me."

Chapter One

-----◆-----

When a man settles on a new course for his life, it's necessary to relinquish the old and learn from his mistakes. When a marquess, disappointed, requires a replacement bride, it becomes absolutely certain that his next choice will live up to his expectations. Kit Reed, Marquess of Taverham, might not understand why his first wife had disappeared without so much as leaving a note, but that departure hadn't been anything to do with him.

He focused on the stage of the Theatre Royal, but his mind was distracted by what he needed to do tomorrow. He had to convince those who mattered that his marriage should be set aside and soon.

He had last seen *The Beggar's Opera* with Miranda, his first and fleeting bride, a few months before their marriage. He thought it fitting to see it one last time before he took the first steps on the path to have her declared legally dead after a ten-year absence.

He drew in a deep breath. There was no possibility she was coming back. He'd searched and hoped for so long after he could have had her declared legally dead that his friends were looking upon him with pity. He was done with the past.

He was done dancing to Miranda's tune

He might not have loved her, but she was his wife and he owed her for the dowry she'd brought to him through their marriage. A fortune that had saved him and their home from the tumbledown ruin it had been on their wedding day.

She should have stayed to see the good their marriage had brought to those connected to the estate. Because of her, every situation had improved greatly over the years.

His gaze flickered across the theatre briefly to where his married friends sat in their own box. Lovers surely, their hands linked, their eyes meeting and soft smiles twisting their lips. He looked down at his clenched fist and forced himself to relax.

There was nothing Miranda had liked better than theatricals, even badly performed ones that made her laugh uproariously and earned her so many disapproving looks. Miranda had been so different in her manner than anyone he knew that he could only conclude he'd been so blinded by her zest for life that he'd proposed before he'd thought the matter through properly. He knew better now.

He turned to Lady Brighthurst to whisper, "How goes plans for this year's hunt?"

A longtime friend and confidant, the recently widowed Emily knew only a portion of his reasons for attending this play. Emily wasn't as enthusiastic about the opera as Miranda had once been, but since she'd come up to town for the season to discuss their arrangement and had no other engagements tonight, she'd humored him by accepting an invitation so he wouldn't have to sit alone.

"It is well in hand, although"—she eased closer—"we have a great many more acceptances than usual this year. I cannot account for the increase in numbers."

Kit smiled, noticing a few familiar faces watching them closely rather than the performance on stage. When he frowned, they quickly turned their attention elsewhere. To Emily he said, "They come this year for the pleasure of your company and because of your renown for designing the most elaborate feasts. Acton's warm and gracious hospitality has always drawn the most avid hunters north, but you are the icing on the cake my dear."

"Thank you." Yet her brow creased into lines of deep concern. "I fear the number of guests this time around may be even too great for us to host."

Kit patted her hand soothingly. "Nonsense, the more the merrier is Acton's motto, and I'm sure with the continued help of staff and funds from Twilit Hill the event will be a merry one. Acton would sulk if I offered my estate as an alternative location for the hunt."

Besides, Kit hadn't hosted a gathering since his wedding day.

"Acton loves you as a brother," Emily continued with considerable feeling. "He would give way should you ask and particularly if doing so made me happy, too."

Kit shook his head. "But I will not ask. I will continue to support the event in my own quiet way. It's worked this way since I inherited the title and there's no need to change anything about our arrangement in the foreseeable future."

Emily laughed softly. "If only you let others see your generous heart and home more often, they would know how truly worthy a gentleman and dear friend you are."

"Thank you," he murmured while thinking he'd been a failure as a husband. Miranda had not thought him worthy in the end.

"She's seated in my place," Miranda's soft voice complained in his mind as if she'd the right to tell him what to do after all these years.

Kit closed his eyes and willed the voice of his wife to leave him in peace. *Miranda's place* at his side had been empty for so long. He had at last reconciled to never seeing her or hearing her voice again. *It's too late now.*

Emily jostled against his sleeve. "I beg your pardon?"

Kit opened his eyes quickly. Had he spoken out loud? He'd been a poor escort so far, burdened by a heavy heart in the face of his decision. "Forgive me, my dear," he murmured to Emily. "My mind wandered and I spoke out of turn."

Emily turned fully to look behind him. "Madam, you are in the wrong box."

Oh. There was always someone blundering into a box in search of friends and vacant seats so he took no notice. He pinched the bridge of his nose and left Emily to shoo them away.

Emily had been a great comfort to him over the years. She alone out of all his friends had counseled patience when taking his next step to secure a wife and heir, especially since his first attempt had been thwarted by Miranda's sudden and shocking disappearance.

She'd understood and accepted his hesitation in seeking to

declare her dead. He could have taken these steps three years ago. No one had heard news of her, but with no body found there still seemed a chance she lived, so he'd continued to delay. The problem was Kit—he was having the devil of a time letting go of her memory. Miranda had made a lasting impression on him, despite their short time together.

Married a day. Not even the wedding night spent together.

It was the two dozen nights spent in her bed before the wedding that made Miranda impossible to forget.

"Unfortunately not." A feminine sigh sounded behind him, one edged with irritation. "I'll allow you to lay claim to the chair in Taverham's box for the night, but the man you cling to so firmly is certainly taken."

The hair on the back of Kit's neck prickled with awareness, but he dared not turn around. It was only a waking dream of Miranda. He had chased after shadows for a very long time.

Emily's fingers tightened over his sleeve in a startlingly strong grip. She gasped suddenly. "Why have you returned to haunt us?"

"Haunt you?" the voice taunted. "I'm not a shade of times past. I merely intend to make sure you understand that he cannot offer for you, even if he wished to."

Kit's heart raced as he stood. He recognized that voice, even after so long apart. Miranda's voice had never failed to send shivers down his spine with just a few words.

The comedic actress on stage faltered and fell silent, her gaze turning to his box. She lifted one arm to point and then used the other to cover her mouth as if she were stunned. With the performance so suddenly halted, the audience followed the actress' direction to stare at his box too. By his estimation, several thousand sets of eyes turned to discover the source of her distress. It was not a pleasant feeling by any stretch of the imagination to be the focus of such widespread scrutiny.

Lady Brighthurst stroked his arm. "I can assure you I am wanted here tonight."

"Tonight perhaps, but come morning the whole of London shall know your efforts to win yourself a marquess will amount to exactly nothing," Miranda's voice said mockingly. "Enjoy the theater, my dear. *The Beggar's Opera* was always my favorite. I am sorry the dowager marchioness has led your hopes on a fool's errand. She was unbelievably blunt about the practicalities of marriage to her son before. I remember his guardians left me with no illusions of marital felicity thanks to your existence."

Unable to ignore what he was hearing, Kit spun around. His breath ceased in his lungs and he took an involuntary step forward when he saw the woman standing behind him.

Miranda!

This could not be real. Not now. How could his wife come back to him when he'd just made the decision to end their marriage?

Even though shadows cloaked her features, he recognized his wife. "Miranda?"

The lady had the audacity to drop into low curtsy and flutter her fan as if she were overcome. *A curtsy of all things!* She rose and stepped farther into the light and the crowd in the theater gasped loudly, the theatergoers beginning to mutter to each other.

The last time he'd seen Miranda, she'd just spoken her vows after a long night of making love to him. That had been ten years ago. Since then, little had changed of her looks except she had become even more beautiful. She was still as elegant as his memory remembered, still as desirable as his fantasies supplied. His eyes lowered slightly from her startlingly direct gaze, skimming along her flawless skin and dipping into the cleavage her scandalously low-cut gown revealed.

He still wanted everything he saw.

"Darling," she replied in a clear, strong voice that must have carried far in the unusually hushed theatre. Her gaze raked him from the top of his head to the tips of his boots with a bold, proprietary eye. "You're looking well, husband. The new fashions agree with you, but I'm not the first to flatter you tonight, am I? Your good friend there was just complimenting you on your boundless generosity with my dowry."

He stared at the woman he'd married a decade before. Same dark hair curling around her ears and nape, same almond-shaped gray eyes that he could lose himself in. Her cheeks were flushed with hot color and her breath was quick, forcing her breasts to rise and fall seductively.

However, her smile wasn't the one he remembered from before their marriage, though that might stem from finding him attending the theatre with a pretty widow on his arm and secret plans in his mind to marry again.

Yet the fact that he was in such a position was entirely her doing. He was not in the wrong. He had finally convinced himself that Miranda must be dead and had made new plans for his life beginning tonight. He folded his arms across his chest and refused to feel guilty. "Where the devil have you been?"

Emily stood and laid a restraining hand on his arm. "Is this the best place for this discussion, Kit?"

He nodded decisively. Miranda might still hold a certain power over his body, but he wanted everyone to know that it was not *he* who had driven her away. He had chosen his wife poorly ten years ago, and he would not be that unguarded, reckless man ever again. He'd paid a high price for her abandonment. Some whispered he'd murdered her for her dowry, though he'd never been outright accused of any crime.

He stared Miranda down. He would not say another word until she answered him.

"Where I was wanted." Miranda's eyebrow quirked upward innocently, and when she glanced at his companion, her smile was full of pity. "I am sure you are overjoyed to be witness to our happy reunion after so many years apart. I regret spoiling your first season out of mourning with my return, Lady Brighthurst, but you still cannot have him."

As the crowd's mutterings rose higher, Emily stepped around him to advance on Miranda. "You turned your back on a great man."

"I'm sure you've been a sincere comfort to him over the years." Miranda smirked as she drew back. "And if he's as attached to you as clearly as you are to him, then you may continue in that vein and skulk about together in private as much as you like. But remember, you'll never be his marchioness now unless he divorces me or kills me."

Kit scowled at Miranda's flippant remarks. Divorce was abhorrent to him, and while her disappearance might have angered him, even worried him, he'd never once wished her dead. He'd had enough subtle accusations of that nature to find no amusement in it.

He slipped around Emily to grasp Miranda's arm, more to

prove her not a figment of his imagination than to pull her close. One touch, however, and that same reckless attraction stirred his heart as it had when he'd first met her, as if her disappearance from his life and their estrangement had never happened. He had the unfathomable urge to pull her into his arms and kiss her right there and then before everyone. He glanced around to clear his head.

Emily was right that their conversation needed a more private location if his thoughts already ran to the precursors of intimacy.

Around them, the theatre patrons craned their necks to watch his marriage resume with a gasping splutter. Tomorrow, society would talk of nothing else but his wife's very public return, and it would hardly be favorable speculation as to where she'd been all these years. "Perhaps we should move our conversation elsewhere. We are drawing attention."

"That was precisely my intention." Miranda did not fight to loosen his hold but stared at him cynically. "I chose the venue for my return well. I wanted everyone to see that I was alive just in case an accident suddenly befell me."

"And I must say that the sight of you fills my heart with boundless joy, Lady Taverham." Lord Louth, a friend of Kit's, stepped into the box behind Miranda, a wide grin upon his face. "I am delighted to see you returned to society at last, fair lady."

"Martin," Miranda cried. "Oh, you darling man."

Miranda pulled free of Kit's grip and embraced Louth with a degree of familiarity Kit found alarming. He suddenly remembered Louth had exhibited a puppyish devotion to Miranda before the wedding, and it seemed the admiration was now mutual. But how could that be?

When she drew back to a proper distance, her grin was the first sincere one to cross her face since he'd seen her. "I was coming to see you."

A pleased smile passed over his face. "That does gladden my heart. Are you all right?"

"I am. Are you well?"

"The same." He squeezed her hand tightly. "I'm sitting across the theatre in Daventry's box. The poor man cannot believe you're alive. Do you know he's married?"

Miranda laughed, a sound that thudded through Kit's entire

being. He remembered that laugh very well, but the last time he'd heard it they'd been making love, laughing through the whole affair as if the real world of responsibilities and duty hadn't existed.

"The whole of England has heard of his marriage and the good he's done for his wife," she said. "I am so happy for Lillian. Such a sweet and kind girl who deserved someone who would spoil her."

Kit moved toward Miranda. Lady Daventry had been a virtual recluse for so many years before her marriage that few even knew she was alive. "How the devil are you acquainted with Daventry's wife?"

"I am acquainted with many," Miranda answered with a shrug.

Louth hooked Miranda's arm about his and held her there. "I had no idea you'd met Lilly until a moment ago. She's very keen to renew her acquaintance with you."

"And I her. Why, this very moment, in fact." Miranda glanced over her shoulder, a smile of triumph on her face when she met Kit's gaze. "I think I've done all I needed to do here."

Then, before he could blink twice, Miranda swept from the box on Louth's arm.

A wild roaring filled Kit's ears and he glanced around, afraid that he'd dreamed his greatest wish. Emily was pale, almost stricken in appearance.

He swallowed quickly. "Given the circumstances, I feel it best to retire for the evening."

Emily's eyes closed. "Yes. I expect you should. Don't worry about me. I am sure I can find my brother to drive me home."

"I knew I could count on you to understand." Kit drew in a shuddering breath.

Miranda lived.

His wife lived.

Kit was still a married man!

His wife had been at his side and then promptly disappeared again. He stared across the theater at Daventry's box. There she sat, greeting Lady Daventry as if she hadn't a care in the world and was an old friend. But Miranda still hadn't given Kit an explanation for her ten-year absence from his life and Kit would have his answers tonight.

He stormed after her, skirting the malingerers in the corridor between his and Daventry's box in order to confront his wife. He cursed under his breath when he found the box now empty of Miranda, Lord Louth, and even the Daventrys. He charged for the theater entrance, determined to catch his wife before she got away. Outside, carriages clattered past but none stopped to take passengers or were pulling away with new ones.

He raked his fingers through his hair. Where the hell had his damn wife gone now?

Chapter Two

Crisis averted. Husband prevented from an act of utter foolishness.

Miranda Reed, reluctant Marchioness of Taverham, hurried to the back entrance of the Theater Royal grinning widely. Her heart beat a wild rhythm, which she knew would take a quiet room and considerable time to calm, perhaps even requiring a dose of the potion her physician had insisted was necessary to calm her heart and maintain her proper health. She snapped open her fan to beat a cooling breeze across her hot cheeks and neck as she walked along.

The distasteful business of proving she was very much alive was behind her, and now all she had to do was collect her son from the tutor she'd sent him to during her long recovery. Then they would make their home in a modest residence in Town and be together forever. She had no intention of living with her husband even a single day, though it was high time he became acquainted with Christopher.

To her regret, the theater's production of *The Beggar's Opera* resumed with no thought to her heart, a cacophony of sound that stirred Miranda's happiest memories to the front of her mind and turned those remembrances to ashes.

And yet Miranda was pleased with her return to society tonight. She'd succeeded in seeing her husband on her own terms without losing control of the situation. How nice to have had the upper hand for a change. It was a rare day when one could control a situation that involved the Marquess of Taverham and his simpering lover, Lady Brighthurst.

She wasn't unduly surprised they were as close now as the day Miranda had married Taverham. The whispers had grown much louder this last year. Society might only speculate on the state of that friendship, but Miranda had seen the truth with her own eyes. Being betrayed on her wedding day was not something Miranda was ever likely to forget.

Her only servant, a burly man with a face scarred enough to frighten the masses, stepped from the shadows to reveal himself. "The carriage will be but a moment, my lady," Peter Landry informed her in his deep, rumbling voice that had once sent a chill through her soul.

She gave him a warm smile. "Excellent."

As a child visiting her grandfather's warehouse on the docks of the London shipping yards, Landry's large body and voice had quite terrified her once. As an adult no longer prone to hysterics, she'd learned to place her faith in him when she wanted something done. He'd dogged her shadow ever since their paths had crossed by chance during the first year after leaving Taverham, and a more faithful and protective servant a lady in hiding could ever want.

"Did everything go as planned?"

"Yes," she promised. "I couldn't have hoped for more but to have Christopher with me."

There was not much that distressed Miranda now. She'd even recovered from an illness that might have claimed her life, although that convalescence had taken over two years. Time wasted and time stolen from her perfect son.

A theater maid appeared to help Miranda slip into her cloak so she wouldn't be recognized as she left. A stab of pity gripped her that no one else would see the stunning gown she'd commissioned from a backstreet dressmaker working in the north of London. The gown was the loveliest she'd owned in years, and Miranda regretted that the seamstress would never garner notice for her work. Under normal circumstances, Miranda had no need for frippery and nonsense. When in hiding from a man and a marriage you'd come to resent and plagued by a title one didn't respect, it did no good to draw attention. She lived modestly.

Every secret she'd learned to snare a husband during her first season she'd reversed so as not to bring unwanted notice to herself.

Miranda spared a smile for the girl when the hood fell over her head. "Thank you and do convey my appreciation to your mistress for her help in setting the scene I wanted tonight. Apologize if the audience remains distracted for the rest of the night's performance and do assure her I had the outcome I'd hoped for."

The girl nodded quickly and departed. Landry retreated to the lane, no doubt looking for the conveyance that would take Miranda away from the theatre and from her husband. She counted his stunned welcome a blessing, for he'd been quite slow to react.

Miranda wished she could forget she was married yet she couldn't place her needs before her son's interests. He was Taverham's only heir. A public and very dramatic return was absolutely essential to prove to the world that she lived and ruin Lady Brighthurst's scheming to convince Taverham declare her dead.

Embarrassing her husband in the process mattered little in the larger scheme of her son's future.

Lord Louth's heavy tread hurried toward her; he was puffing slightly in his haste to catch up with her.

"Your timing was impeccable, Martin. Thank you."

"Your servant. Always." He glanced over his shoulder. "Will I see you tomorrow?"

"Yes, but I must see my cousin, Agatha, first. She wasn't at the theater tonight. After I've seen her we will leave London in the unmarked carriage if you still wish to escort me." She thanked the stars that she could rely upon Martin so heavily. "Landry could take me. I would not have you at odds with Taverham."

"That has always been the case." Martin scowled. "I told you before that I disapproved of your course of action, but I will see this through to the end, no matter the cost."

She gazed up at him fondly, her heart swelling with gratitude at his unwavering friendship over the years even in the face of possible scandal. Martin had become the brother she'd never had, protective and kind, yet disapproving just the same. "What would

I do without you?"

He scowled. "I have gathered everything in readiness. I can come the moment you need me."

Martin's help was essential to set things right. Afterward, she might just need his aid and friendship once more. There was no telling how Taverham would behave when he met Christopher.

As she was about to thank him again, a shape appeared from the shadows, striding from the hallway.

Miranda faced Lord Daventry with a heavy heart. So much for making a clean escape into the dark night.

"Disappearing so soon?" Daventry said cheerfully.

In his day, they said Daventry had more than indulged in his share of fast escapes from a lover or two's bedchamber. Surely he'd be sympathetic. "Have you forgotten how to let a lady make a discreet escape from an unpleasant situation?"

Daventry grinned. "You've been discreet enough. Where are you bound?"

"Home."

"And where is that now?" He cast a curious glance at Martin. His brow furrowed. "I have a feeling it's not where your husband resides."

Daventry was far too perceptive. It was a mistake to have lingered, succumbing to curiosity and the bonds of friendship when Martin had pressed her to meet mutual acquaintances again. She sensed Martin shift closer, as if preparing to defend her from Lord Daventry's questioning. Daventry was harmless in the scheme of things, and she had no doubts she could easily deflect his curiosity by mentioning the one thing he adored most in life. "Where I go is my business. Run back to your wife before she feels abandoned."

As hoped, he glanced behind him.

"I'm here," Lady Daventry said softly as she joined them, seeming to float on air as if she barely touched the ground. "He merely moves faster than I am able and went ahead to delay you."

Miranda studied the deceptively fragile girl with growing annoyance. She needed to flee, not stop and speak to every one of Taverham's acquaintances. Daventry might have chosen love over practicality when he'd wed Lillian, but neither had to contend with difficult connections. They would never understand the obstacles Miranda would face in the coming days. She'd need all her strength, all her patience, all the resilience she possessed to right a wrong of her own making.

She could have stayed and ignored Taverham's faithlessness but she'd been too young and heartbroken to think clearly.

She shook herself from her worries. A carriage was approaching. Her path to freedom was at hand and then she would rest. Tomorrow would be soon enough for stage two of her plan. "I simply must go."

Daventry stayed her flight with a light touch to her arm. "We do not mean to delay you. My wife has grown weary of the theater anyway and I unwisely loaned our carriage to another patron who was feeling a touch under the weather. It hasn't returned as yet. Perhaps you might see us home?"

Her dark carriage, borrowed from Lord Louth's stables, stopped before the open door. Landry rushed to drop the steps and opened the door for Miranda so she could enter. Given Lillian's fragile health, she quickly nodded her agreement. Miranda clambered in without another word. She couldn't delay any longer or Taverham would find her next.

Lillian took the seat opposite and Daventry chose to sit beside his wife. Miranda smiled at their closeness, a subject London loved to gossip over, as if such affection defied belief. Miranda had seen such devotion a time or two herself, and she was rather envious of how content they looked together.

Louth remained without and shut the door firmly. The carriage rocked as Landry climbed up at the rear and called to the driver to move off.

As they rumbled off down Drury Lane, an angry male voice, Taverham's certainly, called out to the coachman to wait. Thankfully, the driver remembered his instructions and did not obey her husband's shouted command but instead continued on their way into the heart of Mayfair via a circuitous route designed to avoid notice.

Miranda was a *little* impressed that Taverham had troubled himself to chase after her. The ordering everyone about was always expected when one dealt with the marquess.

Daventry cleared his throat. "Lovely evening, isn't it?"

Despite her desire not to reconnect with her husband's set too closely, she smiled warmly at her unexpected companions. "Daventry, you really are droll."

"Among friends one can be himself." Daventry caught his wife's hand and pressed a kiss to the back of it. "Taverham will be angry."

"Better angry than a man twice married," she replied.

"True," Lillian said softly, her brow crinkling with worry. "I am sure he would not have cared for that outcome."

Miranda peered out the window at the candlelit windows they passed. Fine exteriors hid the filth and lies beneath. Once Miranda had been oblivious to such deceptions but no longer. "Does he care for anything but his own concerns?"

Daventry leaned forward. "He cared for you."

Miranda shook her head. "Not enough and perhaps not at all. My dowry was all he truly needed from me."

Daventry remained close. "Everyone knew he needed your dowry desperately before you accepted him. That couldn't have been the reason you left him as you did. What did he do to drive you away?"

Miranda opened her fan, stirred the air against her face, then closed it again. She would never tell a soul just how deeply she'd been misled and how much it had hurt her to be so badly used. Surely by now his closest friends knew where Taverham's real affections had always resided? "'Tis not the right time for such a question to be answered. I've accomplished my goal."

"To stop Taverham from starting up with Lady Brighthurst now she's widowed and clearly interested in him?"

"Ah, so you *do* know what's going on between them?"

Daventry winced. "I'm sorry."

Miranda shrugged. The memory of discovering Taverham seducing Lady Brighthurst, his mistress, on *her* wedding day still turned Miranda's stomach.

The memory of her farcical wedding day brought a dull ache to her chest even now. No one had thought to warn Miranda of the unbreakable attachment *before* she'd given her innocence to Taverham. She'd been so naïve. She'd pledged to love, honor, and obey him, hoping he could love her as much as she did him. But there could be no love and certainly little honor in their marriage.

Miranda was older and wiser now, his affair with Emily meant little in the scheme of things. Taverham could have his mistress. She'd not stand in his way as long as she wasn't subjected to the woman's company. She sighed softly. "I achieved all I needed to do tonight. He cannot declare me dead now."

"Never say so," both Daventry and his wife whispered in shocked tones.

Lillian reached for her husband's hand again and tears filled her eyes. Miranda's acquaintance with Lillian may have been slight and years ago now, but the young countess had always been something of a teary girl. Miranda passed over her handkerchief without a word. It wasn't likely Miranda would ever need to use one again. She'd done all her crying and railing at the injustice of having happiness snatched from her grasp by deceit.

This time when it came to dealing with Taverham she would win. She had something he really needed this time. She had Christopher. Miranda smiled. "As you can see, I'm far from dead, though I'm sure there are many who would prefer me six feet under about now."

Chapter Three

Kit pounded on the door of the Earl of Daventry's Orchard Square town house and waited impatiently for admittance. The sun was rising on a new day and his mood was beyond foul. Damn his wife for disappearing so completely from the theater last night that he'd again found no trace of her. She'd made him look a fool.

He'd first thought to find her at their London home, Twilit House, ensconced in the bedchamber she'd never claimed, where she should have been in the first place. But his butler had assured him she had not come there and had looked quite startled by the news that Kit's wife was actually alive.

He wasn't the only one.

Kit had returned to the theater to question the manager and anyone who'd lingered backstage after the performance. After hours of interviews and the occasional subtle bribe, he'd learned Miranda had left the theatre in Lord and Lady Daventry's company, in a carriage headed in a southerly direction.

Clearly a ruse as the Daventry's residence was located west of the theater.

To his relief, Daventry's butler appeared unsurprised to see him and ushered him into the modest town house. He looked about quickly. The house was very quiet. The butler, Dithers, was even more so than normal. Dithers directed him to the earl's study with few words and even softer footsteps without delay.

"Finally," Daventry cried softly as he shot to his feet. "I've had my servants scouring London for you for hours. Where the devil have you been? You're the hardest man to find in a hurry, my friend."

"You utter bastard." Kit strode forward and glared at his friend. "I'll see my wife now, if you please."

"She's not here." Daventry frowned. "The lady dropped us at home some hours ago and went on her merry way without a word of her destination passing her lips. I did try to determine where she was headed first. I had hoped she'd return to you."

Kit smacked his fist against his palm and spun around. "Damn her."

He hadn't the faintest idea of where else Miranda might go.

"I see the feelings between you are remarkably similar," Daventry noted calmly. "Control your temper and lower your voice, please, or my wife will come and investigate our discussion. She's had a restless night again."

Kit grimaced. Daventry's wife was a frail woman. He already felt as if he walked on eggshells around her when they met, yet it was a small price to pay to have her visit on rare occasions. Usually she preferred to travel little as the jostling suffered from even the shortest journeys caused the most horrendous headaches. Her attendance at the theater was rare. Kit took a deep, deliberate breath and let it out slowly.

Daventry gestured to a nearby chair. "Miranda is not the loving creature I saw on your wedding day."

"She was hardly one then." Kit ran his hand through his hair for the hundredth time. If he lost her again, he didn't know what he'd do. "What wife runs off the minute her groom's back is turned?"

"A troubled one." Daventry moved to the sideboard, and although the hour was early—or late when one hadn't slept all night—he poured Kit a sherry. "I must say I can understand her anger at you last night. Not terribly well done of you and Lady Brighthurst."

"Emily is a friend. I've known her for years. Miranda knows how I feel about her."

"Yes, she does." Daventry pinned him with a serious gaze. "If I've learned anything about women, it is not to underestimate what they take offense at. My wife is particularly possessive when it comes to past acquaintances of the female persuasion, and I'd bet your Miranda is just as bad." Daventry shrugged. "At least you did make an effort to chase after her last night. That pleased her. What did Louth say?"

"Nothing, why?"

Daventry regarded him with hooded eyes. "She's with him now, isn't she?"

Kit reared back as if from a blow. "No. She could not be. I cannot believe that of her."

Daventry winced. "Then why did I find them together at the theater door as she was leaving? They seemed rather more friendly last night than I recall them being at the wedding party or any time before."

Kit shifted in his chair uncomfortably as an irrational suspicion surfaced. In the weeks before the wedding, Kit had entertained an uncomfortable feeling about Louth's interest in his soon-to-be wife. Miranda had assured him they were merely being friendly and that if an infatuation did exist on Louth's part, it would easily fade in time. But what if there was more? What if Miranda had in fact fallen in love with Louth? She had used his given name in conversation as if she was used to doing so.

Kit slouched deeper into the chair as the idea of a friend such as Louth being involved with his wife played through his head. Louth had acted surprised to see her last night, but how could Kit know he wasn't being fooled there too? He didn't want to believe the worst of Louth, and yet once considered, Kit couldn't easily dismiss their obvious affection for each other when the earl had appeared in his box. Had the pair run off together, and if that was the case, then where had Louth kept Miranda all these years?

Daventry continued to talk as if the idea of Kit's wife being unfaithful wasn't at all horrifying. It had never once crossed his mind that Miranda could have fallen in love with another man.

The earl tapped his shoulder. "I say, are you even listening to me?"

"Of course."

"I've always been puzzled how you didn't know Miranda was missing for an entire day after the wedding."

Kit licked his lips, trying to remember the exact events surrounding his wedding day and discovering his wife had disappeared. "After so long, my memory is somewhat hazy on the details. But I recall being so exhausted the night of the wedding that I slept alone. When I went to her new rooms the next day, late, I discovered she'd not moved into them. I never imagined Miranda wouldn't be somewhere at Twilit Hill, entertaining our guests while I saw our plans set into motion."

"With her money." Daventry stared at him until Kit grew uncomfortable. "You know, you might have given her the impression that you married her *only* for her dowry."

"I did."

Daventry folded his arms over his chest. "No woman would want that little fact bandied about, least of all by her future husband."

"I hardly think she didn't know why or found it offensive. She knew what I wanted, and it wasn't as if she wasn't compensated. She did become a marchioness."

"A title that she has little used until tonight." Daventry pursed his lips. "Were you really going to have her declared dead so you could remarry?"

"Damn. Does everyone know?" Kit sighed at how fast gossip could spread when you needed to keep a secret. "I suppose my mother started that one. She's been harping in my ear on the subject for an eternity."

"Actually, no. Miranda herself told me and she seemed less than pleased for rather obvious reasons."

He swallowed the hard lump in his throat. He'd resisted the decision long after he could have petitioned for freedom. A part of him had always wanted Miranda back. Now, if she loved someone else, he wasn't so sure what to do about it. He did not enjoy losing to anyone. "How did she find out?"

"She didn't say and I had no time to press for more information. Perhaps Louth told her and suggested she come forward. If so, then you must thank him. Quite a definitive return to society if ever there was one. A performance worthy of the very venue it was enacted in." Daventry crossed the room and passed another sherry into his hand. "What are you going to do?"

"Find her." He swallowed the drink, enjoying the burn as it

slid down his raw throat. He felt like he'd been demanding answers for hours, and with a start he discovered he'd been chasing after Miranda for at least nine. "I'll tear London apart. And if I discover her with Louth…" He let the rest go unspoken. Truthfully, he didn't know what he'd do about that yet, but he doubted the encounter would be pleasant.

"Listen to me. I love Louth as a brother, and if he has wronged you, by all means beat him to a pulp until you feel better. But I suggest some degree of restraint is in your best interest. May I propose you regroup and rest first? You look like you've been to hell and back."

Hell sounded pleasant in comparison to the night that had just passed. "I cannot rest until I find her."

Daventry nodded slowly. "Miranda did not disclose much of a certainty, but she hinted she intended to reclaim her place in society."

A little of Kit's frustration lessened. His suspicions, though damning, were simply speculation at this point. He would find Miranda first and see what she had to say for herself. "That's something in my favor."

Daventry patted his shoulder. "Go home, eat, sleep, rest, and before you know it you'll have all the joy a married man can expect and look forward to."

"I wouldn't know what that is."

Daventry smirked. "Trust me. Once you sort through whatever problems exist with Miranda, you'll feel a whole lot better."

Kit scowled and shoved his glass aside. "Marriage hasn't done you any favors. You're one of those besotted fools we used to joke we would never be."

Daventry's expression grew serious. "You may laugh all you want at my expense, but marrying Lillian was the best decision I ever made. Don't ever think I'd choose to live a different life than the one I have now."

"Good God. You truly are one of them." He shuddered. "Keep this up and I'll have to content myself with only Lord Acton's sensible company from now on."

Daventry smirked. "You'd be lost without us married fellows in your life, giving you hell from time to time. Give yourself a week of marriage to judge for yourself, then come and talk sense to me. You'll sing a different tune, I'm sure."

Kit stood quickly. Marriage was the biggest and only mistake he'd made in his life. How foolish he'd been to marry so young and expect to be content. He took his leave and strode out of Daventry's town house, collapsed into his carriage, and put his head into his hands.

The wild pulse of his blood sounded louder when he was alone. Miranda lived.

Daventry wasn't wrong that she might have had reason to be angry with him tonight. Today he would have petitioned to have her declared dead, their marriage set aside. And then after a suitable period, a mourning period he'd considered it to be, he would have married again. He'd decided that a dowry wouldn't sway him in the least. He didn't lack for funds now. Connections and a sensible approach to life were all he'd require a second time around.

Except, his heart clenched. Miranda had returned. Well, almost.

To his dismay, he was firmly back where he'd always been yesterday—waiting for Miranda to come back into his life. How the devil had his marriage gone so wrong? To this day, he'd never known what had driven her from home, and only Miranda could explain it. Perhaps he hadn't been man enough for her desires.

He slammed his fist into the roof of the carriage, relishing the burst of pain that cleared his mind, then gave directions to Lord Louth's home. He had to know if they were together or not.

Chapter Four

Miranda raised her hand reluctantly and winced as she struck her cousin a soft blow across the cheek to break her from her daze. Agatha, now Viscountess Carrington, had been staring at her with widened eyes for several minutes. Miranda didn't have the leisure to wait much longer for the girl to collect her sensibilities. "Agatha. It really is me."

Her younger cousin blinked slowly and then, on coming out of her stupor, bit her lower lip.

"You are not dreaming. I am here in the flesh and growing cross with your behavior." Miranda drew back in satisfaction as Agatha shook her head.

"Merry?" Agatha shrieked the next moment and caught Miranda in a none-too-gentle embrace.

Miranda hugged her cousin tightly in return. "I had hoped your propensity for overreaction would have subsided by now, but perhaps you'd better sit down while we speak before you actually faint on me."

Reluctantly Agatha released her completely, recovering her poise to a fair degree. But then she all but fell into the nearest chair with a laugh, spoiling the impression that she was anything but the enthusiastic young girl Miranda remembered. "I thought you dead. Or worse, immigrated to America. I cannot believe you've come back to us after all these years."

"You and everyone else." Miranda surveyed the Carrington

town house surreptitiously, noting the disarray and clutter that spoke of a large family living beneath one roof. Agatha could use another set of competent hands to assist her, or better ones than she currently employed. She glanced up at the molded ceiling as a heavy thump reverberated above her head. "You have children, I believe."

"Yes." Agatha's face creased into a stunning smile. "The orphanage Grandfather patronized had to close. Did you know Grandfather died?"

Miranda nodded. "I heard but wasn't well enough to travel."

Agatha clutched her hands. "Are you sick?"

"I was but I am better now."

"Well, after I came to live with grandfather, I discovered he was always willing to help those less fortunate than himself. The Grafton Street Orphanage was an endeavor he allowed me to visit. I played the pianoforte for the children every day and came to love them."

Another thump and then a wail. "Should they be left alone?"

"I have help, and Jeannie can manage them for a little while without me." Agatha smiled timidly. "You'll take tea, of course?"

Miranda eased into a chair close to her cousin, relieved that Agatha seemed more composed now. "Thank you but no. I don't wish to trouble you. I'd rather talk."

"Me too." Agatha frowned and continued her retelling. "When the trustees decided to close after Grandfather died, the children had nowhere to go but back onto the street. The Carringtons were involved with the orphanage, and in the end Oscar and I took them in."

"I wanted to call on you first, to discover how you've been."

"I am well. Oh, Miranda. How I have longed to see you these past years." She inched forward and clasped Miranda's hand. "I was delivered of a child, a son, recently and have only begun moving in society again these past weeks. Motherhood, true motherhood, was such a remarkable experience. You should have been here to see little Elliot come into the world."

Miranda peered at her cousin, noting her eyes glowed with satisfaction. Miranda was familiar with that look and feeling. She had only to think of Christopher to know her life was made whole by his existence. "Motherhood agrees with you, but then you were always the one little children flocked to when we were growing up."

Agatha's eyes narrowed, suspicion flaring in them briefly. "A fact you used to tease me about unmercifully."

"Did I?" She laughed as she struggled to recall their long-ago interactions. "Well, can you blame me? Children never warmed to me when I was younger and you always took everything I said so seriously."

"I looked up to you. Tried to follow in your footsteps." Agatha wrinkled her nose. "Well, up to a point. I did not run away on my wedding day as you did. Why did you?"

Of course Agatha would ask. But Miranda couldn't bear to tell her the truth. Despite her best intentions, she still felt remarkably let down by her own behavior. She should have known Taverham could not love her. And yet she should never have let events drive her away either. But at the time she'd wanted nothing but escape from him and the people who knew his mistress too well.

"I was deceived," Miranda told her finally, squeezing Agatha's hands. "But I'd rather not talk about something that no longer matters. I am so sorry I was not here for you last year when Grandfather died. By the time I heard of his passing, you had already wed Viscount Carrington and had moved. By all accounts you were content. I hope this marriage was what you truly wanted."

"It was. It is." Agatha's eyes grew soft, the dreamy look of a besotted fool if ever there was one. Miranda had probably worn a similar look when she'd spoken to others of her impending marriage to Taverham. "I have loved him since we met. We almost lost each other too, but in the end it all turned out for the best."

The first rush of love is often the most important to a woman. And yet Miranda marveled at the way Agatha had glossed over what must have been an entirely horrendous period in her life. Always looking for the bright side in a bad situation, always hoping for the best when the worst was coming, Agatha rarely let disappointments linger in her mind.

She'd heard Lord Carrington had almost married another. She held Agatha's hand between her own firmly. "I read about the breach of promise in the papers, Agatha. According to reports it was an expensive and protracted business that surely placed a strain on your and Carrington's connections. Is it very bad for you still?"

Agatha glanced down at her fingers, shielding her face from view. "It is not the best, especially with the size of our family. So hard to avoid notice when it takes three carriages to transport us all about, but I would not have it any other way."

A piercing howl rang through the house, loud enough to make even Agatha glance up and laughed. "I love my life and my family."

Miranda patted her hands firmly. "I am glad, Agatha. I would—" She stopped because of a movement at the edge of her vision. When she turned her head slightly, she saw a tiny child, a girl of about seven or so hugging the doorframe as if afraid to venture closer. Miranda smiled. "And who is this pretty creature?"

Agatha giggled and wiggled her fingers at the child to invite her to join them. "This is Jemma, our second-to-youngest daughter. Jemma, come pay your respects to my cousin, Lady Taverham."

Miranda inclined her head. "How do you do?"

The little girl bustled across the room at a spritely pace and then thrust out her hand as gentlemen were prone to do with each other. "My lady."

Smiling at the bold child, Miranda took her hand and was granted three firm shakes.

The little girl's brow creased. "Do you know when Simon and Mabel are coming back?"

Agatha pulled the child to her side. "Lady Taverham likely does not as she has not met them yet. They will be home when Papa is done with his errands. Have you finished with your studies already?"

The little girl looked so incredibly guilty for not being finished that Miranda laughed. She leaned forward. "Can I tell you a secret?"

The little girl nodded quickly.

"Your day will be much more pleasant if you do the things you least like first."

The child's eyes narrowed. "Like eating cabbage?"

Miranda laughed again. "No, I would not suggest eating cabbage for breakfast, but do your studies first, child, and make your mama proud."

The little girl brightened, kissed Agatha's cheek, and hurried away. Agatha swiveled around to stare at Miranda. "Well, it seems you've developed a knack for managing children that you never had before. She is the most difficult to please. I would have spent a quarter hour convincing her to return upstairs to the others. She is always afraid she will miss out."

Miranda grinned, thinking of the tactics she'd needed to learn swiftly to get Christopher to do anything he hadn't wanted to. Her son was not always the most biddable child in existence. "I must have developed the knack from somewhere."

Agatha sighed deeply. "If only half the people we met took so well to them on first meeting. They tend to frighten more timid acquaintances into never calling again."

"Children are meant to be loud. Isn't that what we agreed when we were young?"

If there was anything Miranda could do in the future to help Agatha financially, she would. She had at least ten years of pin money coming to her that might be more use to them than gathering dust in Taverham's now-bursting coffers. A few extra servants, experienced with the demands of managing a large family, might be just the ticket to ease the burden on Agatha's slender shoulders.

"Loud and occasionally dirty, with no thought to their consequence and rank." Agatha's eyes narrowed slightly. "So, you are a marchioness now."

The last time Miranda had been with Agatha was a month before the wedding and they'd both been simply Miss Birkenstock and had played with Agatha's many dolls. Agatha had been quite young then and in awe of the future ahead for Miranda. "I am, my dear Lady Carrington."

Agatha giggled. "When you say it like that I hear the cousin I knew."

"I have not changed so very much. I simply am far less impressed by the lofty and empty titles we both have now."

"How has Taverham taken your return? He must be

overjoyed to see you again. I've not met with him in some weeks, though I sensed the last time we met that all was not well with him. Oscar suggested I was imagining a change. Is he well?"

Miranda was sure she knew exactly what had been on Taverham's mind—having her declared dead no doubt and worrying that he might have to repay her dowry to her father's estate. That must have given him nightmares. "I expect he is irritated. We met last night and I left him to continue on with his own amusements. You'll not find me at Twilit House; I have not returned to my husband."

Agatha blinked several times. "Whyever not?"

"I have some errands to run first, and I prefer to keep my business to myself for the time being. In fact, I should be about them right now." Miranda stood reluctantly. "Do forgive me for rushing off again, but I wanted to be sure you saw me before you read whatever nonsense the papers choose to report today. I am well and indeed alive, and that is all that matters. I will come and see you again soon, I promise."

Agatha stood too, her expression panicked. "The next time you come must be for an entire day, at least. You must. We have so much to catch up on. I'll make sure Oscar is here at first to distract the children, or maybe we could all go on a picnic together. Somewhere the children might run about and exhaust themselves while we talk."

"Such a day sounds extremely pleasant." Miranda hadn't been on such an outing in a very long time. She smiled at her cousin. "I'd like that very much."

Miranda embraced Agatha, held her cousin tightly against her and rocked her from side to side ever so slowly. "You have grown so beautiful, as I was sure you would. I am glad you found your happiness, my dear."

When they drew apart, Agatha studied Miranda's face until Miranda grew uncomfortable. "But you haven't, have you? I've never seen you so unhappy."

Miranda's eyes stung at how perceptive her cousin had become. She'd thought she'd hidden her bitterness so much better. She forced a smile and squeezed Agatha's hand one last time. "I was happy once and in time I hope to be again."

Miranda turned for the door before she blurted out the truth to the one person who might understand. In coming back she'd known she'd need to face her past and the decisions she'd made for her life. What she hadn't expected was how badly she wanted to tell someone about Christopher. But until she had her keepsake safely in her grasp once more, Miranda couldn't dare. No one would believe her without seeing him first.

Chapter Five

Lord Louth's residence on Golden Square was an impressive mansion. As Kit stepped over the threshold at the butler's invitation, he glanced around the entrance, struck at once by the elegance and simple grace of the furnishings around him.

"I'd like to speak with Lord Louth, Gibbs," he said as he removed his hat from his head in the cool interior.

"How nice to see you again, my lord." The older man beamed. "But I am afraid Lord Louth is away from home at present."

Damn. Instead he said, "Did he by chance mention where he was going? Perhaps I can run him to ground at the club or some other destination and ask my question there."

A public discussion wasn't really what Kit wanted, but he could certainly draw him aside long enough to demand his wife's location.

The old man frowned. "He called for his carriage unaccountably early this morning, I believe, but did not expand on his destination. His cousin is in the morning room presently. Perhaps Miss Crewe might be able to shed some light on when the earl will return."

Kit bit his lip and glanced around. What if Miranda was in this house right now? He'd be a fool to rush away without checking. "Yes, that will do for now if she has time to see me."

Gibbs hurried off at a slow shuffle while Kit paced the

entrance hall. Above him, all seemed quiet, and when Gibbs opened a door at the end of the short hall he heard only the faint clatter of silverware on porcelain dishes. Eagerness gripped him. Could Miranda be just a few yards away?

Gibbs appeared. "Miss Crewe will see you now."

Kit hurried forward, eyes darting into the rooms he passed for signs of his wife. He found none between the entrance hall and the breakfast room he was led to.

Miss Crewe stood alone beside the long mahogany board and dipped a curtsy, her bright red hair gleaming in the morning light spilling from the window behind her. "Lord Taverham. What an unexpected pleasure."

He studied Miss Crewe carefully, looking for nervousness. He found nothing in her matter that hinted she was anxious about his visit.

"Thank you for seeing me on short notice, Miss Crewe. It's been far too long since we've met." Kit bowed to Louth's cousin, a woman who'd been part of Martin's household for the last few years.

She smiled, revealing slightly crooked teeth and dimples that gave her a much prettier countenance. "It pleases me to be remembered. I'm so sorry Martin is not here to greet you. I hope you don't mind conducting our discussion while I'm still at breakfast. The hour is early and I simply cannot drag myself away from the paper's astounding news today. Would you care to eat? The coffeepot is still hot if you prefer that over tea. In my experience men often do."

The butler moved to the sideboard in anticipation, but Kit waved him away with the flick of his hand. "Not today, thank you, and please don't let me interrupt your breakfast. I only need a moment or two for my enquiries, and then I will be on my way." Kit drew out a dining chair and sat across the table from her so she might be at ease, noting as he did so that the butler remained, hovering at the door to act as chaperone.

Although he did not care for servants who lingered, it was necessary as Miss Crewe had not married, did not even have suitors as far as he could tell. He'd have to choose his words with care so the butler had nothing to gossip about.

He met the woman's frank stare directly. "Did your cousin say where he might be headed so early? White's, or Tattersall's for an auction? I had hoped to speak with him this morning. It is an urgent though private matter."

Miss Crewe fiddled with folding the paper closed, trying to hide the front page from view. The headlines proclaimed *Marchioness of Taverham Alive and Returned Triumphant to Society*. Kit gritted his teeth. Of course Miranda's return would be celebrated. Half of society had thought her murdered with her body lying in a shallow grave, either by his hand or on his orders. He'd never raised a hand to any woman, but there just might be reason enough to murder Miranda now for this little stunt.

"Martin tells me so little about what he's doing these days." Miss Crewe winced. "He was gone when I woke and his note, slipped under my door during the night, professed to not knowing what time he might return. I was to eat alone this evening too."

Damn. Kit might never find him as quick as he needed. "Is that usual? Being abandoned so much when he comes up to town?"

"That is mostly the case of late, both here and in the country, so I have grown used to it. I have my own interests." She smiled slightly. "Usually I have his company at meals, but he has been so busy this season that seeing him has become an event in itself. My chaperone is quite disapproving of his behavior and wishes he would settle down."

He glanced at the butler, raising a brow at him. Where was the chaperone and who was *she*? "Is that so?"

"Oh, yes. Gibbs certainly worries for his master too," Miss Crewe continued. "We've had many discussions on the topic of finding him a wife. Mrs. Higginstonby claims him too wild still to wed. Have you been introduced to her?"

All of Kit's senses tensed. What a ridiculous name. Could this Higginstonby woman be Kit's wife in disguise? He sat forward eagerly. "No. I don't believe I've had the pleasure."

"It might have a fleeting chance of being pleasurable if the lady could stay awake through the interview. She naps almost all day long. She won't rise before noon I expect." Miss Crewe chuckled at that as if she was pleased and glanced at the butler with a blush. "Oh, don't scold with that look, Gibbs. Lord

Taverham would never spread gossip that my chaperone couldn't keep her eyes open long enough to prevent any indiscretion even if she were right there in the very room while it happened."

Kit ground his teeth. He certainly wouldn't start gossip of that sort, but Louth should be made to employ a better chaperone for his cousin. Surely he couldn't know or approve of that sort of behavior. But since Mrs. Higginstonby didn't sound much like she shared his wife's demeanor, he concluded they would not be one and the same. "Perhaps another time."

"If you are extremely unfortunate, then yes." Her gaze narrowed slightly. "I must confess when Gibbs announced you I had wondered if you might have brought your wife with you."

Anticipation rose again. Miss Crewe had not been a guest at his wedding and to his knowledge had no connection to Miranda. "Do you know my wife well?"

Her lips turned down. "I have not had the pleasure of an introduction, which is why I was so very keen to meet her. The papers say such conflicting things, and it is not every day that I have a chance to meet a runaway bride."

Disappointment slammed into him. Coming here was another dead end. "No, I don't suppose it is."

Her mouth opened slightly. "Forgive me. Martin is always suggesting I curb my interest of the macabre and unusual goings on in society, but it is all so fascinating to me. No doubt that is why his estate has so few visitors. I tend to startle acquaintances with my blunt and often poorly timed questions. It has been an age since Martin has even hosted a house party, so perhaps that is for the best. One less opportunity to embarrass him."

Although astonished by her candor, her response did answer several questions at once. Miranda had not been living at Martin's country estate these past years. Miss Crewe had been in residence there for at least five. "I wasn't offended, but I will admit to you that my wife's behavior perplexes me. I've done nothing wrong."

Miss Crewe nibbled her lower lip and then regarded him, her head tilted slightly to the side. "In my experience, that is the retort of every guilty man. But that matters not to me. I'd rather like to know how you will attempt to convince her to stay this time round. Do you need any advice on winning her over? I am sure that if you lost that put-upon expression, had your valet run a razor over your jaw, and smiled a great deal more, she would melt in a puddle at your feet. You have a nice smile. A lady would be hard-pressed not to grow to like your company." She leaned back, eyes assessing. "I think I should like to paint you one day. Naked perhaps."

Gibbs cleared his throat quite a few times.

Kit began to see why Miss Crewe did not move in society. If she talked so forwardly with all Lord Louth's friends, he'd surely find himself with none at all or an utter scandal on his hands. Such bluntly worded praise would make a man feel they were being led into a willing seduction. But Kit felt uncomfortable in the extreme. He wasn't one to lead a lady on. He was a married man. "I'm sure Miranda and I will come to a mutual understanding in due time."

"Of course." She smiled widely, then laughed. "Just be yourself and do not worry. A woman would have to be mad to turn aside from such a handsome husband."

Was Miranda mad? She'd certainly turned away from their marriage for long enough. He stood and nodded to Miss Crewe. "Thank you for your time, Miss Crewe. I appreciate your honesty and your candor."

"Liar. I've made you uncomfortable, but I can see now your heart is in the right place." She smiled at the butler. "Do show Lord Taverham out, but please be quiet when you close the front door behind him. Remember, we don't want Mrs. Higginstonby to wake. You know how difficult she can be if she doesn't get at least ten hours' rest."

Kit followed Gibbs out. He glanced back over his shoulder as he heard soft humming start up behind him. "Is she normally like that? So outspoken and flirtatious?"

Gibbs smiled awkwardly. "I'm afraid so. She claims she can read a man's mind better when he's caught off guard and makes use of direct speech whenever possible to determine a man's true intentions. She wasn't truly encouraging you, and you're not the only one she has startled by her act. She teased Lord Ettington once the same way, shortly after his marriage."

Ettington wasn't one to suffer fools and Kit shuddered. "How did he take the impertinence?"

The butler stared at him. "He laughed and laughed, so hard he was near to tears for some minutes after. He then invited her to meet his uncle, insisting that Miss Crewe needed a worthy target."

Kit smiled tightly. Ettington's uncle had turned his back on women entirely a long time ago, entrusting his lands and fortune to Lord Ettington, his twin sister's son, on his eventual demise. "Having met the duke once or twice myself, I'm not sure I'd put my money on Miss Crewe to win in that confrontation. He is rather clever himself and just might turn the tables on her."

"One can only hope." Gibbs paused. "I wish you luck in your search for your wife today, my lord. You have not asked directly, but I have read the papers too, as Miss Crewe has done, and we both concluded you might have come here in search of her. Miss Crewe would not have minded the question you wanted to ask and attempted to do discreetly. We have never known Lady Taverham to be at one of Lord Louth's estates."

Kit grunted that he'd been so transparent, said good-bye, and plodded down the town house's front steps. He paused at the base to wait for his carriage to draw up and considered where to go next. Miranda had few acquaintances in London that were not his too. Perhaps she would not go to the normal places at all. He'd have to consider where she ought not to be.

His eyes stung and he rubbed at them in annoyance. Once he could have stayed awake for days but no longer. He was getting old. Almost thirty. Old enough to know when he was utterly beaten. He would not find her by stumbling all over London in exhaustion. When the carriage stopped, he had his coachman take him home.

Chapter Six

The burned-out ruin nestled beside the brook on the outskirts of London sent a chill racing through Miranda's heart. She glanced anxiously at Martin's stunned expression, then started up the overgrown garden path, wishing her eyes deceived her. But it was very clear the occupant she had expected to find in this place might have moved on and long ago. Weeds infested the once-pleasant front garden, and when Miranda craned her neck toward the formerly thriving kitchen garden, she had trouble discerning edible plants.

The front step wobbled as she put her weight upon it and she stopped. "Hello. Mr. Miles Fenning? Are you there?"

Silence, except for the faint scrape of a branch against a blackened window frame as it tossed against the glass in the strong breeze. She took another cautious step and stretched to knock on the charred front door. Slowly, with a creak that sent gooseflesh up and down her arms, the door opened to reveal a catastrophe inside.

The once-cheerful entrance hall lacked its polished and normally rug-strewn floor. Broken plaster walls and ceiling let the pitiful sunlight shine directly through to the ground beneath. A few tangled weeds attempted to flourish around the house footings where the sun reached down to them.

"Mr. Fenning doesn't live here anymore," she whispered in horror. Which meant Miranda had a serious problem. Fenning had been entrusted with Christopher's education.

Martin's arm curled around her shoulder and he squeezed her to his side. "Dear God. Miranda. I am so sorry. I didn't know about this."

"Where are they?" She pushed out of his arms and hurried away toward the carriage waiting at the garden gate. On her way past, she handed the picnic hamper intended for Mr. Fenning to the nearest groom. "Enjoy with my compliments. I will return soon."

Then she turned on her heel and strode toward the nearest cottage in search of answers. This house at least sported no weeds in the garden. An old man halfheartedly cropped at the long grass at the side, pausing occasionally to view her approach. At the gate she stopped. "Forgive me, but I wonder if you might help me." She gestured toward the ruined house she'd just left. "I was wondering if you could tell me what happened over there."

"Fire," the man said without looking up.

"And?" she asked when he didn't elaborate. Miranda fought to keep her panic at bay. "What happened to the man who lived there?"

"You a friend of his?"

"Not exactly. I employed him. He held something of great value of mine that I'd like returned."

The man paused, wiped his brow, and then leaned on his scythe. "Don't know he had more than the clothes on his back by morning."

"Nothing more?"

"Fair broke his heart to leave but there'd not been his line of work needed in these parts. Young folks always move on to greener pastures. Nothing else to do but the same."

Miranda looked at the quiet surroundings with a heavy heart. If Mr. Fenning had lost all she had given him, he would have had no choice but to seek gainful employment elsewhere. She hadn't trusted anyone with her address but Martin. "Do you know where he went?"

"Heart of London, I expect. It's where they all go eventually."

London was a very large place to look for one gentleman and a small boy. "I don't suppose he left a message behind should anyone come to call on him?"

"Not as I recall." The old man sucked on his teeth. "Here now, you're asking a lot of questions."

"I do apologize, but it is imperative I find Mr. Fenning." More important than she'd ever dare let on to this stranger.

The old man hefted his scythe and then laid it beside the house, out of the way. He came closer, his eyes narrowing as he inspected her. He turned his gaze on Martin, where he'd stopped a few feet away to give her privacy. "Is everything all right, Miranda?"

The old man's eyes widened. "You're Miranda?"

She sagged against the gate. "Yes."

The old man snorted. "Should have said so in the beginning. Fenning said to be cautious when it came to strangers asking after him, especially when there was a gentleman involved. I have something you'll want."

He shuffled into the house, leaving Miranda to wait at the garden gate. She anxiously gripped the wood of it with both hands as she waited for her son to appear. Panic crept over her as the time the old man was away lengthened unbearably. She could feel the pulse of her blood as it traveled all the way from her toes to the top of her head. She was too excited to see Christopher again to ever hope to remain calm.

When the old man returned, she glanced behind him eagerly but saw no one in his shadow. He had only a dirty scrap of paper, much folded and aged in his hand. "He left only this. Said I wasn't to show it to none but you."

Miranda snatched up the note but didn't read it immediately. The state of this man's garden and the ruined house beyond brought a realization to her. There were weeds thriving inside the burnt-out house Mr. Fenning had once lived in. "How long ago was the fire?"

He considered a moment before answering. "Spring before last."

Over a year! Miranda's legs turned to jelly. *Christopher.* She clutched the two-year-old message and prayed it contained news that was still valuable to her. Fenning was so long gone that finding him might be impossible. Miranda collected herself enough to smile, but hope threatened to leave her completely. She'd been assured her son would be safe in Fenning's during her recovery. Taverham's guardians had lied to her for so long.

From within her glove, she plucked a coin for the man's troubles and held it out, trying to keep the shake in her hands from his notice. "My thanks, good sir."

He looked at her outstretched hand and then at Martin.

She licked her lips. "For your continued discretion in this matter."

At last he took the coin. "Someone did come looking for Fenning last year. Not him that's with you. Skinnier fellow and a pale-haired woman. Didn't much care for their smiles."

A chill ran over her skin and clamped ice about her heart. "Do you recall anything further?"

"Top lofty fellow, a swell in boots that never seen a speck of mud they gleamed so brightly. The woman was soft-looking. Pampered." He shrugged. "The gent poked a bit in the ruins and then they went on their way."

"What direction did they go?"

"Toward London, same as Fenning."

"Did you mention where Mr. Fenning had gone to him?"

The old man smiled kindly. "Fellow never asked, so I didn't have to lie." He raised his hand to the horizon where dark clouds loomed. "Rain coming. You'd best be on your way."

He caught up his scythe and disappeared around the back of the cottage as the first drops pattered the earth around Miranda.

She gratefully took Martin's offered arm for support and quickly retraced her steps to the carriage. She gave the coachman instructions to return to London and her temporary residence at Mivart's Hotel on Lower Brook Street. As soon as they were underway, Miranda unfolded the note to read Fenning's message aloud, ignoring the distraction of her shaking hands as best she could.

You'll find what you seek where the roads meet and tally seven, one title lower than you married, when the sun is high, and the week at an end.

Oh, good gracious. Fenning had left her a clue to Christopher's location in a riddle. Clever, but an odd thing to do.

"I hate puzzles. Hell, you look about to faint," Martin

exclaimed as he threw his hat aside. He handed her a blanket, a flask of bitter medicinal her doctors insist she drink when agitated, and a fine sherry glass to pour it into. Given the way her hands shook, Miranda would likely spill the lot.

She handed the glass and medicine back. "Would you mind?"

"Not at all." Martin unstopped the medicinal and his nose wrinkled at the scent that filled the carriage. "God, this stuff is vile."

Miranda agreed with him. "Try drinking it."

He shook his head quickly. "No, thank you. My heart beats at the right pace, unlike yours."

Miranda quickly downed the bitter potion. When severely stressed, her heart could beat so erratically and fast that Miranda had fainted dead away more than once. A situation everyone found unnerving and she tried her best to avoid.

"Where could he mean?" She sat back, attempting to slow her breathing and heartbeat while pondering the message. After a time, some of her tension eased. "Meet where the roads meet and tally seven. Seven roads."

Martin grunted.

"Mr. Fenning might have gone to London so he could mean a London location, and perhaps one so well-known to all that we'd be able to guess," she suggested to Martin.

"The only one I can think of is Seven Dials," he admitted. "Surely he could not mean to take the boy there?"

Miranda's heart skipped a beat at the idea that Mr. Fenning had retreated to that location. She was grasping at straws, but that was all she had.

She shuddered. "Is there another place in London with the same feature of seven roads converging?"

"None springs to mind. One title lower than you married," Martin murmured, rubbing his jaw as he stared at the paper. He looked up swiftly. "Earlham Street, off Seven Dials."

"The rest is easier. When the sun is high surely means midday. And the end of the week could mean Sunday." She eased back into her seat, relieved to have new directions for Fenning and Christopher. Her son was still safe. "I cannot wait as long as Sunday to have my son back."

She pulled the blanket tighter about her.

Martin shifted to sit beside her. He took up her hand and held it firmly. "Miranda, I cannot allow you to go into the Seven Dials. Regardless of your need to retrieve the boy, it's no place for a lady."

She pulled her hand free and clutched them together. "It's no place for my son, either. Besides, Fenning will never hand Christopher over to someone he doesn't recognize."

Martin scowled and turned on the bench. "Let me investigate first. Discreetly, and then bring you to the boy when I have found them. You must think of your health. It doesn't do to become agitated, and traipsing about London's worst districts isn't good for you."

"Yet, what if Fenning lies to you? What if Christopher becomes frightened that someone is asking about him?" She shook her head vigorously. "I cannot allow that to happen, so I will go, alone if your disapproval is so strong. This has gone on long enough. It is all my fault for listening to those three devils. Christopher should have stayed with me despite what the doctors warned could happen to my heart."

Martin grunted a grudging agreement and sat back, folding his arms over his wide chest. The three devils were Taverham's former guardians. Grown men with a propensity for meddling.

As the carriage rolled toward London, a brief shower of rain passed over them and promptly disappeared again. Miranda leaned her head against Martin's shoulder and tried not to worry over who had sought out Mr. Fenning last year and especially what they might have wanted him for.

Miranda hoped it hadn't been her husband in that village.

Chapter Seven

---•◆•---

Kit's bedchamber door banged open with neither a knock nor apology, and Viscount Carrington rushed toward him. "Tell me it is true and not a cruel hoax?"

"True. Miranda lives." Kit frowned. "I thought you'd already left for the country?"

"Not yet, thankfully." The viscount, a friend but more importantly related to his wife through his own marriage to his wife's cousin, Agatha, stopped dead in the center of the room and let out a relieved breath. "Agatha will be so relieved to learn her cousin is alive and here once more."

Kit winced. Since Miranda was not actually here, he felt it best to be honest. "I lost her again. Temporarily."

Carrington gaped at him. "What?"

Kit explained what had happened. "Are you sure it was her?"

"Oh, I am sure." He straightened his cravat and took his coat from his valet to slip on. He saw little point of hiding anything now, as he was surely the laughingstock of London already. "My wife appeared and then disappeared from the theater. She made sure everyone saw her make a grand reentrance into society. Quite theatrical. She's not the product of my frustration, I assure you."

"I see."

Fury built in him anew. Miranda was determined to make him look a fool, and he'd let her get away. The papers this morning were damning. That would change. He glared in the direction of the empty marchioness' suite. "If I'd imagined her, I'd be much less irritated."

"Ah." Carrington shook his head. "You've already had an argument."

"How could that have happened? I've barely seen her long enough to get two words spoken. She never gave me a chance to be her husband, and now I have to pay the price for her behavior all over again."

"It's a good thing you never loved her. Agatha will never forgive me for suggesting this, but…perhaps you should divorce her and be done with the pretense of convincing society you want her back. At least now there's proof you didn't murder her as some have speculated." Carrington shook his head. "After that, it shouldn't prove difficult to find a woman who wants to be your marchioness."

Kit bit the response burning on his tongue. After so long, he could barely remember much about his wife, but he did remember a little of the way he'd felt about her before they married.

He'd been obsessed with Miranda. Her warm and teasing smiles had hinted she was eager to marry him, and not just for his title. He'd done everything he could to understand why he couldn't stay out of her bed when he should have left her alone. It was a shock now to discover those disquieting feelings of attraction had never completely gone away.

The absence of her affection last night was further proof that her suitability to be his wife and marchioness was simply a product of his own flawed thinking. "No divorce. I expect to locate Miranda today and resume our marriage forthwith. I'll make sure she knows where her place is this time. She's made enough of a fool of me, and I'll be damned if I'll put up with it a moment longer."

A throat cleared, a childish pitch that made Kit spin around and stare at the door. Carrington had brought two of his children with him, and they were standing in his bedchamber no less, listening to him rant and rage about Miranda's failings. At the door stood the smallest, a girl of barely five and the eldest boy, Simon, gazed at him, wide-eyed in shock.

"Children," he spluttered, reining in his temper quickly.

"Lord Taverham," they said together, one bowing and one curtsying. They looked at him in such a disapproving manner that he felt uncomfortable.

Kit addressed his friend and scowled. "Do you take them everywhere with you?"

"They were with me when I heard the news, so we came straight here together." Carrington made a feeble attempt to appear cross. "They were supposed to wait below."

Neither one appeared to take any notice of Carrington's gentle scold. Kit had never been sure of the boy's age. Some days Simon appeared very young and others, like today, his world-weary gaze made him seem so much older.

"Mabel wanted to ask a question," Simon confessed.

At the mention of her name, the little girl ventured closer. "Do you have any lemonade for Simon?"

Kit shook his head.

The little girl looked at him hopefully and then reached out to tug on his coat. "A biscuit? He does love ginger ones."

Carrington stepped forward and laid a hand on the girls' head, hopefully to halt her impertinence. "Forgive her, Taverham. She is young and we are due to return home and shall have tea soon. I know you must have much on your mind. We won't stay long enough to require entertaining."

The little girl looked so disappointed by the news that Kit leaned down to the girl's level. "Forgive me, Miss Mabel. Unfortunately I have no time today to entertain you properly as I must go out. When I return, I will certainly invite you for tea and we can have all the lemonade and ginger biscuits that Simon likes."

The little girl leaned forward and stared into his eyes. They widened with excitement, and then to his surprise, she kissed his cheek. A little startled by the kiss, Kit touched his face and straightened. Children did not normally warm to him, but these two were an exception. Mabel liked to shock him every chance she got. Simon always had questions about his estate.

He glanced at Carrington quickly. "If she does that to

everyone that offers to feed Simon, you may have a problem there, my friend."

Carrington shrugged. "She is extraordinarily attached to the boy. I swear it's almost impossible to find him alone except when she sleeps."

The boy in question stood silently near the door, urging Mabel to return to him even as his gaze flittered about the room, inspecting Kit's personal possessions. Carrington's children had visited often but rarely ventured beyond the drawing room or his study. In all the times they'd met, Kit had been most impressed by the boy. He was rather calm and sensible and did as he was told. To his surprise, Kit found he didn't mind him coming upstairs and into his bedchamber. "You must be happy that your sister thinks so well of you."

Simon folded his arms across his chest and glared daggers at him. "She's not my sister. She's my friend."

Kit looked at Carrington curiously, startled by the heat in Simon's words. "I take it he still refuses the idea of taking your name. It could only be to his benefit."

"That he does." Carrington strolled over to the boy and put his arm about Simon's shoulders, drawing him forward. The obvious bond of affection was reciprocated as the boy leaned into his would-be father. "We've come to an understanding."

"Oh?"

"Simon insists he belongs to someone and is awaiting their return. When that day comes, he wishes to be free to go with them. He made me promise not to interfere."

Well above Simon's view, Carrington winced. Clearly he didn't agree with the boy. How often did orphaned children cling to the hope their parents would come for them? It made him sad that the child, though intelligent, could not see he was better off as Carrington's son than entirely fatherless. He was about to offer an opinion when Simon's expression changed to one of stubborn fury. Rather than face an outburst, Kit quickly thought better of offering advice and merely smiled instead. "Well, a promise must be kept then."

"Every promise is a sacred vow," Simon said sternly, staring hard at Kit.

Kit blinked. "Has he been spending time with your mother's

husband in the rectory? He'd make a fine sermonizer one day at this rate."

"Simon has a fine mind for many things. He's an avid reader, so he claims the newssheet before I've even seen it and has unfortunately read the gossip and speculation about you and your wife's marriage. He found it distressing to read about someone he knew." Carrington ruffled Simon's hair playfully. "As to a profession, Simon merely tolerates my new papa's sermons but has no interest in the church. He claims to know what his career will be but can never be persuaded to tell me or anyone else who asks what it might be."

Kit grinned, hoping that the discussion could be salvaged. He'd hate to have the boy out of sorts with him when he was the least unruly child in Carrington's brood. "Not everything you read in the scandal rags is true. My wife and I are at odds for the moment, but the matter will be resolved soon enough, I promise you that. Would you tell me what you hope for your life?"

He opened a drawer and idly ran his hand over his handkerchiefs without choosing one while keeping one eye on the boy.

"Not yet." The boy cocked his head to the side and came closer. He peered into the drawer too, reached right to the back, and selected one after careful study. He ran the tip of his finger over the lettering. "You've much to do, you said. You have to recover your wife first and make her love you again."

Kit took the offered handkerchief, noting the boy had picked the only one Miranda had ever stitched for him, one with wildflowers embroidered around the initials of his name. CR— Christopher Reed. He preferred to be called Kit and she had never done that.

Irritation seized him anew and he returned the handkerchief back to the drawer. Love was for fools who could not see the truth beyond pretty trimmings like impulsive gifts, but he would not disillusion the boy just yet. Let him cling to his ideals a little longer before he faced disappointments in his own life.

Kit stuffed a different handkerchief in his inner pocket, affixed his pocket watch, grabbed a handful of coins and notes, and gestured to the door. "I must go. I called on Louth earlier, but I'd missed him. His cousin didn't know when he'd return exactly, so I need to track him down. He seems entirely too much involved in my wife's life and may have information I need as to her location. If you'll excuse me, I'd like to find out if that is true or not."

"Of course." Carrington followed him to the door. "I'm going home now to tell Agatha of her cousin's return. She will not rest easy until she's seen her. Send word at once when we might visit with Miranda."

"Given my wife's capricious nature, I believe that might be wise."

Carrington grinned. "Miranda can meet all the children at once then. We'll be waiting for you."

He called Simon to hurry up and whispered something in his ear. The boy appeared as if he might argue, but then he looked at Kit, his gaze intent. "Remember your promise to bring her to see us."

Taken aback a little by the boy's interest, he simply nodded.

Chapter Eight

———◆———

Kit held out a pound note. "Where is she?"

Mr. Mivart, the proprietor of Mivart's Hotel on Lower Brook Street, took the bribe and leaned forward. "Mrs. Reed went out early with her man and a gentleman who called for her in an unmarked black carriage, but she'll no doubt be back soon. Her belongings are still upstairs, and her rent's paid in full for the month."

Miranda was staying here, not as the Marchioness of Taverham but simply under her married name. At least she remembered she was a married woman. That pleased him somewhat.

"I want to see her room," Kit growled. He'd finally found where his wife had rested her head last night and would discover if she was truly alone or not.

The proprietor's eyes widened in shock and he shook his head. "Please, sir. We have a reputation to maintain. Our guests expect discretion and privacy. I want no trouble."

Kit held out another pound note to the protesting proprietor, knowing further inducement was expected before he'd grudgingly give in.

"Really, Taverham." Miranda's voice shattered his anger like rock striking glass. "Was a pound note all you were willing to shed to find me? You should have offered more and he would have told you what I had for supper last night."

The proprietor snatched the note as Kit spun about to find Miranda, wearing a blue carriage dress and holding nothing but a reticule standing at the hotel doorway. She was alone, but a black carriage was pulling away from the front of the establishment.

Miranda sighed heavily and then turned her attention to the proprietor. "I'll take tea in my rooms if you please, Mr. Mivart. And some of those biscuits you sent up with supper last night would be appreciated."

"Yes, my lady." The proprietor snapped his fingers at a footman, hurrying to accommodate her request, tucking Kit's bribe into his waistcoat pocket as he went off with a contented sigh.

More or less alone with Miranda in the booking room, Kit found himself at a loss for what to say. He had so many questions, but none of them seemed pressing right now. For the moment he was lost in wonder that she lived. "Lady Taverham. So pleased to see you again."

"I am not sure you are. What do you want?"

"You." And that startled Kit, because from the moment he'd laid eyes on her last night he'd been consumed with finding her and never letting her out of his sight again. He held out his arm. "I'll help you pack."

She rolled her eyes and walked toward the staircase without him. "Taverham, you've not lifted a finger in such menial matters in your entire life. Why pretend you would start now?"

Kit followed. "I know how to throw clothes into a trunk and take you home, over my shoulder, too, if necessary."

"But I'm not going to your home."

She started up the stairs and Kit ran to catch her. "Don't be ridiculous. Lady Taverham does not sleep in hotels."

"She most certainly does and has done so on many occasions." She frowned. "Really, Taverham, do you never get tired of having everything your way? What does it matter where I live? You've your own life. As I have lived mine. You should be glad to be spared the burden and inconvenience of a wife underfoot."

He gritted his teeth. If Miranda didn't come home, then how could their marriage resume? "It matters."

He would not pressure her to resume intimate relations, but

he still needed an heir. Only a son could take over the estate after he was gone, and inherit his lands and Miranda's money.

He peeked at his wife's unyielding face, an ache filling his chest. Once she'd been eager for him. Willing to share every forbidden touch and caress until all hours of the night. He'd expected more of that when they married, not a cold, lonely bed for company and a decade of silence.

Carrington's would-be-son Simon had been right. They'd spoken their vows, made promises, and those would be kept. He would make her understand where she belonged.

Two flights of stairs up, Miranda turned down a shadowed hall and stopped before an unremarkable door. She took a key from her reticule and let herself into a bedchamber. Kit followed quickly lest she attempt to lock him out.

As she laid off her bonnet and gloves and set them on a far table, Kit studied what his wife owned inside the plain apartment. Two large trunks hugged one wall and a few personal items littered the space as if she'd not been here very long or traveled very lightly. That gave him his first question. "How have you supported yourself?"

Her lips twisted into a grimace and she rubbed her neck as if she was exhausted. "You haven't changed, have you? Your first question, of course, is about money."

He set his hands on his hips. "Well, what did you expect? You run off without a word ten years ago. Appear and disappear within the space of an hour last night. Why shouldn't I demand answers? You are my wife. Where did you go today?"

Her eyes widened at his irritated tone. "I called on my cousin Agatha, then went into the country."

He narrowed his eyes. Miranda had been a much more agreeable creature as a prospective bride. "Why the country?"

"I needed some perspective." She flicked the paper at him and he caught it, glancing at the first page but knowing what was written there. "The disappointment over my false demise makes for interesting reading, but if I need to explain why seeing you squiring a widow about on your arm would put me out of sorts then there truly is no help for you."

Was she actually jealous of Emily?

"Emily is a friend." He stabbed a finger in her direction.

"Your friend too."

"So you've claimed before but that was a lie, wasn't it?" She drew in a deep breath. "However, the gossip spreading through society speaks of her friendship to you. In particular, a hope for a match to be made and the disappointment that I've returned to thwart your honorable intentions."

"I'm already married."

Miranda shrugged and she looked away. "Having me declared dead would have solved that problem for you. So sorry to spoil your plans." Her hand rose to her chest and it seemed to him she was distressed by what he'd intended.

He moved closer. "Nothing has changed between myself and Emily. If you'd not run off, I wouldn't have had any reason to wonder if you lived or had died."

She moved further away. "Society was already wagging their tongues on the day we married that you'd made a poor match in me. I discovered that after it was far too late."

"What do you mean?"

Miranda paced the room restlessly. "I mean that if I had been in possession of all the facts of your character, of your true intentions, I never would have married you."

The idea that Miranda regretted marrying him was impossible. "Don't be ridiculous. I told you everything that mattered. Of course you would have still married me. You became a marchioness."

"Do you really believe an empty title a balm for an empty life? Constantly told what to do and say, kept to the side and expected to suffer it in silence? No, I would never have chosen you."

Kit stared at her. Their marriage had been based on his need for her money and her ambition for a title. Hadn't it? Time had made the facts in their discussions a little vague. What more could she have wanted from him?

A tap sounded on the door and Miranda turned away. "Now, if you don't mind, I've had an exhausting day and I'd rather be alone than listen to your grumblings."

When she opened the door to the footman, Kit grinned. The tray contained two cups for tea and a plate of biscuits. He wasn't going anywhere just yet. Kit tipped the footman generously and ushered him out. For good measure, he locked the door to ensure no further interruptions were possible.

"In case you've forgotten, black with sugar," he told her.

Miranda sighed and poured for them. "As I said, some things never change."

"And some things do," he said as she added milk but no sugar to sweeten her tea. "I remember you used to take it the same as mine once."

Another shrug of her shoulder was all the response she offered before she sat back in her chair and looked at him. "I have my own mind and intend to use it. I'll not turn myself inside out just to be what you want again."

She'd hardly done what she claimed. Kit made himself comfortable and took a sip of his tea. After a few moments, he set the cup aside and snagged a biscuit. "Come home."

"Why?"

Kit sniffed the biscuit—ginger. Simon would like it here. "You belong with me."

"No, really, why? You have my dowry, doubtless you've already spent the bulk of it these past years. By all accounts the Taverham estate and your interests elsewhere thrive. What more can be gained from joining your household?"

"A son."

Her eyelashes fluttered. "My, we are being straightforward today. You must yearn for the rest of the fortune our marriage granted you. I don't have to live with you to provide you with a son."

"Miranda, you try my patience. You will do as I say."

"That's right. According to your mother the Marchioness of Taverham must never deny her husband, no matter how ill-timed or how rude the request might be worded." She tossed her head. "It must always be your way, and heaven forbid I deny you the opportunity to prove your masculinity."

Heat crept up his cheeks. Perhaps he should clarify. "Forgive me. I didn't mean I wanted to take you to bed this very moment."

"You'll allow me to eat and drink before you ravish me? How generous. At least this time we would be married and it wouldn't be deemed a sin or scandalous." She leaned forward. "You could tell everyone this time."

His temper burst at her insinuation. "I never ravished you."

"Really. Well, I wouldn't call it lovemaking, now would I? You didn't love me even a little when we married, and I cannot imagine you care for me now. What other word fits such a situation? I confess I've no idea." She lifted her cup to her lips and took a slow sip, staring at him over the rim.

Kit leaned toward her. "Are you suggesting I forced myself into your bed before we were married?"

She frowned. "It did ensure I had no choice but to go through with the wedding. What decent man would have had me after your use?"

He stood, jerked her up out of her chair and into his arms. The teacup and saucer she held fell to shatter around their feet. "I did not plan to seduce you before we wed, but I won't deny I needed your dowry. You knew that."

"You do nothing without a reason." She freed one hand and patted his coat pocket, as calm as could be. "I'm sure your little book in there will prove that you always achieve what you set out to do."

"You're wrong," he insisted. But Miranda was indeed correct. Nearly everything he'd set out to do was done. Her money had restored the estate, allowing him to achieve his aims and set things right for the next generation. The only thing outstanding was Miranda, and holding his heir, their child, in his arms.

He glared down at the woman he'd rushed to marry, regret filling him. Miranda still fit snugly in his arms, and although he wanted her, her unyielding stiffness proved she would not welcome the resumption of their marriage in any form. He was not the monster she made him out to be. He had not planned to seduce her before the wedding and would never force himself on her no matter how greatly she provoked his temper.

Desire and mutual surrender to it had happened naturally between them before their marriage, or so he'd thought, despite knowing he shouldn't have behaved so dishonorably with her before she'd taken the protection of his name. She'd made him forget himself in the heat of passion. The accusation that he'd tricked her out of her fortune stung.

He would not stand the lie.

He spun her about, holding her back tightly against his front, facing the tall looking glass across the room. Now, as had once been, they looked good together. The top of her dark head rested against his chin, his arms snaked around her lush body, which begged to be worshiped. Hell, he still wanted Miranda. He quickly reined in his amorous impulses and stared at her reflection in the looking glass. "Just so we are clear, do you believe I forced our match by seducing you and by a cunning plan spent those prior nights before our marriage in your bed just so I could claim your dowry?"

She did not even pause before answering with a resounding *yes*.

Anger filled him, and righteous outrage. He tightened his grip, but not enough to be considered cruel, and lowered his lips close to her ear while watching her every reaction in the mirror. Miranda dropped her gaze from the mirror, turning her head slightly toward him.

His body responded instantly, attuned to her nearness, and the light scent she wore so achingly familiar and missed. "So I forced myself on you, did I? I never asked to kiss you or received one in return? Never once let you decide how we would wile away those midnight hours in your bed? Our last night together, wasn't it you seducing me to remain in your bed just a little longer?"

He skimmed his hands lightly over her body, avoiding her breasts, her most sensitive parts, to help make his point. Miranda's breath hitched, but her body tensed against showing further response. Kit continued to touch her lightly, even while his body craved action. As before, the moment he touched Miranda, the more he wanted her. A pity she still denied his presence didn't affect her the same way hers did to him.

He lowered his eyes to her breasts, pleased to see the tips now revealed her arousal. He smiled at how her body betrayed her. "I never once cared about your pleasure. I took mine first and often. If I was such a beast, are you not in fear for your virtue now?"

Her breath panted from her lips when Kit slid his hand till it rested against her ribs and paused beneath her breasts. This desire was their undoing. The cause of his misery. He cupped her breast and her breath left her in a ragged gasp. He lightly kissed the column of her throat as she squirmed against him, pressing her bottom against his thickening length. She'd always been a temptress. Everything about her set his desires alight.

She must remember how insatiable their appetite for passion had been, but for some unfathomable reason she now meant to deny its existence. How many couples married for money and provoked each other like this? It wasn't rational or normal. It was extraordinary. Kit brushed his arousal against Miranda just once.

Then he dropped his hands and stepped back, pleased to see she had lost her careful composure and staggered a step. She met his gaze and her eyes glowed with a lust he remembered well. "If that is what you recall, Miranda, then I challenge your memory, because all I remember is the sweetness of surrender, yours and mine. Good day to you. Don't think you can escape me again."

Kit snatched up his hat and Miranda's reticule for good measure and strode out, his trousers too tight, his passions too high. He would not force Miranda, but he'd be damned if he'd let her forget the truth of how right they had been together in bed while she tarred him with the brush of an utter scoundrel.

Chapter Nine

---◆·◆---

Three breaths into the morning, Miranda discovered she wasn't alone. Soft steps crossed the room, approaching the bed in a stealthy manner. Her heart hammered in response. She'd specifically told the maid she would call when she was ready for company. After the events of yesterday and her encounter with Taverham, she was feeling rather delicate and unsettled. "Have you never heard of knocking first before entering a lady's bedchamber?"

"My husband said knocking spoils the surprise."

Miranda levered herself to a sitting position to stare at her old friend. Since they'd last seen each other Virginia had married Lord Hallam, a man with no discernable sense of humor, and borne him a daughter. Or so her informant had told her. "Ginny."

"Merry." She came closer and they embraced. "What in heaven's name are you doing in a hotel?"

"Bracing myself for Taverham's next visit."

"He's outside." Virginia smiled a little sadly. "I could not believe my ears when I heard of your return after so long with no hope. I had to come see for myself that the tales were true."

Knowing it was beyond useless to remain abed with Virginia around, Miranda unwound the sheets from her body and peeled the remaining covers back from her legs to dangle them over the side. She discreetly placed her fingers over her wrist to count the pulses of her blood as doctors had suggested she do first thing in the morning and then again later in the day to see if there was any serious change before standing. The beats seemed steady, at least for the present. "What is the gossip this morning?"

"That you created such embarrassment for Taverham that he's not receiving callers."

Miranda rubbed her wrist, then brushed her hair from her face. "Are those turned away not to be considered lucky instead to be spared his tiresome company?"

"Merry," Virginia said, chiding her. "This doesn't sound like the girl I knew all those years ago."

"The Miranda you once knew trusted more. She was a fool." Miranda stood and faced the window, noting the day was as gray as the one before. It suited her mood and the gnawing ache filling her as she thought of Christopher somewhere out there. He was the only good to come from marrying Taverham. "I was a simpleton with stars in her eyes and whipped cream in place of intelligence. I ought never have been persuaded to marry so young."

Virginia frowned. "At the time, I didn't think anything would stop you having him."

And there was the rub. Despite the time that had passed, she had desired her husband then and she still desired him now, apparently. The annoyance of that and the manner he'd left her in, aroused and furious to be feeling so strange again, had kept her awake until all hours of the morning. The tangled state of her bed sheets was proof she'd not passed a restful night for thinking of him.

But she would resist his demands and not return to his house until she was free to do so with her son as leverage. There was no choice. She couldn't become confined beneath Taverham's roof until she had found Christopher. After she'd retrieved him, she didn't much care what happened in her life as long as she was allowed to see her son. She would be at peace at last and done with hiding his existence.

Miranda began to dress. There was only so long she could count on having privacy before Taverham forgot he was supposed to be a gentleman and barged in on her unannounced.

Virginia helped dress her hair without a word and then held out a ring to her. "Taverham thought you might like this returned to you."

The ostentatious Taverham family heirloom, more emeralds and diamonds than she'd ever seen on anyone's hand, gleamed in Virginia's grip. Miranda had left it behind when she'd run away, and she'd not missed the silly, heavy thing one bit.

She took it with a weary heart. She'd sworn never to wear it again and wouldn't until her mission was complete. "I expect it's merely a means of reminding me of what he brings to my life. Gilded chains. Rules and obedience. I hope for your sake your husband is in love with you."

Virginia blushed. "He wouldn't dare not be. Put it on so we may go?"

Miranda placed the ring into a drawer instead. All she'd had with Taverham was misguided passion and that was merely a passing sensation. Lust was fleeting. Only love lasted and they were certainly not in love and had never been. In time, she'd learn to dull her senses to his touch and ignore the reminders of what she'd imagined they'd once shared. "Then you are fortunate. Where are we going?"

"Taverham wishes to spoil you and insists you need a new wardrobe."

Miranda's wardrobe might not be in keeping with the latest fashions, but there was nothing wrong with her gowns in the least, not for the retiring life she preferred to live. She'd not been entirely without resources these past years to be considered an object of ridicule in her manner of dressing. Taverham would have to take her as she was or go to the devil. Let Lady Brighthurst continue to delight him with her appearance. "I don't think so."

"Oh, come now. Madame du Clair will triumph if her establishment is the first business Lady Taverham choses to patronize after her return." Virginia linked their arms. "It also gives us an excuse to send our husbands away, and you know we can talk openly before Madame. She's been worried about you too, so expect to be completely smothered in delight by the little Frenchwoman."

Madame du Clair had been the kindest soul during Miranda's

short and only season in London. Miranda had genuinely liked the woman and had soaked up every scrap of advice offered on how to present herself to her advantage. That advice had won Miranda a proposal from a marquess, but her prize was a man she could never fully claim. "Very well. For Madam's sake only, but I will not be returning to Twilit House at the end of the day."

"If that's what you want, I will do whatever I can to help."

Miranda followed Virginia out into the hall with a heavy heart. She might have had a chance to slip away from her husband, but her chances now were much slimmer if she didn't want Virginia taking offense. She shut and locked the door, then looked up straight into her husband's eyes, so like Christopher's but a much deeper shade of green. A little startled by the resemblance, she eased away.

"Good morning, wife."

Miranda held on to her temper and tongue by sheer force of will. She didn't need reminders of her role in his life. Not yet. She addressed Virginia's husband instead of responding. "Lord Hallam. A pleasure to see you again."

"Not so surprising to see you. Took you too bloody long to come back."

Hallam's blunt remark had no power to hurt her, so she merely smiled tightly and contemplated how on earth the kindest woman she'd ever known had come to marry such a fustian ogre. He must have well-hidden positive qualities somewhere that only the most patient of souls could uncover. That explained why he'd proposed to Virginia. Virginia was entirely too softhearted.

Taverham thrust out the reticule he'd taken from her yesterday, possibly in the vain hope of preventing her escape. Miranda kept little of value in it, scarcely enough to identify her to anyone, but she took it so he wouldn't know. The purse felt heavier and she concluded he'd provided her with pin money. Her first.

Although she hated giving in, the money would go a small way to repay Martin's expenses as he searched for information about Mr. Fenning's whereabouts. Martin was right that she couldn't go into the Seven Dials unprotected, especially if Fenning might have moved again. She would take Peter Landry and maybe hire another man as a bodyguard for her protection. Someone loyal to her and to her money.

Before she'd gone too many steps, Taverham caught her hand and spun her about to face him. His grip was cruel as he jerked them up to look at her bare fingers. "Your ring?"

Miranda gestured behind her to her room.

His jaw clenched. "Get it and wear it now."

Miranda glared at him in answer rather than refuse. Oh, she could easily find more reasons to hate him when he told her what to do. Bossy and stubborn were not character traits she found admirable in any man. When Virginia slipped the key from her fingers and returned to the room, Miranda kept her gaze on Taverham. Frustrating, demanding fiend. What did she need jewels for?

She needed their son at her side more than new dresses or any diamond ring. She wanted to tell him to get out of her way so she could retrieve Christopher, but the words stuck tight in her throat. He'd never believe her without proof, and Martin had that.

When Virginia returned, eyes downcast and apologetic, she handed the ring to Taverham because Miranda's hands were clenched into fists. Taverham pried her fist open. "With this ring…"

Knowing resistance would lead to a worse scene, she opened her fingers and let him place it on her, uncomfortably aware that the piece fit her hand better now than it had when she'd first received it. Clearly pleased with himself, Taverham held out his arm. Miranda strode forward without his aid. There was only so much idiocy she would endure so early in the day.

Together they started down the stairs and swept out into the street where Taverham's newest gold-crested black carriage waited to take him wherever he wanted to go at a moment's notice.

Once outside, her gaze darted down the street and she spotted Martin, frozen several feet away. She shook her head the tiniest amount to warn him back, hoping Taverham didn't see him and wonder why he was there. Martin disappeared into the crowd, and to her relief, it was clear after a few anxious moments that Taverham hadn't seen her friend.

But once she was at Madame's place of business, she would send Martin a message and arrange to meet somewhere else. Although her arms ached for Christopher, it might take an hour until she could escape her husband again.

For now, she would suffer Taverham's company, gleaning what information she could to help Christopher adjust to his future life.

Aware that eyes everywhere had turned in her direction, she entered the carriage and took a place beside Virginia.

Silence reigned. Not one word was spoken until the carriage stopped on Bond Street. When they stepped out, Taverham caught her hand and wrapped her arm around his. "My dear, this way."

"Actually, no," Miranda interrupted brightly. "Our appointment is this way, and I have no need for your aid in picking out my fashions if you don't mind."

He frowned. "Mrs. Denning's salon is, I'm told, highly regarded. Everyone says she is the best in Town and I have already arranged an appointment. Lady Brighthurst and my mother raved about her just the other day. Why not a fresh start?"

"Good grief." Miranda pinched the bridge of her nose as her temper climbed. Taverham intended to restart their marriage without mercy. She would not do things the same as everyone else in his life. She would patronize the shops she liked and to hell with Lady Brighthurst's suggestions.

Miranda freed herself from his grip. "I already have an exquisite modiste in Town who knows my tastes better than anyone. I'll not change just to please you or the women in your life."

Miranda would fight with him right here on the most popular street in London just to prove he couldn't order her about. She would make him see she wasn't a brainless ninny without opinion and opened her mouth to do so.

Lord Hallam began to laugh, cutting off her tirade before she could start. "Well, I'm not going in there. It's all pins and lace and yards. Does a man's head in. Besides, I like the surprise that comes later at the private unveiling of new garments."

Hallam's face softened when his gaze turned on his wife and

Virginia blushed a little. Miranda made the mistake of looking directly at her husband. Judging by the change that had come over Taverham's eyes, his mind had turned to private unveilings of intimate apparel too.

His brow rose expectantly. "Something to look forward to?"

Miranda shook her head quickly. No matter what she had imagined might happen on her return, it was clear she hadn't anticipated Taverham would still desire her. He clearly thought that once bedded, Miranda would fall straight back into his arms without hesitation. This time around making love to him was something she did not intend to do. But he still imagined he needed a son so she would keep him at arm's length.

Hallam kissed Virginia's cheek. "Send word when you need me. We'll be at Hoxham's Coffee House for the next hour."

When Taverham made no similar move to say good-bye but stood there staring at her intently, Virginia tugged Miranda toward their modiste's shop. At least there Miranda could look forward to an uninterrupted hour or more, discussing everything from fans to muslin and every speck of gossip between before she'd need her wits about her again. When she could, she'd scrawl a note to Martin that they'd go collect Christopher.

With that thought before her, she could move on.

The little shop was exactly as she remembered—cozy, warm, and a bustle of activity that paused as the bell on the door twinkled.

Madame glanced up from her patterns and her eyes widened. She clapped her hands together in delight. "*Chéri*, so it is true you have returned to set the city *enflammé*?"

Miranda laughed at the idea and drew closer. "Hardly. It is good to see you again."

"The pleasure is with me." Madame beamed and glanced around her shop to her workers. "Is it not correct that the Marchioness of Taverham should seek out the best seamstress in London immediately on her return to *société*? *Magnifique*. We shall be beset by orders within the space of a day and entirely run off our feet."

Miranda exchanged a glance with Virginia and saw the merriment glittering in her eyes. Miranda allowed herself to be drawn into the excitement of meeting friends and to the corner where comfortable chairs waited for customers to take tea and eat little cakes while important decisions were made. Miranda had spent hours here on her first visit and easily found herself comfortably at home once more.

Madame clapped her hands and the women returned to their sewing and cutting. She perched on a delicate chair facing them, her hands clenched tightly together. "It is so good to see you after so long a time apart. Are you in the great city for long?"

The workers paused.

Miranda shook her head. "Not too long, I imagine."

Madame's face fell and she clutched her hands to her chest. "We are *désolant*. We must talk of the gown you wore to Covent Garden last night. They say it was a *triomphe* even if I did not sew a stitch myself."

Madame regarded her with a raised brow. It was a well-known fact that she did not like to see her customers wearing another seamstress' creations. Miranda patted the woman's hand soothingly. "The gown came from a small shop far north of London. It is beautifully made and I wish you could meet the seamstress. In fact, I would be happy to offer you a letter of introduction today. I fear the woman is struggling a little and she is quite young. She might value the guidance of an astute businesswoman to aid her. I told her all about you when we met and I thought she looked a bit wistful about being so far away from London."

"It is a possibility I am willing to entertain. A shop such as mine requires the correct management to ensure our clients are well tended. You may write her indeed."

Madame fetched a tiny writing table and Miranda quickly wrote her notes, including one to Martin, without Virginia being any wiser. She sealed them and a footman dealt with them on her behalf.

Madame smiled warmly. "How may we help you today?"

Miranda fidgeted as Virginia discussed her needs. A nightgown of the finest pink silk, a robe to match, and lacy garters completed the order. Madame scratched down her requests with a murmured word of approval as they selected fabrics and embellishments. "Oh la la, Lord Hallam has a *tendré* for the softest rose on you."

Madam loved to gently tease her clients over their many admirers and Virginia blushed as bright as a new bride. "The color suits me."

"*Absolument*," Madame agreed. She then turned to Miranda. "And for you, *chéri*?"

Miranda winced at the turn of conversation. She hadn't really intended to have anything made, but she could see Madame and Virginia expected her to order at least something. "What do you recommend?"

"The soft blush of rose is not for you. Not with your complexion."

"I remember you telling me that before I married," Miranda murmured.

"*Chéri*, you are favored to wear an *intrépide* hue of blue, or chartreuse. There is a lovely spun silk just arrived, very bold. Very original, I think."

Madame disappeared into a back room and returned with a material so light but full of exquisite color that Miranda's resistance teetered, then disappeared completely. "Yes."

Patterns appeared next, spread out before her to choose. It had been so long since Miranda had access to such a superior modiste that she couldn't decide which she liked best. She shook her head at the choices. "They are all lovely."

Madame leaned forward and tapped a print. "That one to begin."

Miranda lifted the print to study it. "It's a bit daring, isn't it?"

Madame clucked her tongue softly. "A decade married and still so unsure of your charms, *non*? Your husband will be ravenous before the first dance is over. My word, *chéri*. You will beguile him again with just one glimpse of your lush body in what I create for you today."

"I don't think...," Miranda began, but the modiste had whipped out her measuring tape and was studying her intently.

The Frenchwoman's gaze lifted to hers, a question in her eyes. "I must take your measurements again before we begin."

Miranda stood still for the measurements, watching Madame's face grow even more serious as her hips and breasts were measured twice. Yes, her measurements had increased since she'd last stood here and she began to feel uncomfortable about that. She'd had a child. Every woman gained a little more flesh after such an event. "Too much cake?"

"Perhaps." The modiste's expression cleared, replaced with an amused smile. "*Monsieur* will be nibbling cake from your palm before I am through. *Absolument.*"

Miranda wasn't sure she needed Taverham to be any hungrier for intimacy than she suspected he already was. The way he watched her, studied her with such direct attention, reminded Miranda of a caged lion. Miranda might have been his supper once, but she wouldn't be consumed willingly now.

As she selected undergarments in similarly bold colors and styles to complement the gowns, she wondered if she knew what she was truly doing. Baiting Taverham with seductive garments, especially undergarments, without intent to show him seemed cruel.

She'd never intended to share his bed again. Teasing him a little though seemed a fair punishment for the deception he'd carried out once if she didn't take it too far. He was right when he'd claimed them equally attracted to the other. Yet that desire had been built on a lie. He didn't, couldn't, love her when he was still attached to Emily.

She could not give her body to him knowing he was deeply in love with someone else. Besides, there was no need. Once Taverham understood he already had an heir in Christopher, he'd turn away from Miranda instantly.

Chapter Ten

"That woman does not like you very much," Hallam pointed out before too many minutes had passed in the busy coffee house on Bond Street.

Kit swirled the coffee around in his half-empty cup and frowned. Despite yesterday's favorable reaction to his touch, Miranda was in no way warming to him that he could see. "So it seems."

He gazed out to the busy street where he could just see the dove emblem on the front door of Madame du Clair's Salon. He was desperate to know Miranda hadn't disappeared out the back door already. The only thing keeping him seated was his belief that Lady Hallam would return to her husband if Miranda did in fact run off. He glanced down at his cup, fighting to keep his anxiety contained and hidden.

Hallam nudged his arm. "Does she know how widely you've traveled in your search for her all these years?"

"I don't know. I can barely get a straight answer from her, and we've not spent too much time talking about the past, although I've tried."

Hallam snorted and then drained his cup. "Perhaps that's the problem. You should only discuss the future and the present moment most of all."

"How?" Kit glanced around the coffee house to check that

they were more or less alone. The faces around them were unfamiliar, and that eased his mind. Kit needed a friend to talk to, one who might see the solution in a logical and clear manner. Hallam was something of an intellectual man and largely discounted emotional responses. "She won't come home with me."

Hallam's brow rose at his embarrassing confession. "Then the answer is clear. You will have to go home with her."

Could it be that simple? "I won't force my way into her bed."

Hallam's lips curled in disgust and the look he sent was rather frightening. "I should hope not, but there are other ways to win her over. The solution is obvious. Take a room at the hotel where she is staying. In my experience, proximity makes the heart grow fonder. Woo her, Taverham. It worked for me with my Virginia. But don't expect the process to be quick or even easy."

Kit spluttered. That was the last thing he expected a man of Hallam's intelligence to suggest. "She is my wife already. I should hardly have to seduce her to make her understand where she belongs."

"Women belong where they choose to belong, and there's not a damn thing we *poor besotted fools* can do about it." Hallam set his cup aside.

Kit winced at hearing his complaints of yesterday repeated. "You spoke to Daventry?"

Hallam's expression turned pitying. "Didn't have to, but thank you for confirming how you view marriage for me. We've all had obstacles to overcome—most have been our own pigheaded prejudices."

That didn't make any sense. Hallam and Virginia's marriage might have startled everyone, but once known, it seemed a sensible arrangement. "What obstacles did you face?"

"Pure loathing." Hallam gestured for another coffee while Kit stared at him in shock.

That was the last thing he'd expected to hear from Hallam. The man worshiped his wife and the feeling seemed entirely mutual. What the devil had he missed?

Once Hallam had his coffee, his expression turned thoughtful. "If you ask me, you're going about this all wrong.

She left you. She won't return home with you to take up her life as your lawful wife. You cannot force her without building further anger in her and making yourself look like an ogre. This time you need to follow her and let her know why you're doing so."

"She knows I want her. I always have."

"Do you hear yourself? The woman is not a possession, you clod. She is your wife. You could be talking of a whore for all the affection in your voice. Do you understand the difference?" He leaned close. "What do you really want, anyway? A marriage like most of our generation have, cold lives lived mostly apart, or something better? Drag her home to have the marriage you planned in the first place and be miserable. Strive for something more and listen to her for a change."

In the face of Hallam's verbal challenge, Kit sank deeper into his chair as mortification struck deep. After ten years apart, perhaps it couldn't hurt to be a little more obvious about his desire to just be near Miranda and hear her speak. He thought he'd been doing that already.

He took a deep breath and let it out slowly. Maybe this time he'd have a chance to explore how deep his feelings for his wife went, but if Hallam disbelieved his intentions, then he could hardly blame Miranda for having some doubts about his motives for wanting to remain married. They'd already spoken of his need for an heir. That couldn't be put off indefinitely at their age, but perhaps the discussion had been more than a little ill timed. "I'm trying to listen. But what more can I do to convince her?"

Hallam glared. "Do I have to explain everything? What did you do the first time, before you married?"

"I..." Kit spluttered to a stop. They'd met and... His mind blanked. For the life of him, he could not remember what he'd done to win his wife. He drew out the little book he always carried, the one he used to record his goals and his successes. On the first page it said marry, but no other details. He shut the book slowly. What exactly had he done to win Miranda's hand in marriage? There wasn't even any evidence to prove he had. "I don't recall."

"I see." Hallam shook his head sadly. "A beautiful woman

with an enormous dowry just fell into your lap, and you took what was offered because you could have her. You deserve what you got then, my friend. Congratulations. You've only yourself to blame for her resistance if you don't remember the most important occasion in your lives together—meeting and getting to know her. No woman wants to think she isn't wanted for herself."

Damn. Maybe he was to blame in part, but was there a way to fix their marriage after all these years? He'd never been able to imagine marriage to anyone else. That was why he'd avoided making a decision about her absence for so long. Miranda was his wife. The only one he'd wanted once they'd spoken. "I don't see how to fix this. What do you remember most about Virginia?"

Hallam swallowed coffee. "She threw eggs at me and I didn't duck fast enough."

Kit gaped. Virginia wasn't the kind of woman he'd ever suspect of such violent behavior. "She did? Why?"

"She was fourteen and angry. I'd told her she'd be faster than Jack in a footrace if she wore breeches instead of skirts. Apparently that wasn't the compliment I meant it to be."

No, it probably wasn't. "Well, you're married now, so it's all turned out for the best."

"That wasn't the only memorable clash in our relationship, but the most important. Never underestimate what a woman will do if pushed past her limits."

He shifted in his seat. Miranda appeared to hate him now. Could he expect to dodge eggs instead of eating them? "I'll remember that."

"We had to earn our happiness. Me, Ettington, Daventry. Carrington most of all." Hallam nodded sagely. "Since you appear clueless, I'll help just this once. Here's a list since you like making them so much. Take her driving in the park, attend the theatre, a soiree if she cares for dancing. Discover what she likes, and more importantly, stop doing what she doesn't. Prove to her that her company is what you want most of all. Too late to explain you didn't want her for her dowry. I imagine the bulk was spent years ago."

Heat crept up his cheeks and he looked down at his hands.

Without Miranda's money, he'd not be where he was today. Where *they* were. Their future was secure save for lack of an heir. "I can do that."

"Put your life, and the contents of that book, aside for a while."

Kit put his little book back into his pocket. There was but one thing left to accomplish from his book of plans and he knew it by heart. *To have a son.* For that, now Miranda had returned to resume the position of his wife, he needed her participation and agreement. Kit was ill used to failure, so he latched on to Hallam's first suggestion in absolute desperation. He called the proprietor over and paid for paper and pen to scratch out two brief messages. A coffeehouse boy was dispatched to make the deliveries, and he returned to watching the front door to the modiste's shop. Anticipation built as the first hour apart drew close to completion. He needed Miranda to see his intentions were sincere. Yet for the first time, Kit feared getting what he wanted might just be at the limits of his reach.

Chapter Eleven

Miranda shifted her gaze to the man walking silently beside her. Something had changed in the past three hours, and she couldn't put a finger on what that was. Taverham seemed more thoughtful now than bossy. She'd expected more bluster and orders from him once they'd left Bond Street, where she'd requested his driver take her from shop to shop after Virginia and her husband had left them.

To see how far she could push Taverham's newfound patience, she'd run up bills all over town, most for gifts to be sent to her cousin and her brood of children. Only things they had needed and a few small treats. No greater expense than her husband might wager over a game of cards among friends. Taverham made not one complaint.

They were headed back to Mivart's Hotel now and the quiet and solitude she craved. She had so much to do yet. With Taverham hovering, she'd had no chance to meet with Martin or even decide which London square she might wish to live in. Something at a short distance from Taverham would be perfect: close enough for Christopher to visit yet far enough away that Miranda need not see her husband's comings and goings.

She had hoped he would leave her at the hotel, yet Taverham didn't appear in a rush anymore, not even to mention returning home with him once. He had become silent and watchful, and that completely unnerved her. A biddable husband she didn't know how to manage.

She stepped through the front door of the hotel, nodding to the doorman she passed and crossed the tiled floor toward the staircase. Miranda kept her gaze forward, hoping her husband would take the hint and go away. He followed a step behind. His silence was making her tense and profoundly weary. Every day without knowing where Christopher was worried her. She wanted her son desperately, but she also needed to lie down and rest her weary heart a few moments. She couldn't do that with Taverham lingering.

The proprietor hurried toward them with a welcoming smile. "Everything is in order, my lord. Welcome to Mivart's, and may we say how honored we are to have you stay with us for this visit?"

Taverham took possession of a key, one very similar to Miranda's. Her blood boiled in her veins. No wonder her husband had left off demanding her return to his London town house. The nerve of the man to move into her room without a word to prepare her for the surprise.

She continued on her way without a word, walking swiftly ahead of her husband and toward the staircase. She'd fool him; she'd leave and stay elsewhere. Maybe even scandalize the *ton* by accepting Martin's generous invitation to become his guest for the duration of her stay. She'd originally declined due to its proximity to her husband's residence and the potential to fuel harmful gossip that she was involved with Martin in a romantic way. His cousin was also in Town and that gave her pause too. She wouldn't cause problems for anyone but Taverham. There had to be another establishment that he couldn't find her in so quickly.

As she reached her door, her hands shook, but Taverham merely leaned against the wall beside her and gave her a lopsided grin. "Have supper with me this evening?"

Spending time with her husband, even for a simple meal, was not part of her plan. "You'll give me time to eat? How charitable of you."

His brow furrowed as he followed her inside. "I'll collect you at eight. The hotel boasts a private dining room, and I've made arrangements for its use."

Miranda checked the room. When she looked about, it became clear that none of Taverham's things had been moved into her room during her absence. Relieved, she dropped her reticule on her bed. Taverham shutting the door behind them gave her no satisfaction. She removed her hat and gloves, then shifted to stand before the fireplace while her pulse raced. Reluctantly, she lifted her gaze to his. "I see. And what else have you arranged?"

His smile widened, a flash of teeth that made her heart leap at the playfulness behind it, but he was still standing beside the door and she considered him no threat yet. "A bath to refresh you after your long and arduous day. The servants should arrive momentarily and will give you anything your heart desires."

A bath would be wonderful and just what she needed. But the fact that Taverham had organized it made her wary of seeming too pleased. Her gaze narrowed on him, looking for flaws and finding few besides his nature. "Will they toss you out if I ask?"

"Not a chance." His relaxed stance disappeared as he drew closer. "You came back to be seen, and I intend to see you."

"You've seen enough."

He laughed at that and reached for her hand. Although her heart clattered against her ribs, she allowed him to play with her fingertips. "I've not heard your voice and opinions anywhere near enough to be satisfied."

His head tilted a little to the side, as it would if he intended to lean in for a kiss. And yet he merely watched, fingers restlessly shifting over hers. She caught her breath and he smiled softly. Very gently, he lifted her hand and rained light kisses over her knuckles.

The warmth of his breath across her damp skin made her anxious for an entirely different reason. Her body hummed in anticipation of where he would kiss her next. And kiss her he would. He would drown her in desire before she'd realize she was thoroughly seduced.

With his head bent over her hand, Miranda's eyes flickered over the only dark hair she'd ever run her fingers through. Despite her first impression being that her husband hadn't changed, she saw tiny strands of gray peppered through the top.

They were both growing older. Too old for games and

pretense. She jerked her hand back finally, embarrassed she'd allowed him so many liberties already. She refused to let him think he was welcome in her bed.

Instead of the protest she expected, he merely shook his head somewhat ruefully and took a pace back. "Your effect on my senses hasn't changed. Until later, my wife."

He gave her another lopsided grin and turned away, heading for the door. He left it open as he stepped into the hall and crossed it. When he reached the opposite door, he inserted the key he carried into the lock and swung that door wide. Beyond, she saw signs of new and rushed occupation. Trunks were thrown open and in varying stages of being unpacked. As he was closing the door behind him, he glanced at her one more time. She saw devilry light his eyes and her heart plummeted. He was staying across the hall? She would not have believed he of all people would occupy a room in this establishment.

Miranda hurried for her door. She pushed it closed with more force than intended, and the sound was accompanied by his laughter. She leaned against the door for support, scowling. The fiend meant to dog her steps. She would make him look a fool for the assumption that he'd neatly trapped her. Her room had a daring exit she wasn't afraid to use if necessary to meet with Martin tomorrow. Taverham would never know she'd gone until it was far too late.

Chapter Twelve

Kit tapped firmly on his wife's door at Mivart's Hotel and waited, listening to the low murmur of female voices within but unable to understand any of the conversation. He glanced along the hall as a door opened farther down toward the stairs. An elderly gentleman escorted a young woman, no more than a slip of a girl really, quickly toward an exit. He smirked. Why that dirty old fellow, bedding a woman not even a quarter of his age.

Kit wished he had half the old rascal's luck when it came to his own wife.

Waiting had never been his forte, much preferring swift and decisive action to get what he wanted, so he tapped on Miranda's door again. Waiting for Miranda seemed his lot in life though, as she kept him standing at the door some few more minutes. When the door finally did open to admit him, an elfin-faced maid blinked, then squeezed past with a muttered *excuse me* as she fled down the hall.

He ignored the maid and focused on his wife, who was dressed in a gown of deepest blue, black gloves in place and not a hint of tempting flesh visible below her collarbones. Her eyes flashed with barely concealed hostility toward him. Definitely no chance that she'd softened toward him.

And yet he again found himself pulled toward her against his will. With a sudden burst of clarity, he remembered feeling exactly the same way when they had first met. At the time he'd been so certain that Miranda was meant to be his wife.

Despite the difficulties, he wasn't a fool to ignore how much he wanted her, and not just in his bed. He wanted to know why her eyes flashed with such fire when he spoke of the past and of their future together. He desperately wanted to learn where she'd been keeping herself these past years and why she wouldn't tell him of it. "Miranda. You look lovely."

"Taverham. You look the same."

He prowled toward her. "Irresistible?"

Her eyes swiftly flickered over his appearance and a smirk curled her lips. "Hardly. I'd describe you as being as pretty as the peacocks strutting the grounds of your estate if that wouldn't malign the peacocks."

He blinked at her words, taken aback by the notion his physical appearance offended her. "Pretty?"

"Well, yes. I daresay you spent more time before the looking glass than I have tonight, but then I've learned from experience that the surface only reveals part of a man's true character and cannot be swayed by elegance."

He swallowed back the retort begging to be spoken. He would not be goaded into a fight with her. If she found fault with his manner of dressing and his character now, she would have to learn to bear it. At nine and twenty, he wasn't planning to change much about his life until she gave him the time of day. He held out his arm. "Supper is waiting."

Miranda glanced at his outstretched arm and ignored it. She stepped around him and stopped only when she'd gained the hall, key in hand. Kit gritted his teeth and followed. He closed the door, held out his hand for her key with which to lock the door. Miranda bit her lip briefly then passed it over. Would every decision be a battle of wills?

When he was done, he slipped it into his pocket beside his own key as she did not carry a reticule with her. "The dining room is this way."

"I know the way. I was a guest at Mivart's Hotel long before you."

"How long have you been here?"

"A few days this time."

He absorbed that, including the idea she'd been here before.

"When were you in London last?"

"Last year when I learned of my grandfather's death. I was too late for the burial but not too late to lay wildflowers on his grave."

Thomas Birkenstock's passing had been sudden and a sad event. Kit had never won his approval, certainly not when Miranda had fled their marriage and disappeared so completely that she couldn't be found. He'd felt sorry for Agatha the most and hadn't even considered how Miranda might feel about his death.

Had Miranda missed her family, or had they kept in touch secretly all these years? He really had to know how big a fool he'd been. "Did you see your cousin, Agatha, when your grandfather died?"

Miranda slowly shook her head. "There was no need to bring further complications to her life by making myself known to her again. By all accounts she was content in Viscount Carrington's care, and I knew Lady Carrington would comfort her in her grief. Estella was always kind, and I understand they've become like mother and daughter since the marriage. My cousin did not need me."

Kit peeked at Miranda. For a woman not moving about in society, she was remarkably aware of the most important events in their circle and her family. Was Louth her only source of intelligence or were there others involved in keeping her location a secret from him?

He paused inside the dining room and glanced about the quaint hotel room set aside for private dining. The table was set with the finest the establishment had to offer, silverware and glassware gleaming beneath two candelabras set at equal distance along the oval table. Four footmen in hotel livery stood at the ready to serve them whatever their hearts desired. A large mass of crimson roses was the centerpiece he'd chosen to brighten the room and soften his wife's heart. The setting and the menu planned was as close a match to their wedding breakfast feast as it was possible to recreate at such short notice. Miranda did love roses so.

"Wonderful," he said as he smiled down on her.

Miranda sneezed and then stared ahead. "Yes, the hotel is

very keen to please their guests in every respect. I see you've recreated the dining room from your home and the wedding breakfast."

"Our home." He'd insisted the hotel arrange the room to his liking and was well pleased with the results and that Miranda remembered too. It wasn't a precise recreation, but then again the room was exactly one-third the size of his usual dining room. He wanted to give Miranda a reminder of how things would be when she came home to him.

When she went to sit, Kit waved away the footman who stepped forward eagerly to hold her chair and seated her himself. He touched her shoulder, a brief caress over the top of her gown to prove her real. He couldn't seem to help such touches and stood back quickly lest she demand he stop.

Miranda murmured her thanks to her plate.

The fact that he could unsettle her with a simple touch pleased him. He wanted Miranda to remember that she'd once lapped up every caress between them. It had been almost impossible to keep his hands to himself when they'd been courting, and more difficult now when he should be able to do so at any time he pleased.

Kit took his place at the other end of the table and signaled for the meal to commence being served before he got too far ahead of his new plan. The four footmen were sufficient for the task, and he sat back and threw a pleased smile in Miranda's direction. Almost immediately he perceived his error. As he looked along the table length, he discovered the center flower arrangement and candelabras concealed all but the tips of her elbows from his gaze. After a few frustrating minutes, Kit concluded he would have little choice but to lean to the side to speak with her. Had this happened on their wedding day? Perhaps that occasion hadn't been so perfect after all. He peered around the roses. "How do you find the soup? I hope it's to your liking."

"As excellent as always." Her gaze flickered to the footmen standing closest to her and she smiled warmly. "Do pass my compliments along to the chef and staff for their hard work tonight. The marquess may be used to such preferential treatment as an everyday event, but this is exceptional. They have outdone themselves and should be very proud."

The man stood taller, soaking up her praise. "Thank you, madam. I shall happily express your satisfaction below stairs."

Kit straightened in his chair, annoyed that Miranda gave compliments freely to servants and spoke meanly to him. It wasn't fair. This dinner was his re-creation. Didn't he deserve some praise too? He was trying to win her regard, not become an object for her to ignore. What did a husband have to do to win a genuine smile from his own wife?

When the soup course was cleared and the next served out, he realized his plan for getting closer to his wife needed adjustment. He'd moved into the hotel so as to spend more time together but had inadvertently placed further obstacles in his path when he'd organized this dinner. Dinner for two should be cozier than a normal setting allowed. There was room for two empty place settings between them. He needed to move if he wanted a chance to get to know Miranda again.

He stood and every servant froze before swiveling to stare at him. Miranda glanced at him at last, her face inscrutable in the candlelight. He gestured to his place setting and then stood back. "Move my setting to a place at my wife's side and be quick about it."

The four servants rushed to do his bidding, quick, efficient, and blessedly silent in the wake of his abrupt request. They would be talking about this strained affair for days at this rate, but what was one more rumor where his wife was concerned?

When he sat again at her side, Miranda addressed the servants behind him. "Thank you."

Kit glanced behind him too, slightly abashed that he'd overlooked speaking to them. It was Miranda's fault. Attempting to win her over unsettled him more than he'd known it would. "Yes, thank you."

Miranda reached for her water glass and sipped daintily, then returned to her meal in silence. Kit ate too, more comfortable with a clear view of his wife. She picked at her pork and ignored her full wineglass in favor of water, sniffling occasionally. Puzzled by the sniff, he leaned forward to see her face better. A single tear slipped over her pale cheek. "Are you crying?"

She scowled at him. "I have not cried in years."

Undeterred by her warning tone that he might be prying, Kit leaned closer yet. Her eyes were rimmed red and glassy bright; she twitched her nose as if it tickled. "Well, if you are not crying then what is the matter with you?"

Eventually, her gaze flickered along the table. "Roses do not agree with me. They never have."

That stunned him. "But you loved them. I had an arrangement sent to your room every day before we married, and you said not a word about disliking them."

She shrugged. "They were already present so why complain?"

Kit reared back as she succumbed to a sneeze. Why complain? Why *not* complain? A marchioness did not suffer discomfort when it could be avoided. That was one of the benefits of being a peer. He pointed to the table. "Remove all the flowers and wait outside until called."

As the footmen filed past with the large arrangements bobbing before them, Miranda sneezed again and again, dabbing at her nose and eyes as they watered horribly. When she slowly calmed from the sneezing fit, he caught her hand. "What else did you not tell me?"

"I imagine many things. You were too busy planning everything without consulting me." She jerked her hand from his grip as if he'd burned her. "There's no need to concern yourself."

He gestured to the plate and wineglass. "I take it by that you must also dislike pork and wine too."

Her nose wrinkled. "Those are recent dislikes I've not managed to conquer as yet."

He caught her hand and pulled her to her feet angrily.

Miranda steadied herself against his chest. "Must you manhandle me?"

"Oh, I have not even started." He dragged her toward the sideboard where the remainder of the meal had been placed, ready to be served. He uncovered each dish to show her. "Does anything else here displease you?"

Her glance flickered over the silver and glass dishes and she smiled. "No. I'm fond of everything there."

"Good." Kit caught her chin in his fingers and tilted her face upward. Her eyes were still irritated as he stared into them.

All of a sudden, they softened from their usual coldness and

Miranda stumbled back a step, far out of reach. "I'm fine now."

Kit wasn't so certain that was the truth, but he felt better for knowing the rest of the meal would be acceptable to her. He ushered her to her chair, called the servants back to them, and watched his wife carefully all through the meal. He didn't understand her in the least, but he knew three more facts about his wife. He would give her anything she wanted if only she spoke truthfully from her heart.

His parents had never hesitated to criticize each other's decisions and tastes in all things little and great. Their blunt honesty had been the basis for his life. Yet his parents had spent a great deal of their later years apart, which did go a long way to explaining why he was an only child. He had never wanted that for his own family.

In the back of his mind he considered what else Miranda might have omitted to tell him before their marriage. Had she really believed herself set up so she could not refuse to marry him? At the time he'd believed them a fair match when it came to their likes and dislikes. Had they only been a match in bed and then only in his mind?

Chapter Thirteen

⸻ ◆ ⸻

No matter how loathe Miranda was to admit it, there was something compelling about being more or less alone with her husband. An indefinable air about him that drew her close while her mind shrieked at her to run away before he captured her heart again and crushed it to dust. He was an enigma she couldn't help but be intrigued by. Handsome, but proud. Cold, but possessed of a cheeky, warm smile.

Where she'd imagined him furious over her absence, he expressed only mild concern now. He hadn't laid out any plans beyond sharing a meal with her, and he'd stopped delivering ultimatums.

Unless he'd decided it was a foregone conclusion where she'd spend the remains of the evening. She groaned softly under her breath.

Miranda thanked the footmen as she turned for the door to the dining room and avoided touching her husband at all costs. He seemed amused by that; the corners of his eyes creased, adding a touch of wickedness to his face.

Miranda lengthened her stride so she wouldn't have to see any more of his good looks. The evidence that he'd gone out of his way to look his best tonight when she hadn't irritated her unbearably.

"Miranda," he called and she drew to a stop like a puppet on a string outside their chambers. She hated he could still do that. She hadn't felt so under another's control in quite some time.

Kit smiled down on her. "In the absence of a drawing room, I hoped you might join me in my room for tea."

"Tea?" Surely that wasn't what he intended.

"It's already arranged. A servant will be here directly." Without waiting for a response of any kind, Taverham unlocked his bedchamber door and stood aside to let her pass.

Ahead lay a room of similar proportions to her own: a bed, chaise lounge, washstand, and countless traveling trunks stacked neatly in one corner. There were a few other pieces of furniture, but likely nothing to the luxuries found at his London home. Her husband did not normally skimp on life's little comforts, and she was surprised by how frugal he appeared today.

The only luxury appeared to be a chaise lounge without a back to rest against. Miranda didn't have one of those in her room, but it was the kind one could escape from in a hurry from almost any direction if imposed upon.

Miranda crossed the room and took a position on the edge of the chaise, closest to the empty hearth, to await the promised tea being delivered. If Taverham so much as twitched in her direction before or after that, attempting to *get his heir*, she'd bash what little brains he had with the fire poker.

She observed him discreetly as he closed the door, shutting them inside where he had control and privacy. He placed his key on the table beside the door, then laid hers beside it neatly. Miranda made note of the position of hers for later. He strolled toward her and Miranda's heart pounded fiercely. Yet he passed her, stopping at the covered window and peeking outside. "We'll have rain tomorrow."

"Certainly." Anyone with sense could tell the cloud-filled sky boded rain on the morrow. She fiddled with her glove, then scolded herself for showing nervousness around him. She wasn't afraid to refuse him his husbandly rights. He wasn't completely irresistible.

A knock on the door brought tea and a brief respite from the tension building inside her. When the servants were gone and he hadn't moved, Miranda took it upon herself to pour as if she were the hostess and tonight's meeting was an everyday event.

"Have you finished reading *Tom Jones*?"

Henry Fielding was one of her favorite authors. Christopher's too. "Yes. Many times."

"It's still my favorite. Haven't found anything to surpass it while you've been gone. Have you?"

"No." Miranda shrugged. Enjoying the same book meant little. It wasn't enough to base a marriage—a life—on when there was no hope for more.

He sighed and took a place beside her on the other side of the chaise, facing the blanketed window. Close but not so close as to invade her personal space. Her skin tingled as if he stared at her face. "You have more lines about your eyes now," he said suddenly.

Miranda stiffened at the accusation she was growing old. "So do you."

He laughed then, a bitter sound that, despite her best efforts, made her even more aware they were alone. "Yours are laugh lines, I think, rather than worry."

She faced him. "How could you know that?"

He shrugged and turned away, brushing imaginary lint from the fabric straining across his strong thighs. "What did you have to worry about? There was only you, and you knew what you were doing when you left me."

Miranda stiffened. How dare he sound hurt when he was the one at fault in their marriage? He'd thrown away any chance for happiness by keeping Emily as a mistress. "You don't know a thing about me."

He turned his head slowly, green eyes completely lacking any warmth. She shivered.

"I know I failed you somehow," he said slowly, brow furrowing. "I've spent the years since our wedding looking for some sign you existed, always fearing the worst and hoping you'd come back of your own accord, even if only to ask for your freedom. Were you happy, Miranda? Was being so far away from me what you truly needed?"

She stared at him and the urgent need for the truth glittered in his eyes. He'd looked for her and not just to drag her back to where he thought she belonged. A dull thud began in her chest and she forced a smile to her face to hide her confusion at how that pleased her. She couldn't have stayed to watch him and Lady Brighthurst together, so she'd left to save herself the misery of seeing every day what she'd lost. "So many questions."

He leaned toward her, his gaze boring into her and setting her heart racing at a mad gallop. "Would you prefer it if I didn't give a damn whether you lived or died? Answer me."

Miranda shook her head to clear away her sudden feeling she should ask for his forgiveness. It wasn't his heart that had been broken ten years ago, but hers. Actions spoke louder than words. He'd betrayed her even before the wedding breakfast's last dish was cold. "I left of my own volition, and yet circumstances gave me little choice."

"I don't understand."

"No. I doubt you would."

He drew in a deep breath. "Now that you have shown yourself to be alive, you must know I will never let you go. I will never agree to a divorce and our marriage will never be annulled. We were intimate once, and I cannot as a gentleman forget that you are already my wife in every way that matters to me."

Miranda closed her eyes. That was her one remaining fear extinguished. Returning had prevented him from declaring her dead and annulling their marriage so he might start over with another woman. A divorce after her return though could have ruined all her plans and Christopher's future. She couldn't let him know she was pleased that they would remain married. That would lead to more questions she couldn't answer. "That is for you to decide, husband," she told him, adding sadness to her voice rather than the exaltation and satisfaction she felt building inside her.

He leaned closer and his hand rose to brush against her hair gently. "I have decided. I decided long ago. I wanted you to be my wife from the moment we met, and that feeling hasn't changed. I didn't seek my freedom the moment I could because I clung to hope."

His brow creased as he continued to touch her. A thousand thoughts flittered through her mind, but the most pressing was the discovery that Kit was desperately unsure of himself. They were strangers to each other again. Married strangers, admittedly.

"Kiss me good night, Miranda."

Miranda swallowed. A kiss wasn't part of her plan. There was no need to encourage him when she wouldn't fall into his bed again. He had his heir, yet didn't know it. Miranda turned her face away and the fingers ghosting over her hair firmed. Could she tell him of Christopher now and be believed?

Kit turned her face back to his and closed the distance between them.

The first brush of his lips was soft. Tentative. When Miranda would have drawn back, he wouldn't let her. He pulled her tighter against him, his fingers digging into her hair, but not brutally. His lips hovered beside hers and his warm breath panted across them. "Another kiss won't hurt you after the many we've shared."

Except Miranda remembered the power of his kisses. They made her forget herself and all thoughts of any sense. She met his gaze reluctantly and swore under her breath. If she ran now, he would know she wasn't as immune to him as she'd hoped to be after so long apart.

But if she stayed and gave in, he would think he'd won.

Retaining the upper hand in their marriage was vital. He would not be the one to dictate the terms of their intimate encounters if she couldn't avoid them. A kiss was a kiss, unless she allowed it to be more.

Daringly, Miranda leaned forward to kiss Kit first, hoping to prove to herself that she could withstand his magnetism.

As their lips touched, a thousand suppressed emotions swirled and fought for prominence in her mind.

Need—possessive, raw, and unflinching—brought out her aggression. She hungered for him, cradled his head too, and possessed his mouth as if not a day had passed since their last kiss.

Anger that she could not hold on to the feeling came next. Taverham wasn't a faithful man by any stretch of the imagination. He would never want only her and would break her heart if she let him. She would not be a victim again. What was she thinking to believe his lies? He would not have given her a second thought after she'd left except to curse her for not giving him the son he needed. A child he would rip from her arms the moment he could and refuse to give her one say in the child's upbringing. By leaving, she had not allowed that to happen, and Miranda was proud of that fact.

To show him what he'd missed, taunt him with what he'd thrown away, Miranda forced Kit down on the chaise until he lay helpless beneath her.

A tactical mistake.

His arms closed about her, holding her tightly against his body until his warmth penetrated her gown. In her desire to best him, she'd forgotten that Kit was rarely helpless. His lips devoured hers despite his seemingly weak position. His tongue slipped between her parched lips, possessive and hungry for victory. Miranda held his shoulders tightly, aware that their legs had aligned even while she shifted over him restlessly, unable to help herself. She imitated the intimacies they'd shared before their marriage, and she couldn't remain still. He was her husband. Her lover once. Her body remembered how he felt and acted of its own accord.

He groaned once then flipped them over until Miranda lay beneath him. His weight bore down on her, pinning her beneath him where she hadn't been in so long. He stared into her face until Miranda's grew hot.

"My wife," he whispered. He kissed her again while his fingers caressed her face. The soft touch frightened her because it muddled her mind and made her forget what she was here to do.

She pushed against his chest to gain some space. "That was more than one good-night kiss."

Chest heaving, Kit appeared ready to devour her but smiled at her observation. Miranda wriggled beneath him, noting he was aroused and hard against her sex. He did not draw back his hips and give her space.

His eyes softened and he grinned wickedly. "And yet less than one kiss for each day of our marriage. I mean to claim them all, Miranda. Everywhere I can."

He dipped his head to the side and his lips caressed the sensitive skin of her throat. The tender kiss forced a gasp from her lips. Kit had always kissed her in the strangest places and made her senses fly high from the experience. Once he'd spent half an hour kissing her elbow and claimed the act and watching

Miranda attempt to squirm away on the bed had excited him.

Miranda allowed her hand to slide from his shoulder to his waist. The muscles beneath her fingers flexed as he rubbed against her body. Kit could always make her enjoy every touch and sensation. He'd clearly not forgotten how to excite her best.

Miranda arched her back as he lightly nipped at her throat. She groaned helplessly and slid her hand beneath his coat, pressing his body closer to hers. Burning warmth scorched her fingers and her skin everywhere they touched.

Kit shifted, his hand wriggling between them urgently. Warmth and his firm touch cupped over her quim.

"That's not a kiss," she gasped.

His chuckle against the damp skin of her neck gave her gooseflesh all over. "It could be. Eventually."

He wriggled lower. His breath skimmed her collarbone, continuing the shivers that assailed her. His lips followed, and then he attempted to slip her gown lower, though he was thwarted by the modest design. He pressed a hard kiss to the apple of her shoulder through the material.

Miranda struggled not to feel desire, but with her husband worshiping her body so tenderly it was easy to forget he'd betrayed her. Desire was one thing she'd never doubted he'd felt for her, but an unequal marriage to him would only cause her pain.

Knowing she had to end this unexpected reminder of their past, Miranda shoved hard against him.

He released her but hovered over her. His expression when their eyes met was stubborn. "I will make you want to be my wife again."

Miranda scurried out from beneath him, slid farther along the chaise so they didn't touch any longer. Kit's chest heaved and the look he sent her brought out new panic. Would he allow her to end it or force his husbandly rights?

She hadn't meant things to go so far, but she definitely didn't want to grant him victory. Miranda shot up from the chaise and backed some distance away from him. "Good evening."

"No, Miranda, it certainly is not looking to be very good at all. You've become a tease." He drew in a deep breath, then made himself comfortable on the chaise, lounging on one side as he smirked at her. Her eyes slid to his groin helplessly. The fabric of his trousers strained at the seams. He chuckled softly. "Just so we are clear about what happened, I didn't force myself on you. I waited for you to come to me, and I'm certain now it will happen again."

Miranda gaped at him. He was right. He had goaded her to take control of the situation and in doing so retained control himself. She spun for the door, slapped her hand over her own key, and stormed from his room. Beast. Bastard.

"Sweet dreams, Miranda," he called.

She'd prove to him how weak he was too. She just needed time and Christopher's presence to bring him to his knees.

"They will be."

Chapter Fourteen

———◆———

Kit rolled onto his side and stared at the door of his hotel bedchamber, which he was currently occupying alone. After a restless night, he'd woken early with a feeling of loss so intense he couldn't breathe. He'd been dreaming of Miranda, her teasing smile as they'd made love had filled his heart with unmistakable warmth, but then she'd been ripped away.

Though he'd looked for her in the dream, he'd found no trace, much as he had ten years ago when he'd searched in vain in every ditch and pond on his estate. The similarities between the dream and reality were horribly blurred after last night's promising encounter.

The one thing he knew beyond a shadow of a doubt was that he needed to see Miranda. Immediately.

He stumbled from the bed, threw on what clothing he could find, and eased his door open, little caring what he looked like should anyone walk past. At this hour, the hotel guests should still be sleeping anyway. Luckily for them, the hallway was deserted and they would be spared his less-than-decent appearance.

He crossed the hall and pressed his ear to the wood of Miranda's door.

Not a sound could be heard within. He tested the handle and found the door locked still. She was likely sleeping, unlike him. Perhaps Miranda was not plagued by any doubts stemming from her desertion and return and the possibilities running through his mind after last night's wild kisses. He wished he could make her see that their marriage didn't have to be an endless battle. Before she'd disappeared, he'd been content. Optimistic even.

As he turned away, he heard the faint scrape of a window rattling. He smiled. Miranda was awake but ignoring him. He tapped lightly on the door, eager to see her even if she only scowled and tried to pretend she didn't know every inch of his body intimately. He would not let her do that forever. A woman of her passionate nature couldn't deny her impulses forever, but he would do as Hallam suggested and properly woo his own wife and let any intimacies happen as they may. Surely it would not be that hard to make her remember what might have been had she stayed with him.

When she did not immediately answer the door to his knock, or even tell him to go away, he tried again, knocking a little louder this time in case she had not heard him.

Still nothing.

Could she not see that gossip of any public disputes would follow them for years? It was bad enough to have abandoned him years ago, but to come back and then snub him still would only make things worse for the family reputation. Would he have to wake the whole hotel to have her open the door to him again?

He glanced along the corridor as a maid hurried down the hall in his direction, bucket and cloth in her hands to begin cleaning. At her hip hung a set of keys, jingling softly with each step as she moved toward him. Luck was with him at last.

He pointed to the door. "Open this."

"Oh no, sir, I may not. It's against the hotel's rules. Mr. Mivart would surely end my employment for entering a guest room without invitation."

Damn rules. He thought quickly. "This is important. I heard a noise, a cry for help perhaps, and fear the lady has fallen and hurt herself."

The maid's eyes widened and she rushed to find the right key. As soon as the girl turned the lock, Kit was inside Miranda's room, wildly triumphant.

Yet Miranda was not in her bed, beneath it, or hidden behind the dressing screen. She'd gone. *Again.*

He glanced around and inspected the chamber more carefully. Her bed had been slept in, her nightgown lay neatly across her pillow. He picked up the matronly garment and crushed it in his fist. Her remaining clothing resided in much the same place as yesterday, trunks and hatboxes stacked in the corner. But the lady had vanished into thin air.

He frowned, puzzled by how she'd managed to depart the hotel without him hearing her door open and close. Then he remembered the window rattle and groaned. When he inspected it, he discovered the window unlatched and a set of rickety stairs crisscrossing the rear of the building, guaranteeing her a discreet escape route. No wonder she'd chosen a room unfit for a woman of her station.

He cursed and thrust his head out the window, studying the filthy lane below. Just then, a black carriage turned out of the lane and merged with the traffic on the nearest cross street.

"Damn that woman to hell and back." He spun about and met the maid's horrified gaze.

"Did she fall? Oh. Oh dear. Mr. Mivart always worries a guest will fall down those stairs. But the lady specifically asked for this room, even though it isn't the best Mivart's has to offer. She was ever so nice to me. A real lady. Let me dress her hair too and never worried how long I took."

Kit pinched the bridge of his nose as the girl waxed lyrical about how kind and gracious his wife had been during her short stay. She'd thoroughly won the girl over and had used her time to get to know the hotel well. No wonder Miranda had smiled at the idea of seeing him this morning. She hadn't planned to be here and wanted him to look a fool. "What's your name, girl?"

"April, sir. On account I was born in December." She blushed. "Madame said she wished she'd thought of that."

Kit shook his head at the logic of the lower classes. He would not allow Miranda to name their child in such a way when they finally had one. He studied the girl. Clean, but talkative. Miranda clearly didn't travel with staff but for the one large fellow who was likely with her now. This girl was all he had to work with. "Do you like working for Mivart's?"

"Yes, sir." She looked at the door quickly. "Mr. Mivart's a fair employer to everyone."

Kit heard her words but didn't believe her for one moment. She was saying what was expected to a guest of the hotel. She had a harried look about her even though it was so early in the day. Surely meeting the needs of one would be better than working for many. "How would you like a new position?"

She drew back, staring at him as if he had three heads. "I'm not like that."

He laughed and gestured to the room. "My wife is in need of a personal maid, and since the two of you are already acquainted I see no need to look any further afield."

"Me, work for her?" The girl clutched her hand to her chest. "Me mum isn't going to believe I could be so lucky. She'll think I made it up."

"Not once you've been paid. In advance." He dug a coin from his pocket and held it out, pleased when she snatched it up quickly. At least the girl was enthusiastic. "Well, there is much to do first. I want my wife's possessions packed back into her trunks and ready to be transported within the hour."

"Where is she going?"

Determination filled him. "Home. My valet will give you the particulars when he and several footmen come to the door to collect everything."

April peered at him. "You're not a regular husband are you?"

"What do you mean by regular?"

The maid looked him over critically. "You've deeper pockets than most and servants to order about. Most of our guests don't have houses in London so they have to stay here instead. Are you really Mrs. Reed's husband or trying to trick me? I'm a good girl."

Kit shook his head and ran his hands through his hair, almost ripping it out. "She never even bothered to use her bloody title once, did she?"

The maid backed away as his voice rose and he worked to keep his temper in check.

"My wife, Miranda Reed, is the until-now-absent Marchioness of Taverham. I am the marquess. What money we have is our business. Now, do you want the position or not?"

April nodded with great excitement. "I do."

"Then pack her things and your own, say farewell to Mr.

Mivart, and be prepared to devote all your energy to making my wife happy. At least one of us must have a chance to do so." He muttered the last one bitterly, then spun on his heel and marched for the door.

If Miranda had no love for the title her dowry had bought her, then why the devil had she married him in the first place?

In the hall he encountered his valet, returned from Twilit House with a new shirt, waistcoat, jacket, and other things splayed over his arm for him to wear today. "Change of plans. We're going home. Pack everything and introduce yourself to my wife's new maid, April. I didn't catch her last name, but she's in there. She'll be returning with you, and after working here will likely need guidance on how the house runs in the beginning."

The valet's eyes widened but he wisely held his tongue, which was a good thing because Kit was in no mood to explain himself further. He found the proprietor, settled his debt and his wife's, and extracted a promise from Mr. Mivart not to rent Miranda another room no matter how much she pestered him. He also advised the man to find a new maid, and quit Mivart's in a mood so foul he hoped not to meet with anyone he knew.

So much for getting a chance to know his wife again and putting her needs first. If she'd stand still he'd have a chance. Was divorce, as everyone suggested, the only way he'd be happy?

He shook aside the idea as the carriage stopped before his home. Divorce was unthinkable. He and Miranda simply needed time to figure things out.

He took the stairs two at a time and found his mother still abed but awake and reading the daily scandal sheet. "Mother."

Her eyes narrowed and then her gaze flickered to the empty air at his side. "Still no luck?"

"None."

His mother shrugged and turned the page. "As I expected."

Kit glared. She could at least try to be sympathetic, but concern had never been his mother's way. "Miranda will be home today."

Her brow rose as she glanced at him around the paper's edge. "Will there need to be an abduction to go along with that claim?"

"Of a sort. Her possessions will be here shortly."

"Ah." His mother's lips curved into a satisfied smile. "Now

that is what you should have done from the start. Give her no choice but to come to heel."

Kit bristled. He'd never much cared for the way his mother spoke of Miranda when they were alone. He'd hoped this time she might mind her tongue, but clearly she wasn't above flaying his wife for her abandonment. "Miranda will return soon, and I would like your promise to make her feel welcome."

"I put myself out once for no good reason and will not do so again. A pity she came back. Lady Brighthurst is much more reliable when it comes to keeping one company. At my age, I have no need of new acquaintances or the renewal of old and distressing ones." Her glance flittered over his rumpled appearance, eyes narrowing in disapproval. "And neither do you it seems. Have you spent the night in a hell?"

"No."

"Then you need a new tailor. Go put something on befitting your station. That gel has always had a lowering effect on your consequence."

He suddenly understood some of Miranda's reluctance to return home with him. After all the good Miranda's dowry had done them, his mother continued to speak so dismissively of someone who'd saved them from the prospect of a difficult future. He still remembered how matters had stood upon his inheritance. His father had run the estate to the brink of ruin. If not for Miranda's dowry, there would be no new suits from his tailor, and his mother would not have led so comfortable a life these past years. When she continued scorching his ears over Miranda, his blood boiled.

"Mother! Enough. Miranda might be in the wrong to have left me, but that problem is ours. I will get to the bottom of the strife without any assistance from you. You will do nothing to offend Miranda. She is my wife and marchioness. Whatever troubles we have are not for you to stick your nose in."

Her gaze grew flinty. "Well if that is the case, then I believe I shall return to Twilit Hill."

Kit sighed in relief. Without Mother here there would be one less source of friction to deal with. For both of them. "That is an excellent idea. Thank you."

Mother looked startled a moment before she calmly folded

the paper and set it aside. "Next week. I shall of course greet your wife properly today and see what she has made of herself. Reports say she is quite unremarkable still. I don't know what you ever saw in her."

Kit almost groaned aloud. He'd heard of her dowry first, but the rest of her was equally as attractive to him upon introduction. "As you wish."

The dowager shook her silver head. "Miranda will be woefully out of touch with what matters. I suppose I will have to *show her the ropes* again."

Something that Hallam had suggested finally made sense. Women chose where they wanted to be and how they would live. Once he'd urged Miranda to follow his mother's advice without question and that suggestion might have been another factor to turn her against him. This time round he would do things much simpler. He would have to learn to trust Miranda's judgment if he wanted to make this marriage work.

"Mother," Kit interrupted. "Miranda is no longer a new bride nor a young woman without the wits to hold her own in society. She will make her own decisions anyway and decide how to go on without interference, yours or mine. You will not need to take her under your wing."

His mother slapped her hand on the paper. "You would let her ruin us. Drag our name further through the muck and insist we give her leave to do so?"

"She saved us once and cannot ruin anything else. Things must change now she is back. Perhaps for the better. I will devote my time to seeing her restored to her rightful place as my marchioness. After all, this is her home and I would like her to be at ease here."

"And if she parades her lovers beneath your nose and humiliates you beneath your own roof, will that be to your liking too? I suppose then you'll eventually want to cry on my shoulder and curse the day you married her."

Crying on his mother's shoulder was so ludicrous he laughed. He'd been raised by servants and only been presented to his parents once a week when he'd been a boy, twice if he'd misbehaved. "I'd never dare do something so vulgar."

Her gaze grew troubled. "She will have had lovers. Women of

her background always do."

Kit did not want to think about that, not when he held suspicions about a friend's loyalty in the back of his mind. If Miranda had taken lovers he wouldn't like it, but he'd put a stop to her affairs one way or another until he had his heir. "Just as many ladies of rank do, as you well know," he mused.

Her gaze turned pitying. "Just don't complain when she leaves you for another man again. The woman is as flighty as they come. I cannot contemplate why she should come back now of all times. You were just about to start over."

"I am married to Miranda and look forward to being her husband." He met her gaze directly. "Just so there can be no misunderstandings between us, I am not sorry to see Miranda again. I once liked her very much."

His mother's face turned a startling shade of pink. "Please, share your delight in your wife with someone else. My sympathy is with Lady Brighthurst. She's devastated by Miranda's return."

"Why? Emily is our friend."

"But you would have married her if not for Miranda." His mother protested. "How can you be so unfeeling toward her?"

Not Mother too. Kit folded his arms across his chest. "Even if Miranda had not come back, I assure you I would never have married Lady Brighthurst."

His mother clucked her tongue. "Of course you would have. You know your duty to the family. Lady Brighthurst was the wife you were destined to have all along, even if she did not have a dowry large enough to please your guardians. I've been grooming her to take over from me for years now."

That was startling news to him. He would never marry Emily. He'd never considered it, even before he'd met Miranda. "That is where you are wrong. Emily and I understand each other. We are no more than friends. That is all we will ever be to each other. I've no patience for your ridiculous and far-fetched notions, madam. Do excuse me."

Kit might find his mother's insistence he was destined to marry Emily mildly alarming, but he had more important matters to occupy his thoughts: how to woo his wife and keep her satisfied so she might not look for affection with another man.

Chapter Fifteen

———◆———

"This is the place," Martin assured her, but his disapproving expression spoke volumes.

Miranda slid toward the doorway of the carriage, her heart racing eagerly in hope. They had searched the area for hours since dawn's rays had first lightened the great city. Taverham's extravagant pin money loosened the tongues of all they met. This was where Mr. Fenning was last known to be according to their enquiries, although he moved from place to place constantly as work came and went, or so they'd deduced.

Martin held out his hand to assist her from the carriage. Miranda joined him on the street, looking up at the shabby building's windows, in search of her son's face peeking out. Fenning had taken rooms in a run-down boarding house that made Miranda's skin crawl and her eyes fill with tears. To think he'd brought her son here and not come up with better made her furious and equally guilt-ridden too.

She was to blame for this.

Once inside, the staircase creaked underfoot alarmingly as they moved upward, unopposed and unseen. Landry and the other fellow Miranda had hired as help took up positions on either side of the door where Miranda believed Fenning resided.

The door to Fenning's chamber hung poorly from the hinges, and when Martin hammered on it, the wood rattled wildly as if in danger of splintering apart. That door had no hope of keeping dangerous men out, and Miranda's concern grew. If any great evil had befallen Fenning or her son while they'd been here, she didn't know what she'd do.

Inside, heavy footfalls drew closer and when the door did open, she barely recognized Fenning. His hair needed trimming and his shirt collar hung open without cravat or neck cloth to lend even a little respectability. His unstarched shirt draped across his thin chest, which spoke of horrible poverty and dissipation. He'd not dressed for company, and it was clear to Miranda how bad his straits were.

Martin pushed his way inside and Miranda followed, leaving the servants at the door to ensure their privacy for the conversation.

"Mr. Fenning."

"Oh, God," Fenning groaned as he backed away from Miranda, tumbling over fallen chairs and discarded shoes. "You found me."

"Of course I would find you." She looked around at the debris littering the tiny room. Enough empty wine bottles to make her uneasy lay abandoned in all parts of the room. A padded chair had been tipped against the wall, and a mouse peeked at her from beneath papers and scurried away again into the cold hearth. She took a deep breath to stifle her scream. "I understand an accident befell your house some time ago and that coming to London was unavoidable."

"Yes, my lady. I had no choice but to seek other work."

"I see." Miranda righted a chair that appeared sound and gingerly sat in it. "And did you not consider returning to your employer?"

"I couldn't." Fenning shook his head violently. "Bad things would happen if I did that. I couldn't go against them."

Miranda gasped. "Against whom?"

Fenning covered his mouth and glanced toward the door anxiously. After a moment his shoulders slumped. "Guess it doesn't matter much anymore. Don't know who they were. Never saw them before or since, but they were a rich pair. Determined to flush out the boy. I had to pretend I didn't know the boy but it didn't matter what I said."

Miranda leaned forward. "A pair? Describe them."

"Woman as pretty as a picture. Man who'd likely never worked a day in his life." Fenning drew in a deep breath as tears slipped over his grubby cheeks. "Paid me ten guineas to set the fire and step outside. I refused of course, but they had a pistol aimed at me and I had no choice in the end."

"What?" Miranda gasped. "No. No. No."

Fenning shook his head quickly. "Oh no, Master Christopher wasn't killed in the fire. Clever child. Heard it all and knew what to do without a word from me. I saw him slip out a back window and flee into the nearby trees before the fire truly caught hold. Didn't find him till morning though, long after the swells had gone. I was about to give up when he came up to me and told me we were bound for London."

Miranda set her hand to her chest as relief slammed into her. "Well, I'm here now to take him back."

Mr. Fenning's skin paled and he hugged himself. "I wish you'd not found me."

When Martin moved to stand behind her and settled his large hands lightly on her shoulders, Miranda's heart began truly to race. The room was too small for her not have heard him. "And why is that?"

"I don't have him anymore. He ran away."

A scream bubbled in her throat and Martin's grip tightened, effectively holding her in place and curbing her hysteria. It was too much. She broke away from Martin's touch and curled over as unbearable pain filled her chest. Her worst fears had come true. She should never have been persuaded to part with her son.

Martin's hand smoothed over her back as he questioned Fenning over Christopher's disappearance.

Fenning's chair scraped and she looked up quickly. The fellow sat across from her like a naughty schoolboy, hands pinched between his thighs and a mournful expression on his face. "Came to London after the fire as the boy wanted. He said it was safer to be one of many than sticking out like a boil in the quiet countryside, but I'd lost almost everything to the fire. Had some money so I wasn't desperate at first. I left a note behind, which he was sure you would return to collect."

Miranda nodded as dismay filled her, numbing her senses until she couldn't do more than sit and listen.

"Everything was fine for a few weeks. Had a nice place, food, and tricked my way into a good position because the man's daughter fancied me. I thought it was going well until one Sunday a month after our arrival. I turned my back for just a moment and then found myself alone."

Miranda sobbed, and her body swayed of its own accord despite Martin's attempt to contain her movements.

"Breathe, Miranda," Martin begged, but her chest burned with pain and her eyes filled with tears. "It's not the end of the world," he promised. "Calm down."

"How can I be calm?" She stared hard at Fenning, hating that they had all failed. "He lost Christopher. He almost got my son killed and now he's lost him too?"

Mr. Fenning swallowed and he looked near to tears too. "I didn't lose him, my lady. I swear to you," he insisted. "The boy up and ran away. He stepped out of the carriage we were traveling in with only a few pennies in his pocket. I thought he was happy with me. I thought coming to London was what he wanted."

Martin left her side and leaned close to Mr. Fenning. "Explain where you lost the child and do not leave one thing out. Start with where you were that day."

"Near St. George's. We'd just come back from taking a peek at Asterly's. The young master insisted on seeing all the sights of London from the start and was having a grand time. I indulged him because he looked more excited than I'd ever known him to be."

Miranda pictured her son, barely nine years old and seeing London for the first time and then shook away the vision as tears toppled down her cheeks. "Do not think to blame my son for this disaster. He was your responsibility."

"Begging your pardon, Lady Taverham, but the boy told me what to do and never the other way round. He's very clever at getting people to do what he wants."

Martin threw an annoyed glance in her direction. "Much like his father."

Miranda shifted, thinking of her husband's determined nature of late. "So it seems. Despite keeping them apart, you suggest temperament is the result of parentage rather than upbringing."

Fenning nodded. "Maybe you shouldn't have told him he was

bound to be a marquess one day. He's unlike any child I've ever tutored before. Bright, resourceful. Willing to work hard to achieve his goals. He's got an air of command about him, no matter where he is. I've had time to think about it, and it is my belief he didn't take his decision to leave me lightly. He was always cautious around strangers, even more so after the fire. We were in London a month, had covered many sites and neighborhoods before he vanished."

If that were true, what on earth had Christopher been thinking? He knew Miranda expected him to be with his tutor and not to attempt to return to his father until absolutely necessary and she was with him to prove who he was. The fact that Kit remained unaware of their child's existence so far hinted Christopher had not made his way to his father's house and was now lost somewhere in London. She couldn't believe this was happening.

Martin turned from Fenning and patted her shoulder. "Let us hope the traits he inherited from his father have kept him safe," he added grimly.

Fenning leaned forward suddenly. "My lady, I promise you I did search for him. For six months if I wasn't working, I prowled the district where he left me, in search of some sign he lived. I even enquired at your grandfather's abode, circumspectly of course, and had no success there."

The weight on Miranda's chest grew heavier.

The secrecy she had covered her son's existence with was a double-edged sword. Few in her current life knew of her son's existence. Martin had not even seen Christopher since he was a babe in arms. She didn't have the faintest idea where he would have gone if he had in fact chosen to do so of his own free will.

Martin eased her up from the chair and placed his arm around her back to support her first steps. "Remaining here will gain us nothing more. I am certain Mr. Fenning has told us all he can by the sound of it. He can make his way back to his family by the stage tomorrow if he'd prefer. I must get you back to where you belong now."

"And where do I belong without my son?"

Desolate, Miranda allowed Martin to place her, unresisting, into the carriage and order the driver to take them away, back toward Mivart's Hotel and the cold comfort of her memories and the few things she'd tucked away in her traveling trunks. That was all she'd had of Christopher for the past two years. Mementoes and keepsakes of a happier life.

But it wasn't enough if she couldn't have her son too.

She needed his laugher in her ears and his smiles to light her days.

Once the carriage began to move, the tears began to fall and she couldn't hold them back. Her son was lost. Martin passed her a large handkerchief, then caught up her hand and squeezed it tightly. "You belong with your husband. It's time to go home."

"I cannot go without Christopher at my side."

Martin chafed her hand. "Today's the first time since your return that you've said the boy's name."

"Christopher is never far from my thoughts. Saying his name causes me great pain. I have missed him dreadfully." She brushed tears from her eyes and fought for breath to speak. "I don't think I will ever forgive myself if he's lost forever. Who do you think came to Fenning's door two years ago? Who could want to harm Christopher?"

"I don't know. Maybe Taverham found him."

Miranda shook her head immediately. "No. I'm sure he has no idea about Christopher. He wouldn't want me to come home so badly if he thought he had an heir. He wouldn't need me."

Despite the impropriety, Martin put his arm around her and she sobbed even harder. He rocked her gently until she pulled herself together and set herself away from him. "I'm sorry."

"It's quite all right. Do you not think that taking your place as Lady Taverham in society might bring the boy to you? It seems clear to Fenning that Christopher left of his own accord."

Miranda had told Christopher time and again that she would not return to the Taverham estates without him. Now she might have no choice because she couldn't think of another option at this moment. Christopher was bright. If he read of her return in the newssheets, surely he would try to reach her if he could. "There is hope in what you suggest. I'll pack tonight." She shook her head. "Taverham must remain in the dark though about why I've chosen to return to live under his roof."

"Are you sure that is wise? He is better placed to search for him."

Miranda dabbed at her eyes. "He will never believe Christopher is his if I just say he exists."

Martin patted his pocket. "I do have these letters as proof too. He'd be a fool to dismiss the claims of his own former guardians when they were the ones who watched over you from the day after you married."

Miranda bit her lip. The Earls of Applebee, Sorenson, and Watts were the most devious lords she'd ever been acquainted with. Alternatively kind and ruthless, the trio of crusty bachelors had at first grudgingly conspired with her to help her temporarily escape her marriage and her hurt. By sheltering her in their own homes, places her husband would never willingly visit, they had taken on the role of doting uncles since her own father cared nothing for her distress. But when it became obvious some months later that she carried Taverham's child, a fact they'd never doubted, they had embraced the roles as substitute family completely. When she'd gone into labor, they had even remained to witness the event despite protests that it wasn't proper. "Have you seen them?"

"From time to time." Martin grimaced. "They don't have the child in their care, I'm sure of that. They would have said something about him to me if they did, brought the boy back to you since you were finally on the mend, or to Taverham himself. They're meddlers, not monsters."

Kit would not be pleased his guardians had kept her location and Christopher's existence a secret all these years either.

She shook her head restlessly. "The letters are meaningless without Christopher standing right there in front of Taverham to claim his place. But where has he gone? I've no doubt Applebee, Sorenson, and Watts would swear it to the king himself that the boy was Taverham's son and heir, but that means nothing without Christopher. I cannot tell him until our son is found."

Martin stretched out his legs. "You play a dangerous game. I don't think Taverham will forgive you the deception easily."

"I never thought he would. The only thing that has ever mattered is Christopher's happiness." She shrugged. "What happens between myself and Taverham is inevitable."

Chapter Sixteen

---◆---

Silence could be a comfort or pain. Today's silence proved to be the latter. It was almost eight o'clock and Miranda had still not returned to Twilit House to berate him for the theft of her few possessions. He poured another whiskey and swallowed it in one gulp. In truth, Kit was beyond disappointed. As the hours progressed, his hope was fading and he'd begun to worry for her well-being instead.

Despite their unresolved separation, he couldn't seem to stop feeling concern for her. She had not returned to the hotel at midday. She had not even returned by the fashionable hour. No one had laid eyes on her since the night before when they'd left the dining room and gone to his hotel bedchamber. *He* was the last person to see Miranda before she'd fled from him and desire.

He glanced outside at the darkened skyline and fretted over where she was now, and more importantly who'd collected her from the lane behind the hotel that morning.

"Better you give up than look any more the fool," Lord Acton advised as he joined Kit at the sideboard and poured himself a refill. "Looks like the lady has vanished again."

Acton sounded so sure she wouldn't come back, as he had been all along through the empty years of Kit's marriage. Kit continued to stubbornly cling to hope. But could he do that for the rest of his life?

"She will come." She had to. He had all her clothes. Everything she owned. A surprisingly small amount for a marchioness. When his mother traveled, a second carriage had always been required just to transport her clothing. "Supper is not late until nine o'clock."

"As you say," Lord Acton said, a look of irritation passing over his face as he glanced about the room, his gaze settling on the ticking clock. "I suppose we must put our lives on hold until her arrival then, as we have done these last dozen years. Care to play cards while we wait?"

"It was only ten. Ten years, ten months, and a handful of days." Kit knew the number by heart, and even understanding that their estrangement had halted, he was still so anxious he could barely keep still. He wouldn't rest again until Miranda was beneath his roof, sleeping in one of his beds, preferably his own, though he would not force that issue. Perhaps he'd have to go so far as to fetch her from Mivart's himself. Was she sitting there stubbornly on the front steps as staff tried to shoo her away?

He shook his head to clear that image away. Surely Miranda couldn't be that mulish, but he had to acknowledge that her mind was very much a mystery to him. "I think not. You'll only line your pockets with the spoils of my distraction."

Acton smiled and looked over at his sister. "There was that bonus for me."

Emily, ever the peacemaker, glared at her brother in disapproval even while she wrung her hands. "Everett, behave yourself. Can you not see Kit is beside himself for his wife's disobedience? This will be all settled tonight and then we need not think of it again."

Acton patted her hand. "Let us hope you are right, but can you not imagine a better distraction than watching Taverham lose so completely to me?"

She shot him a warning look. "Bend your mind to swindling funds from some other source; pick someone you dislike rather than a friend. Perhaps Kit would be kind enough to show us the book he offered to explain more of the other day. I find Italy fascinating and cannot wait to travel."

Kit groaned. "Forgive me. Showing you the book entirely slipped my mind. You are both so keen to travel, but I am afraid our plans for next year must be put off. I'll get it at once."

Acton groaned loudly and shook his head.

Emily shot to her feet, eyes wide. "We're not going now because of *her*?"

"How can I?"

Emily's face fell and Kit winced. She of all of them had been most looking forward to their adventure, a delayed grand tour for Kit, but Acton and Emily's first opportunity to leave England's shores too. She moved toward him, her face switching from desolation to acceptance quickly. "I'd be happy to accompany you to the library. Will you join us Everett?"

Her brother smiled and arched a brow. "No, I'll stay here and wait for Kit's mother so I can tell her the latest development. I trust you two not to misbehave while you're alone."

Kit laughed. "No danger of that."

He waited for Emily to gather up her shawl and precede him from the room. Once in the hall, she wrapped her arm through his and sighed. "The trip would have been just the thing for us. You've been very upset of late."

"Forgive me. Miranda's return has me at sixes and sevens." He patted her hand. "We'll muddle through."

Once inside the library, she lifted her face to his. "I apologize for Acton. He is terrible at waiting around on most days, and you know he finds your lack of action concerning your wife unfathomable."

"Don't I know it? He's no patience for waiting for anything, least of all my wife." Kit chuckled. "I hate even attending the races with him. Barely possible to gather one's winnings before he's off to look over the next pretty filly, but it is entirely different when one waits for one's wife."

"My brother's eye does rove quite a bit." She smiled shyly. "I cannot understand what keeps her from you. If you were my husband, I'd never let you go."

Kit sighed wearily and released Emily's arm. "I thought she'd be here long before this. I did take all her clothes and possessions from the hotel."

"And what did you discover among her belongings?"

He shook his head. "Nothing. A maid packed and unpacked for her. I've no idea what Miranda owns beyond the few gowns I saw her wear these past days or what she purchased yesterday."

"Whyever not?" Her shawl slipped from one shoulder as she shrugged, revealing a low-cut gown that showed a great deal more of her cleavage than she likely intended. "Are you not in the least bit curious about her life? You said she lives very spartanly. A man in your position would be undoubtedly curious about what items of importance travel with her. Any letters she kept could tell you a great deal about her character now."

She smiled and rested her hip against a tabletop, her manner changing to boldly provocative in the blink of an eye. Kit moved away from Emily, disturbed at how uncomfortable he felt in her presence. They had been alone many times in his life and never once had he been truly tempted by his widowed friend and neighbor.

Was his mother right that Emily had expected he would pursue her once he was free of his marriage? Was society gossip that they were involved based on Emily's secret hope for more between them?

Kit dug his finger into his cravat as unaccustomed nervousness filled him, and he eyed the door longingly. "I would never violate Miranda's trust by going through her possessions without her permission. I never cared for my mother's when I was a lad. She will confide in me in due course."

Emily frowned and straightened again, drawing closer. "If Miranda does not come tonight, you would be well within your rights to be sure her behavior brings no further shame." Emily circled him before she looked about the room as if for listeners. "I could peek for you and no one would know but us. Besides, you need to know if her character is still suitable to be your marchioness. For that you would need some sort of evidence should you wish to petition for divorce."

Kit pressed his lips together. Divorce again, and from a source he'd never suspected would consider that an option for him. He'd thought Emily had understood that he wanted Miranda as he'd never wanted another woman in his life. He shook his head. His mother might be entirely correct in that Emily had assumed a closer relationship was possible between them without Miranda in the way.

He met Emily's gaze firmly, hoping she understood his wishes clearly by what he said next. "If I didn't attempt to declare

Miranda dead before she returned, then I certainly would not trouble myself to divorce her now she's back. I am married to Miranda and wish to remain so."

"I see." Emily nodded slowly, then looked about the room again. Her shoulders lifted as she sighed. "Where did you say that book was?"

Relieved that the conversation was over, he pointed across the room. "Over there on the lectern. Let me collect it and we can return to your brother to see what mischief he's gotten himself into."

As she turned, the shawl around her slipped and fell to the floor. Kit bent to pick it up and hand it back, but she appeared oblivious to the loss and had moved away. He hurried after her, shaking it out. "Your shawl, madam."

"Oh, thank you, sir," she said with a smile that made her eyes glow with unmistakable warmth, proving she'd not given up hope. "What would I do without you?"

Kit stepped back quickly. "Perhaps its time to find out. You've been a widow long enough, don't you think? I know of several fine gentlemen who always have a ready smile when they see you at parties."

She laughed softly. "Do you now? I told you that one love was all I have room for in my heart."

But whom did she love? Kit was almost certain her marriage to Brighthurst hadn't been a grand passion. Their relationship had been for mutual gain. Kit had never much cared for the man himself but had kept that to himself.

She turned back the cover and paid fierce attention to the new book he'd found in Gilbert and Hamilton's charming bookshop. The pages had entertained him for hours, and he had considered allowing Emily a chance to borrow it. Given his suspicion that Emily had been pining for an offer of marriage from him, he decided to withhold the invitation.

He would persuade her to look elsewhere for romance.

Chapter Seventeen

—◆—

Miranda hated her husband with a renewed passion that eclipsed her previous ill feeling toward him. He'd stolen her possessions from Mivart's Hotel and brought them here of all places. He had every keepsake of Christopher's childhood beneath his roof. He'd have proof of Christopher's existence should he look closely at the contents of her trunks. He would ask questions. If she couldn't distract him and he learned she'd borne him a son, he would demand to see him immediately.

She stared up bitterly at the façade of Taverham's London residence. Martin led the way, helping her out of the carriage and uttering soothing words of encouragement and cautioning her not to worry too much. He'd endured without complaint the brunt of her temper and despair that afternoon since the discovery of Christopher's disappearance and the shock of Taverham's theft, only muttering an occasional reminder that she needed to calm herself.

"Remember what I said." Martin drew closer so his words would not carry. "If you feel threatened in any way, you may come to me no matter the hour. I'll alert my staff to shelter you should I be away from home."

Miranda gripped Martin's hand tightly. "I will. Thank you. I will endure the first night."

Martin snorted. "Hardly your first night in Taverham's bed, is it?"

She smacked his chest as she saw the humor lighting his eyes. She had of course confided in him about sharing a bed with the marquess before marriage, and when Christopher had come along he'd never judged her for being a silly fool. "Mind your manners. That was the past, not the future."

He shook his head. "My dear, you are the most confusing woman I've ever met. Behave and all will be well."

"Am I not always a proper lady?"

"Always, and I will challenge any man who dares besmirch your character by saying otherwise." He let her go. "I will send out more inquiries tonight and I will call on you tomorrow to strategize our next step. Now go in, smile at your husband, and don't let him see how upset you are unless you plan to be truthful at last."

Miranda drew in a deep breath. "He won't fool me into confiding in him. He'll never even notice my distress."

Martin shooed her toward the stairs without another word.

Miranda climbed the stairs to Taverham's house, Peter Landry trailing behind, and before she could even knock the door was flung open. Beyond the butler, Taverham stood waiting. She crossed the threshold and let out a breath, surprised to find herself relieved.

She handed her bonnet and gloves and reticule to the butler. He was familiar to her—Addison, she thought his name might have been, but couldn't be sure. "Thank you."

When she raised her eyes and met Taverham's, her world tilted just the slightest amount. Last night she'd made him wild for her and retreated before he could claim more intimacies. Tonight? Miranda didn't think he'd let her escape him twice. She was too tired, too upset, to worry about what he might do next.

A growled *wife* was all the greeting she received.

She curtsied and pasted a smile on her face. "Husband. Did you pass a pleasant day?"

"No, but that was your intention anyway." He walked toward her and held out his hand. "Come. Supper has been delayed long enough while we waited for you."

"Wait." She gestured to Mr. Landry, who'd followed close

behind her. "See to it that my man is given a place."

Taverham appraised her servant from head to toe, his expression critical. "A groom?"

"No. A place in the house. I would have him above stairs where he can be of greatest use to me."

Her husband's brow rose at her request, but eventually he nodded in agreement. "Addison, see to it immediately."

She smiled in relief as Peter Landry moved toward the servant's stairs. "Now that's settled, I should change first."

He stared at her, his eyes narrowed as he inspected her. "As you are is good enough. Come, I'm hungry."

He drew her toward the dining room she remembered from a previous brief visit. Nothing had changed too much since her last time to this house. Taverham's ancestors still looked down on those passing before their disapproving faces. Haughtiness appeared ingrained in each generation of Taverhams. What would they make of her son when his portrait was hung upon their precious walls and he was smiling?

Taverham paused a moment, his gaze darting in each direction of the hallway. Suddenly Miranda was in his arms again, her lips claimed, her length pressed tightly against Taverham's heated body. He devoured her mouth, tongue sliding against hers in a sensual dance as she belatedly remembered his intention to claim ten years' worth of kisses every day. Miranda had mistakenly thought he'd wait for the privacy of a bedchamber before he attempted to claim the next. She wasn't to be so lucky.

He released her as a footman appeared then disappeared. "You taste unbelievably good," he whispered against her lips. "Good enough to eat."

Miranda swallowed the hard lump forming in her throat. Compliments came easily to his lips and she wouldn't fall for them. Compliments she'd once believed as truth, especially when they were alone and he whispered them with a soft smile lighting his eyes, had once made her think he cared. To hear them now hurt and she looked away, squeezing her eyes shut to block him out. She couldn't bear Taverham's attempts at seduction coming so soon on top of finding Christopher missing. She wasn't a good mother nor a compliant wife. She was failing on all fronts, and there was no one to blame for the mess but herself.

"Miranda? What's wrong?"

She couldn't be fooled by Taverham's concern. He just wanted her available to kiss and make love to when he wanted. He wanted his heir. Well, so did Miranda. She swallowed and glanced up, hoping her eyes didn't give away her feelings. "Supper?"

For a moment, Miranda thought he'd hold her there in the hall and question her. But then he smiled ruefully, held out his arm for her to take, and dragged her toward the dining room. Miranda had dined here once with her father and Taverham's three guardians, who had arrived unannounced and insisted they had every right to stay. Taverham had been furious, but when it came to his guardians, he had not had the ability to send them away at that time. At least tonight's dinner couldn't be as uncomfortable as that one.

A footman in sharp black livery opened the double doors smartly, and Kit dragged her through. She stopped and looked at the table with a sinking heart. What she hadn't expected was to find the room filled with three familiar and unfriendly faces. The faces she'd most dreaded to see were already ensconced in Taverham's household. She smiled at them, hiding just how much she detested both Lady Brighthurst and her brother Lord Acton, not to mention the Dowager Marchioness of Taverham. Had one of them discovered her secret and conspired to remove Christopher from the succession?

The dowager marchioness sat at one end of the table and nodded regally, though her gaze flittered over Miranda from head to toe. She'd not been given a chance to change for dinner, so Miranda was sure she looked less than presentable to that lady's exacting standards. It was Taverham's fault, so she beamed at the woman. The dowager's eyes widened only a fraction in shock at her response to silent criticism. Miranda was sure her face would split apart if she ever encountered something that pleased her and turned away.

Lord Acton and Kit's lover, Lady Brighthurst, stood on the far side of the table, leaving two places empty for Taverham and Miranda to sit near each other. At least no one else was expected to dine with them. The siblings, Taverham's dearest friends, would be bad enough. The pair had been close at the time of her marriage and appeared to still be in each other's pockets to this day. As she inspected them, she wondered if Acton and Emily were the well-dressed couple who'd discovered Mr. Fenning had harbored her son and forced him to burn down the house.

Neither spoke.

Taverham held out a chair for her on the unfilled side of the table, set closest to him, and then took his seat at the head of the table. "Supper can be served."

The footmen went about the task of filling glasses and laying napkins on laps while Miranda's skin crawled in the heavy silence. The dining room was so opulent and reeked of so much power that she felt adrift and very shabby by comparison.

The dowager sniffed the air as if a bad smell lingered in the room. "Where have you been, madam? Explain yourself."

Miranda sipped her water, aware that Taverham had groaned softly. She didn't expect any help from him and it seemed he still allowed the old dragon to rattle about in his gilded cage. She drew in a breath and let it out slowly as the footmen laid out the first course. She would not give the servants fodder for the gossips as answering honestly surely would have done. She picked up her soup spoon and ignored her mother-in-law.

The dowager marchioness slapped her hand down on the table. "I will not be ignored in my own home. You will answer to me and do it now."

"Mother," Taverham growled but said no more on the subject.

"Well, I for one have had enough of this lady's scandalous behavior," the dowager complained.

Miranda set her spoon aside and pressed her napkin to her lips. The servants were listening, every ear trained for her response. She met her mother-in-law's gaze with unwavering confidence, as she hadn't been able to do as an expectant bride. "This is Taverham's home, is it not, and supper, not an inquisition. I have no intention of answering any question you demand of me, or anyone else's, for that matter, when they are so rudely put. I owe you nothing."

"You will answer to him," Lord Acton said then scowled fiercely, attempting to intimidate her as he bounced in his seat as if about to leap across the table and do her harm. Unfortunately it worked. After discovering someone had attempted to harm her son, she had little trust left. There could be a cruelty about some men, hidden for the most part but certainly felt when they were denied what they wanted most.

She did not know what Lord Acton was capable of, and she could not let down her guard around him. She turned her gaze from Acton and tried to slow her breathing to normal.

"Come now, Miranda, surely you can appease our curiosity a little," Lady Brighthurst pleaded, her eyes skipping to Taverham's with a soft smile that didn't bother to hide how highly she regarded Miranda's husband. "Kit has been very generous and patient with you."

He'd been generous? Hardly. Miranda wanted to scream.

The pair sickened her. It was too much even now after ten years of knowing about their affair. Her chest tightened with the old pain she'd thought lost and long buried. Try as she might, Miranda could not sit by and watch the pair flirt. She was no longer the daughter of a merchant but a marchioness. It was past time to put her title to good use. "I do not recall ever giving you leave to address me by my given name, Lady Brighthurst. I still do not."

"That was unkind, Miranda," Kit protested.

Miranda ignored him and stared the woman down, little caring that she was now making the scene she'd promised not to have. Coming home to Taverham was bad enough without seeing his lover here, flaunting their mutual affection across the mahogany of what was supposed to be her home too.

Emily patted his hand. "It's all right."

"Please," he begged. "Let's all just eat our supper and enjoy having Miranda back where she belongs."

Miranda turned her head slowly to glare at her husband as the soup bowls were cleared away and new plates placed before them. He appeared almost as uncomfortable as she felt but likely for far different reasons. Miranda did not care if she offended his lover. She was no longer interested in pleasing anybody but her own son, and until Christopher was here, she would make all the waves she liked.

When she glanced down at her own plate and saw pork had

been served to her without regard for her dislike of the meat, she knew how little she still mattered in the scheme of things. She pushed back from the table and tossed her napkin aside. "Would you excuse me?"

Miranda stood and, before Taverham could insist she stay, walked from the room as regally as she could manage. Her hands shook and she gripped them together before her churning belly. She would not ask him for directions even if she had no idea where she was going. The marchioness' bedchamber had to be upstairs someplace. She'd find it eventually.

At the foot of the stairs, Taverham caught her and spun her about. "I apologize. Mother must have changed the menu when I was busy elsewhere. She does that from time to time if the housekeeper can't find me. Please come back and I'll have something else prepared for you."

His hands stroked up and down her arms but did not soothe her.

"I will not. The meal is just a small portion of the problem between us. Your friends will never accept me, and your mother is determined to put me in my place. I warned you how it would be. I don't need to live here to be married to you."

"You belong with me." He bit his lip, a gesture of uncertainty that she'd never seen him wear before, and then slipped her arm through his. "I won't lose you over a mistake. Things will become more settled soon, you'll see. Let me help you get situated for the night. You don't know this house, do you?"

Why couldn't he just leave her be? She wasn't interested in a house that best resembled a palace. "There was no need to worry about what my money saved from ruin. Your staff have done you proud."

"Our staff," he corrected.

Miranda shook her head. "Nothing here requires my attention when the dowager marchioness is in residence. Let us leave it that way."

"No." He tugged her to the steps and started up them, one arm lodged behind her back so she couldn't resist. "Everything must change or there was no point to our marriage. I will not accept that outcome and neither should you be willing to."

At the top he curled her arm through his and they strolled

through the upper-level hallway. Taverham pointed out rooms and amenities previously unknown to her congenially enough, but Miranda tensed anyway. When they came to his bedchamber, he walked her past the door without opening it. He stopped at the next one, an adjoining room. "Your room was ready hours ago, though I must confess I did leave it to your maid to unpack your trunks."

Relieved but unable to show it, Miranda rubbed at her temple as her head began to throb. "My maid? I don't have a maid."

He smiled. "I noticed the lack, so I took pains to employ one. I hope you've no objections when you see her."

Not returned more than an hour and he was already trying to smother her in how things must be done his way. Miranda did not take his presumption well. She dug her nails into her palms to keep from screaming. She could have purchased new dresses very cheaply to make up for what clothing had been stolen. There were other hotels in London that wouldn't rudely deny her entry as Mivart's had done that afternoon.

He nudged open the door and allowed her to walk in first. Miranda feared what she would find. Another of the dowager's cast-off servants who cared nothing for her but the gossip she could supply to the other servants of the house. Yet when she looked, Miranda saw no haughty abigail across the room but the tiny girl from Mivart's Hotel. The one that talked far too much. The one Miranda had instantly warmed to.

Taverham nudged her arm gently. "She said her name was April. As for the rest, I've no idea. Her suitability and experience I leave for you to judge, but I thought you might like a familiar face, someone you'd already met, taking care of you over a complete stranger. She can be taught to do things your way."

Miranda's throat tightened and she swallowed the unexpected feeling of gratitude. Taverham had actually done the right thing for a change. She wouldn't have believed it possible without the proof grinning at her from across the room in a new dress. April might be a little lax in her manner, but Miranda had requested her over others at the hotel during her stay because she had potential. How had Taverham discovered that preference and why had he bothered to care? It was difficult, but Miranda decided she had to say something. "Thank you."

"My pleasure." He kissed the back of her hand, a lingering kiss that promised so much more than it might appear to the maid. Then he turned her hand over to kiss her bare palm and his tongue skipped across her skin lightly. He lifted his head suddenly to peer at her hand and the burn scar resting here. Miranda closed her fingers over her palm, hiding the unsightly blemish from his view. The burn had happened so long ago that she had almost forgotten how she'd come by it. The reminder was all she needed to regain her bearings.

Christopher had given it to her with a hot fire poker. An accident, of course, when she'd not watched what he was doing with enough care. He was missing because she'd done it again.

Taverham's brow rose as she sucked in a sharp breath, but then he smiled quickly, asking nothing of the scar. "Now you must excuse me. I had better return to my guests. Until later, dear wife."

A ball of dread filled her as he hurried for the door. His title was all she managed to choke out before he was gone again to be with his best friends. Later would be when he returned and joined with her in bed. She didn't think he would let her sleep alone, not when he'd already had her before. She hoped he was with his friends for a very long time so the night might be as short as possible. Tomorrow she had to set out in search of Christopher and find him before another day had passed.

Chapter Eighteen

---◆---

Kit normally enjoyed the company of friends and encouraged them to accept his hospitality for as long as they liked. Tonight though, he was torn between good manners and the urge to suggest they leave. Mother should never have invited guests on such an important night. He and Miranda had a lot to talk about, and they could not begin until he was free.

He also suspected she was much more upset with him than she let on.

Perhaps he'd been in the wrong for taking her possessions without permission, but damn it all, she was his wife and he wanted to watch over her here and not in some third rate hotel.

He turned aside the suggestion of a third port and checked the time on his pocket watch. Would Miranda be asleep already?

An exasperated sigh reached his ears and he glanced across to the source. His mother stared at him, her expression thoughtful. "I believe I will take my leave of you young folk and retire for the night. There seems to be an issue with the staff that I must attend to."

"Miranda and I will take care of any staff issue in the morning, Mother." He stood when she did. Mother likely would take issue at Miranda's man joining their household, not to mention her chattering maid. He did not want to make Miranda feel she could not employ anyone she pleased, although she could have picked someone with a less frightening appearance for a footman. "Pleasant dreams."

She scoffed at that. "Dreams are for the young and foolish."

"You're not so old as to have none at all, surely, Lady Taverham," Emily soothed, glancing between them quickly. Emily was always the one to cajole his mother into lighter spirits, although some days she had little success.

Today it seemed Emily was unequal to the task as his mother did not soften her expression one bit. Her brow rose haughtily instead. "There is but one dream I have, and it preys on my mind. Taverham's need for an heir under his roof."

When she strolled from the room, murmuring a blunt good-night, Emily's face grew red.

After a few minutes where Kit struggled for something to say in the embarrassing silence, Acton rose to his feet and held out his hand to his sister. "Come, Emily. You will have to leave him at some point. Any goose can see our presence is not what he needs right now. Man's hardly been able to hold up his end of the conversation all night, and I'm sure he has much to... to discuss with his wife tonight. I don't envy him the chore."

Emily's skin turned an even brighter shade of red. Kit glanced at Acton in annoyance. Meeting Miranda in their marriage bed would not be a chore to Kit but a joy. Yet that could only happen if she wanted to be there of her own free will.

"It's been a stressful day," he murmured softly so Emily would not feel slighted.

"I imagine it has." She grimaced. "I do find myself weary too. Good evening, Kit. Perhaps we will have a chance to talk again tomorrow at the Huntley soiree. You promised me a dance if you recall, although your wife may not like to have your attention diverted."

"Yes, of course we will dance," he quickly assured her. "Just because Miranda has returned doesn't mean I cannot dance with my friends. We shall have a great time."

She smiled brightly then, her eyes flaring with anticipation, and he cursed that he might have made a mistake in saying that.

He saw them headed for the door, waited a few minutes longer, then climbed the stairs to his bedchamber. His valet was waiting and silently assisted him in changing out of his evening clothes. Once he was alone again, Kit strolled toward the adjoining bedchamber's door. His stomach was in knots, uncertain whether he should disturb Miranda at this hour to say goodnight. He had no idea of her sleeping habits, although she'd seemed to retire early when she'd been a guest at Mivart's Hotel.

He felt very guilty for the poor welcome she'd received, and if nothing else he wished to ask if there was anything she needed.

He lifted a hand to knock and let it rap against the wood softly. Her response to come in was immediate and that surprised him. Usually she made him wait. He stepped through and approached the bed. Finding it empty was a surprise. He turned around in a slow circuit to search for her.

Miranda was sitting in a chair by the window, gazing out at London instead of sleeping.

"I thought you'd be asleep or at least in bed."

"Your mother paid me a visit and sleep is impossible," she told him.

He winced. "What did she have to say?"

"Oh, nothing I'd not heard before: show the proper degree of respect to the family."

"Ah." Kit drew closer to her but stopped when she stiffened. "I remember the lectures she gave me as a boy. Quite terrifying to live up to her expectations and to those who came before me."

"Imagine what she might say to a wife who bucked at adhering to your noble family traditions and hasn't delivered the heir."

Kit pinched the bridge of his nose. There would be no son at this rate. "Is that why you're not asleep yet? Forgive me, but I would have thought you'd not care what any of us had to say. It's late. You should get some rest."

"The bed is unfit for sleeping in."

He took offense at that. The beds in his house were of the finest quality. "I doubt that."

When Miranda held out her hand to him suddenly, Kit took what she offered. A jagged lump of stone rested in his palm.

"Another quaint family tradition you kept secret? I am so happy to have missed this experience on our wedding night. I suppose you might enjoy the discomfort, I know not your tastes now, but I assure you sleep in that bed is impossible."

"I don't understand."

She waved her hand toward the bed. "By all means, disbelieve me and see for yourself."

He tested the bed, ran his hands over the sheets, and then stripped them back to touch the mattress. He discovered a split seam and nothing more. "You're mistaken."

"Try lying down and see what you discover."

Still detecting nothing untoward, he humored her by climbing up to lay flat on his back along the closest side. The next moment he jerked upright with a curse and stared at the mattress. The bed was full of hard lumps. Miranda was right that she could not be expected to rest well in that bed. He doubted anyone could. "Who the devil did this?"

Miranda returned to her view out the window. "I assumed you were responsible. A little discomfort to punish me or perhaps ensure I could not sleep at all."

"Mother." He growled. "I would never do such a mean-spirited thing to you."

Her gaze raked over him, her eyes softening slightly. "I believe you now, but the end result is still the same."

"You cannot sleep in a chair all night."

Her laugh was a dry chuckle in the night, whispering across his senses like a lover's caress. "Why not? It wouldn't be the first dawn that has found me this way."

"Well, there is no need for such extremes. You will simply sleep in my bed and tomorrow we will have that mattress removed and dealt with."

"As I said, the result is the same. Your mother wins and I'm forced into your bed."

"Oh, for heaven's sake. I refuse to have such a ridiculous conversation about where you will sleep or will not." He gestured toward his room angrily. "Bed. Now."

She stood slowly and walked toward his bedchamber door with her head high. Defiant, as if she were on her way to the gallows for a crime she hadn't committed. "As you command."

Kit threw his hands up in the air, then scowled at the bed. "I will not fight with you."

"No of course. You don't have to in order to get your way." She stared at his bed. "Which side must I lie upon?"

"Whichever side you bloody well like."

Kit moved to the side Miranda did not take. He extinguished the nearest lamp, then removed his robe and slipped naked beneath the cool sheets. He faced away from his wife. When she slipped into bed with him, he did not turn, did not stray toward her even an inch. He didn't dare push the issue of even suggesting a good-night kiss. There would be no heir for the Taverham estates in the near future. Never at all unless his mother stopped helping him get his wife into his bed.

Miranda must think him obsessed with sex, he was interested in that, but only if she wanted him too.

He bore the silence for about ten minutes before rolling onto his back. "I'm sorry I snapped at you. I don't know what my mother was thinking, and your accusations offended me. I never asked or wished for her to interfere in our marriage. I specifically asked her to leave you be. I can understand how it would seem a way to have you forced into bed with me."

Miranda shifted slightly. "Your mother is determined to acquire a grandchild, and she's not above trickery to have her way."

Kit grunted and rose up on one elbow so he could look more closely at Miranda's face in the dim light. "So it seems. Just so you understand that such deceptions are not my way."

Her lips turned down. "Yes, you have always been direct."

"As were you. A character trait I admired." He licked his lips. "May I say good night properly?"

She scowled again. "Is there a point to protesting?"

He grinned to ease her mind. "About kisses, no. Everything else can be debated."

Before she could answer, he captured her lips and kissed her gently. He had his wife in his bed for the first time in his life, in their marriage, and he would not waste a moment in showing her how pleased he was. He stroked his tongue across her plump lips and her gasp allowed him to taste her.

Miranda was a drug to his senses. He could kiss her for hours and never get enough. He sampled her lips a long while, then moved lower to her throat and nipped her skin lightly. He growled against her throat and she moaned softly. The long-missed sound sent his senses soaring. They were unbelievably attracted to each other. He'd like to think that if she had stayed and not run away that they might have made love every night, or near enough, and woken in each other's arms every day too.

He'd hoped for that and lost. Now he had another chance to make the future the way it should have been. He could not take things too far unless she asked him to.

Kit curled his fingers around her waist and pulled her closer to him. Miranda rolled until they were side by side, her cold toes pressed to the top of his feet, her nightgown the only barrier between them. The barrier could stay. He would let her keep her modesty if it gave her peace of mind. Kit only wanted to kiss her. He just hadn't told her where.

Miranda's hands were light against his side and chest. He caught one and brought it to his lips. "You have a burn on this hand. How did you come to be injured?"

"An accident."

He found the rough patch of skin and pressed a kiss to it. When he'd glimpsed the wound earlier, Kit had found himself furious that she'd been hurt. He buried those feelings again. Now was not the time to question her and demand she be more careful. Now was the right time to convince his wife to give him another chance to be her husband in every way that mattered.

He slid beneath the covers, fingers catching the hem of her nightgown to raise it up her legs. Miranda shifted restlessly as she likely guessed his intent. He'd loved to taste her with his mouth while his ears were filled with the sounds of her excitement before their marriage. Her desperate cries for completion had always driven him wild. Tonight would be the same, he hoped.

He inhaled her scent, pressed butterfly kisses along her thighs until she parted them at the gentle urging of his hands. He kissed her curls, once softly, the next firmer still. Above his head, Miranda was quiet, offering no encouragement whatsoever. Puzzled, he opened her lower lips with his thumbs and blew softly over them.

Miranda's hips bucked high in the air as she tensed. Not a word passed her lips. Was she silent to punish him? It wouldn't matter to him if she was. Her body betrayed her excitement. Every muscle was tense. The scent of her arousal filled him with glee.

He rested his head against her inner thigh and touched her body intimately. Miranda, despite her silence, was wet enough to make him ache. He eased his cock away from the friction of the bedding, coming up onto his hands and knees between her parted thighs. "Pillow," he requested, and received one quickly.

Kit gently eased it beneath her bottom, lifting her pelvis to his hungry mouth for more kisses. He hungered for her taste, so he held back nothing. He stroked her lower lips, teased the hidden bud of her clitoris until her hips rocked against his mouth. He paused a long moment, savoring the joy he found in that simple acknowledgment of the effect he had on her.

Miranda caught his head by his hair and pushed his face back against her.

Laughing, Kit teased and sucked and savored each quiet command she gave. He didn't mind doing her bidding when the reward was so sweet. Softly, as if the sounds were unwillingly made, his wife moaned to every touch of his tongue as he slid against her. In the past Miranda had always come fast and hard, yet tonight she held back. Kit doubled his efforts. He caught one delightfully full breast, squeezed and kneaded the flesh until she thrashed. He sucked her clitoris hard.

Miranda bucked against his mouth, her incoherent cries loud in the dark of their bedroom. Kit savored every sound and sensation as if it might be his last, storing them with past remembrances. With Miranda, tonight just might be his only opportunity to love her.

He stilled, warming to the idea that the sensations she stirred might have a name. Had he loved her before she'd run away? He couldn't remember ever ascribing his fascination for her with that deeper feeling, but he couldn't deny it was a possibility now. He had missed her, waited for her, and once she'd been found couldn't be lost again without pain. Was this love or merely lust fooling him once more?

He kissed her thigh and stayed close until the very last tremor shook her, then crawled to his side of the bed, flopping onto his back. He would not consummate their marriage without her explicit invitation, and not just a desire-shrouded encouragement either. He would have her say she wanted him in the brighter light of day where she could not pretend or claim she'd been tricked into it.

As for the other, tomorrow would be soon enough to assess his emotions, with a cool head and not the fog of desire clouding his mind. The chances of him being in love with Miranda were slim and utterly impossible if she continued to resent being his wife. He wasn't about to admit how that might hurt. It would be terrible to love and not have that love returned.

Kit whispered good night and rolled to his side, facing away from Miranda so he stared into the darkest corner of the room, hoping and dreading that the morning would come soon and his aching cock would know when to give up hope on its own.

Chapter Nineteen

—◆—

Miranda continued to feign sleep as Taverham went about his morning routine. Before their marriage, Taverham had skulked away the moment he was done with her. Well before the sun had risen so he wouldn't be caught leaving her bed. Last night she'd listened to him fall asleep for the first time.

The sudden absence of restlessness on his part and steady, even breaths had not allowed sleep to come easily to Miranda, though. She pondered his actions for hours. Why hadn't he claimed her? It wasn't as if he'd not entered her body before. She'd borne his son, after all.

Her body hummed disturbingly at the memory of his touch even now, and she fought not to think of how eagerly she'd encouraged his ministrations last night.

Today Taverham had woken, stretched, called for his breakfast and the day's newssheet, all while prowling the room in a state of half-dress. Miranda found his ease this morning so different than she'd anticipated. He'd drawn the curtains around his bed quietly just before the servants had arrived and had opened them again when they were gone. Now he stood near the windows, likely out of sight should anyone dare look up. His expression was pensive.

His countenance painfully handsome.

She cursed her traitorous emotions as her heartbeat quickened. Could she not keep straight that she disliked him?

Her body too was making her decisions fly from her mind the moment he touched her anywhere.

Knowing she couldn't maintain the charade of sleeping indefinitely, she decided to make an effort to be at least civil to her husband this morning. He *had* behaved during the rest of the night after his scandalously placed *kisses*. He'd remained largely on his side of the bed, only waking her when he turned over and his arm or feet strayed close to her side. But when his breathing had evened out again in sleep she'd relaxed but couldn't shake the feeling that lying in his bed wasn't exactly the worst thing that had happened to her. They were married and he wasn't at all repulsive.

"Good morning," she said softly, breaking the silence around them.

His head turned and he scowled. "I thought you'd never wake."

Miranda was growing used to his expressions and didn't bother to find offense in his abrupt tone. It seemed to be his way now. He'd once smiled so much more. "I was awake. I was watching you."

That seemed to catch his interest. His scowl disappeared and he took a step in her direction. His bare chest swelled as he took a breath, and Miranda couldn't keep her eyes on his face. She'd never seen him undressed by daylight, and the sight took her breath away.

His face lost its grouchy appearance and heat filled his eyes. "I don't know if you care for tea in the morning, but there is still some left. It might be hot enough."

Aware he'd noticed her being distracted by his body, Miranda sat up quickly, settled some pillows behind her back, and drew the sheets up to her chest so she was decently covered. As she smoothed the soft sheets in place, she brushed over her breasts, finding the nipples hardened to little points. She shifted in discomfort, hoping he hadn't seen. She'd not like there to be any misunderstandings about why she lingered in his bed this morning. She had very good reasons.

Miranda never threw herself from bed at first light if she could help it. Her heart couldn't stand the strain. "Let's see."

He quickly passed her a cup and when she tried it, it wasn't completely stone-cold. "Thank you."

"You're welcome." He stood back, hands falling to his hips. "I expect we will have many callers today."

Miranda tried to keep her eyes away from his midsection. With him dressed only in loose drawers of a kind she'd never seen on him before, Miranda's face grew warm. The area his fingers pointed to had begun to grow. She jerked her gaze up. "Gawkers would be a more apt description."

"Likely you are correct. It cannot be helped, but I will stay with you every moment I can to discourage the worst of impertinences." He bit his lip a moment. "Miranda, did you mean it last night? That you're willing to keep whatever difficulties we have between us? I, too, should like to keep those concerns away from public consumption."

She tilted her head, trying her best to hide her amusement at his request. She didn't care what society thought of her or their relationship. She'd happily be an example to any young heiress on the verge of marrying a penniless peer. Without love, lust wasn't worth the trouble to risk your heart over. The feelings Taverham stirred in her were only lust, proven to be fueled currently by his state of undress. "And how do you propose to manage that?"

"I should like you to continue your promise to only discuss the past with me." He rubbed his hands together and the muscles of his chest flexed in a disturbing way. "I do not want a repeat of last night's supper debacle. I don't want you made upset again."

She shrugged as her attraction to his body grew despite her best intentions to keep her mind on the discussion at hand. Supper had been his fault, but not even that memory could seem to pour ice over her growing lust. "Then perhaps you shouldn't expect me to dine with your friends and family."

He nodded slowly, as if agreeing. "I should also like to know where you are, where you're planning to go, and who you spend your time with when I am not with you."

Any desire she'd felt in his presence vanished. "You mean to be my keeper."

"I mean to have the intelligence any married man expects." He came closer, close enough that she could almost reach out and touch the hard flesh that was tempting her to crawl into his arms. "If you accept an invitation, I should like to know so I may fit my plans to yours and vice versa. For example, before your return I had accepted an invitation to the Huntley soiree tonight. I should like your presence on my arm."

"I see now why so many gowns were required and in such a rush." Miranda slipped from the bed before she did something truly stupid and showed him how he disappointed her. The night ahead he planned would be awkward and uncomfortable. Strangers joking about Taverham's need for an heir would be tedious when she couldn't speak of Christopher's existence to anyone. She headed for her bedchamber. "I can manage the farce that we are happy together instead of what we really are: strangers that married for my dowry."

Taverham stormed after her. "It wasn't just that."

Miranda picked up her hairbrush from the dresser and gripped it tightly before she slapped him for lying to her face about his lack of feeling. "Please do not insult my intelligence."

"Damn it, woman, as impossible as it seems to you, I did miss you."

He stared down at her and then his gaze shifted to her lips. In the face of Taverham's scrutiny, her mouth grew dry. "Not soon enough. It was not as if we were a marriage of equals, not with only my dowry and common connections to recommend me."

"I tried so hard to find you." His lips crashed against her suddenly, bruising and bold. His tongue demanded entry to her mouth, and the feelings he had stirred in her before from just looking at him returned to shake her to her core. Taverham could still blind her to the truth with a single kiss. The only thing that mattered to him was her money and satisfying his lust. Any moment, she expected him to cart her back to his bed and finally claim what he believed was his.

When the door to the hall opened, they both glanced at it quickly. Miranda's new maid squeaked an apology, blushing furiously, and jerked it closed again. Miranda closed her eyes, knowing that within an hour the whole household would be talking about how they were discovered, with her undressed and in his arms, about to make love.

"Ignore it." Taverham kissed her again and drew her close, curling his hand around her head and the other over her bottom.

He forced them together, and Miranda could not miss the signs of his arousal pressed low against her belly. His fingers dug into her bottom brutally as he ground her pelvis against his length. Miranda fought not to be affected, but after last night her resistance crumbled all too soon.

She wanted him and she hated herself for falling for his charms in the bedchamber again. He made her crazed with inexplicable lust.

When he spun her about to face away from him, she whimpered. Yet he didn't immediately whip up her nightgown to take her from behind as he had done on one occasion before their marriage when speed had been his aim. He touched her legs possessively, moving aside her robe and finally inching her nightgown higher so that he touched the bare skin of her inner thighs.

Miranda couldn't think. Couldn't reason with herself to end this before he went too far. As his fingers skimmed higher to touch the curls between her legs, her eyes closed of their own accord. Taverham had always gotten what he wanted when it came to the bedchamber. She was still as powerless now to tell him to end it as she'd been at seventeen. He was right that he'd never forced her into bed with him. One touch and she was lost.

His fingers dipped inside her and he groaned. "For a woman who claims not to want her husband, you are incredibly aroused."

His hand closed over her breast and squeezed. His lips and breath scorched the skin of her neck and shoulder as he slid her nightgown aside with his teeth. He penetrated her with his fingers deeply, and she shuddered at the pleasure of it. She couldn't help it. He excited her and she was unable to prevent the moan passing her lips. It would not take long to climax, given how intent he was on arousing her needs to fever pitch.

There was nothing her body liked better than moments when she had his undivided attention, especially with his fingers sliding over her clitoris in little circles and dipping inside her body.

When she was close to coming, she clamped her jaw shut.

"No." He released her breast to cup her face, fingers sliding gently over her jaw to break her resistance even further. "There's no need for silence now that we are married. I've waited a long time to hear you scream my name. Say it at last, wife. I need it."

She couldn't say it now. She wouldn't do it.

Miranda closed her eyes as he brought her to the brink time and again, fingers sliding in and out of her body firmly. He played with her clitoris until she thought she would come, but then he'd stop and focus his attention inside her body, his cock bumping against her bottom restlessly. The fingers of his other hand stroked her throat softly, then drifted down to her breast again.

He pinched her nipple suddenly and Miranda's control shattered. She screamed his name—Kit—and sobbed aloud to discover herself so weak against him.

He turned her to face him and kissed her mouth hungrily while she shook and shook, his hot body crowding hers against the table behind them. The pressure of his cock against her sex brought on more shudders of pleasure. She caught the edge of the table with one hand, bracing herself for whatever position Taverham demanded next for further intimacies. She touched Taverham's chest with her other hand and discovered his skin was scorching hot and slick.

He drew back, his green eyes bright with passion, his face flushed. Miranda had never made love to him in the daylight, and he appeared utterly unlike the careful aristocrat she'd left behind all those years ago. His wide chest rose and fell rapidly, and she couldn't look away.

He caught her face and lifted her gaze to his again. Miranda dug her fingers into his shoulders, grasping for purchase.

He kissed her soundly before drawing back again. "This is the passionate woman I married," he murmured softly against her lips. "The one I've waited my whole life for. Don't ever leave me again."

He jerked away suddenly, storming back into his own bedchamber and slammed the door behind him.

Without Kit for support and no notion of when or if he'd return, Miranda settled to the floor in an untidy heap beside the dressing table, little caring how she looked should her maid come back. Her body trembled. Her breath wouldn't settle. Her heart raced frantically.

Passion had never been their problem. It was what happened outside the bedchamber that made them an incompatible match.

Chapter Twenty

If all men had sex on their mind, then all women must secretly wish their contemporaries ill couplings. One hour into morning calls, Kit found himself thoroughly disgusted by their many exuberant callers. Throughout the long morning, Miranda had shown remarkable restraint given the thinly veiled queries, more insults and sneers, aimed at her and the resumption of their marriage. *Oh, you have no children do you? So sad that you'll never understand what a worry they can be* or any variation on that theme was fast growing tedious.

Clearly they had no children. They'd barely had a marriage.

He folded his arms across his chest as yet another woman spoke of her children so fondly as she departed. "Take the knocker off the damn door, Addison."

His mother gasped. "You cannot do that. I have friends coming specifically to call on us today."

He glanced at Miranda's drawn face and joined her on the long chaise lounge where she'd perched. "As my wife pointed out last night, it's my house. *Our* house. We can do whatever we want. I, for one, am sick of visitors, and I think Miranda may be too. I'd like a quiet hour with my wife if you don't mind."

He stretched out on the remaining space around Miranda and sighed. A cozy afternoon couldn't be guaranteed, but he'd certainly try for it. "Tea, Miranda?"

"Yes, that would be very welcome," she said hesitantly.

Kit twisted to look at the door where the butler hovered, apparently torn over whom to take orders from—him or his mother. The fact that this still continued to happen after a dozen or more years as marquess irritated him. He was the Marquess of Taverham. His mother lived here by his invitation and good grace. "Addison. Bring tea for my wife and me. Perhaps Mother, too, if she wishes it, but we are done accepting calls for the day."

His mother huffed and straightened in her seat. Any stiffer and he could attach a sail to her and have her glide away. "Sit up, Taverham," she ordered. "Show some respect for your position."

Kit let his mother's thoughts on how a marquess should behave in his own home go in one ear and out the other. He watched Miranda instead and saw a small smile lift the corners of her lips when he didn't move to accommodate his mother's wishes immediately.

Interesting.

He crossed his feet at the ankles and laced his fingers together behind his head. "Mother, do stop your nonsense. When do you leave for Twilit Hill?"

The dowager sniffed. "Not for several days yet, I suspect. I'm needed here."

Miranda glanced down at her hands, the beginnings of her smile vanishing. *Blast.* For a moment she'd almost been happy. "When shall we leave, wife?"

She whipped her head around to stare at him. "Leave London?"

He wondered at her surprise. He'd never spent more than a month or two in London each year and never together in a row. She'd told him once she'd been pleased by that as she liked the country better than Town. Had that changed? "I've no need to be here for the season, and I'd rather spend my time with you than suffering through parliament. I thought you might be keen to see Twilit again. Our home is very different now. I'd like your opinion on the improvements we've made."

Miranda licked her lips. "I'd like to stay and see more of my cousin Agatha. I wanted to go to her today, but with so many visitors…"

He recalled she'd made mention of going out today a few times, and so far he'd managed to put her off with one distraction or another. She must have missed her cousin, but the notion that the outside world and her family held more appeal than being with him stung a little more than he liked. Must he reconcile himself to becoming her shadow if he wanted to keep her happy?

He huffed at the thought of being second in her good graces but could see no reason to deny her wish to remain close to her cousin for the time being. The estate ran itself now, allowing him freedom to come and go at will. There was really no reason to rush home to the country. No reason to rush anywhere at all. "Of course. The Carrington's customarily do not remain in London for terribly long. Perhaps when they have returned to the country we can too. I've no objections to that. Mother can go on ahead and prepare the servants for our return. I'd like a smooth transition and no awkwardness about your removal to the dower house, Mother. You may request any staff member to join you there, and do write to us with your requests for additional comforts. Miranda will want to change things, as is her right."

When his mother began to protest, attempting to change Kit's mind but failed to make headway, Miranda smiled for the first time at him, with more warmth than he expected.

Happiness trickled through him. At last—a small thawing of her resistance. He ignored his mother's furious departure to drink in the contentment he found in pleasing his wife. She was the marchioness, and he would support any changes she wished made.

Before he could put those thoughts into words, the butler slipped back into the room, clearing his throat in a manner Kit found extremely irritating. "I said we were not to be disturbed."

"Forgive me. Lord Louth has called to see the marchioness and will not take no for an answer. He's become rather cross in fact."

Miranda sprung to her feet. "I'll see him at once, Addison."

She took a few steps away but then clutched the backrest of a chair tightly and squeezed her eyes shut. Kit watched her, uncomfortably aware that she was eager to see another man.

Kit rolled to a sitting position and nodded to the butler, anxious himself to see how the pair greeted each other.

When Lord Louth strolled in, he shook Kit's hand firmly, then his eyes narrowed on Miranda. "My lady, a pleasure to see you again."

"Lord Louth. So nice of you to call on me here."

A deep vee formed between his eyes. He took her gloved hand in his and brushed his thumb across her clenched fingers as he looked at her face closely. "Please sit," he murmured, then led her to a high-backed chair and eased her into it. Miranda settled comfortably, and when Louth nudged a footstool in her direction, she accepted the fussing wordlessly and placed her feet upon it.

Kit stared at his wife, noticing the rapidity of her breathing, a sign her nerves were beset by strong emotion. Kit glanced down at his hands as disappointment filled him. Her connection to Louth was a strong one and unabated by her return to be his wife. Miranda could not love him even a little when she clearly cared for Lord Louth so much more.

But Kit would not be driven away from Miranda in his own house. She was his wife, and he'd never given up hope of her return despite the many years apart. If that return came with a price, they'd both bear it. She could have Louth when she'd given Kit a son. Until then, Kit wouldn't allow them to be alone one single moment.

Miranda spoke first to Louth. "I understand your cousin is with you in Town this year. I'm sorry not to have paid her a visit yet."

"Think nothing of it. She will understand you have other more important obligations than calling on her." Louth's lips twisted into a grimace. "She's driving her companion to distraction actually. I hired the woman to escort her about town, thinking Whitney would attend balls and such. All she does is walk in the park and visit the art gallery each week. I should have hired a companion with a creative flair so they'd have more to talk about."

Kit didn't like the way Miranda's gaze softened on Louth as he spoke. He sat forward in an attempt to draw Louth's attention from Miranda. "Does your cousin not wish to be married?"

"Ah, you've forgotten the old gossip." Louth winced, appearing uncomfortable in the extreme. "Whitney was disappointed in love during her first season, cruelly played and embarrassed when the fellow married someone with better connections, her best friend actually. It broke her heart. Her aunt made the situation worse by speaking of it repeatedly until her death. Whitney hasn't had much time for gentlemen since. She claims there's not one worth the trouble of keeping."

Kit frowned, not remembering the specifics of the incident mentioned, only the fact that it had occurred. As far as Kit could recall, Whitney's connections and dowry should have been sufficient for most men who were not weighed down by debts. His eyes flew to Miranda's. He'd thought he'd been lucky in finding Miranda, a woman he'd desired from the moment they'd met.

Miranda nodded. "'Tis difficult to forget such a disappointment. A woman's heart, her belief in her desirability, is often the thing she values most, and when abandoned, recovery of her confidence can take time."

Louth eased back and crossed one leg over his thigh. "That is what I suspected. She's vowed never to marry and we have a pact of sorts."

Had Louth made a similar agreement with Miranda? "What sort of pact?"

"I'm not to ever suggest she needs to marry and she'll do the same for me."

Kit rubbed his hand over his thigh. "It's high time you did."

Louth grimaced. "Now you sound like Miranda."

Kit glanced at his wife in surprise. "*You* recommended marriage?"

Her eyes were fixed to the leg that he'd rubbed, and she jerked her feet from the footstool and smoothed her skirts over her knees as if discomposed. "Most find it agreeable enough. Some even like it so much they marry many times over."

Kit held her gaze, aware of a rising of her color. Her eyes slipped from his to scrutinize his chest. When he rubbed his leg again, she followed the movement as if mesmerized. Kit struggled to hide his satisfaction. Miranda was aware of him, his body particularly, even from across the room. That had to be good news. "Once is enough for me," he said softly.

Miranda blushed a deep shade of pink as she looked away to

Louth. "I quite agree."

She did not, Kit was pleased to see, give Louth the same level of inspection as he'd just enjoyed when he moved in his chair. Her glances were quite cursory now Kit paid more attention, and he sat back at ease, delighted with this discovery.

Louth glanced between them, his lips curving in amusement as if he suspected there was more going on than said. In fact, he looked ready to laugh. "I should take my leave," he said quickly. "I merely wanted to pay my respects and ask if you were attending the Huntley soiree tonight or not."

"We are," Miranda told him quickly. "We'll look forward to seeing you there."

Louth smiled. "I'd like that. I'd attempt to claim a dance, but I'm sure your husband has already claimed them all."

Kit hadn't thought once of dancing with Miranda tonight and felt a momentary pang of embarrassment when she spoke of not being inclined to. He'd persuade her to glide across the ballroom floor with him one night soon. He'd give anything to hold her close in his arms while they danced for the first time. It had to be a waltz or nothing.

When she made to stand, Louth gestured for her to stay where she was. "Don't trouble yourself."

Kit followed Louth into the hall as he took his leave, his heart a little lighter. Miranda had used the term *we* to describe them, not once but twice. It was a small victory admittedly, but just the same he felt better about his marriage than he had in years.

"Is Miss Crewe coming to the ball tonight too?"

Louth shook his head. "Cannot convince her. Even had new gowns ordered in secret from her modiste and that didn't even tempt her to venture forth. I suppose she's afraid of being hurt again."

"That's a shame. I think many gentlemen would find her an interesting conversationalist. When things are settled here, I'll ask Miranda to consider a dinner and we can invite you both to join us along with a few eligible men."

"Only if you don't mind your friends being shocked when she points out their foibles in a clear, loud voice that carries to every corner of the room." Louth set his hat on his head. "Whitney does not suffer fools."

"You sound very fond of her. Maybe you should marry her yourself. It's not unheard of for cousins to marry."

Louth spluttered and coughed. "Are you mad? I have less in common with Whitney than I do with your wife, and that, for your information, isn't much at all."

"What don't you agree upon?"

"A great many things but I usually possess the ability to keep my opinion to myself even when I know she's making a huge mistake." Louth nodded and strolled out without explaining further.

Kit remained in the hall, thinking over what Louth had hinted at. As far as he could sense, his wife and Lord Louth were not lovers. By his own admission, Louth had claimed little in common with Miranda. That assertion comforted him greatly.

Thinking of her waiting, he returned to Miranda quickly. She reclined casually into her chair, lids closed over her remarkable eyes. Her face in repose brought a smile to his lips. She was exactly as he remembered. Breathtaking, even at rest. Kit yearned for her presence in his arms with a powerful ache. Perhaps this was what love felt like. A driving need to stay connected to Miranda had always been part of their relationship.

"Miranda," he whispered as he drew close and sat on the edge of the chaise nearest her.

"Hmm," she mumbled sleepily, the sound at once irritated and amused.

"Could I convince you you'd be more comfortable if you were to come over here with me and lie down?"

Her eyes fluttered open, head rolling slowly in his direction. He smiled at her drowsy expression. At least Louth's visit hadn't excited her passions.

"Is there enough room for me?"

"I'll make room." He scooted further into the corner.

Miranda placed her hands on the arms of her chair and anticipation filled him that he might just claim the intimate afternoon he'd hoped for. He patted the empty space beside him. After a long moment, Miranda crossed the room and settled on her side, her face pillowed on his outstretched arm, her back resting against his chest.

Kit drew her to him, arm curled over her hip so she'd not

worry about falling off the chaise. As Miranda sighed deeply and burrowed closer against him, he promised himself he'd take care of her.

They might not be in love, but touching like this clearly didn't disagree with her present mood. Kit pressed a kiss to the top of her head, loving the feel of her soft hair brushing against his lips. "We'll stay like this for the next unwanted visitor. What do you think?"

Miranda's grumbling answer made him chuckle. No more interruptions. The next person to visit when not wanted would have Kit's shoe thrown at them. Miranda cuddled closer, fingers of one hand touching the arm she used as a pillow. Then, because he really didn't want to spoil the moment by further talk, he closed his own eyes and let sleep claim him too.

Chapter Twenty-One

In the years of her self-imposed exile, Miranda had not missed the false affection so blatantly bestowed on her by the people she met at social events. She was sure none but a few kind souls present at the Huntley soiree had worried over her absence or were truly happy to see her returned to take up her role as Taverham's wife. Public sympathy was clearly with Lady Brighthurst, and their disappointment that Kit was still a married man seemed acute.

None of it mattered.

Miranda leaned close to Martin so he would hear her words over the din. "I believe we will be in London as long as the Carrington's remain in Town."

"That gives us a week at most." Martin frowned. "I spoke to Carrington yesterday and he mentioned the date for their return to the country had been set."

Miranda bit her lip. "Perhaps I can encourage them to remain longer. I simply must get away from Taverham soon."

"You could try, but I've a suspicion he's not going to make it easy. I had no chance to tell you when I called earlier today, but I spoke discreetly to Viscount Wade about your situation and the difficulties we might face in tracking a missing person."

Miranda gasped. "I've heard of him. Doesn't he usually investigate murders?"

Martin nodded. "Sometimes, but he also has skills in finding people who don't necessarily want to be found. Wade has offered to take your case for a reasonable fee without knowing the exact particulars yet. You can be assured of his utmost discretion. He's an old hand at keeping his enquiries out of the scandal rags." Martin procured her a glass of punch from a passing waiter. "I feel confident he will be of great help to you. He did ask if the one we sought might know anyone in London. I didn't believe that to be the case."

Relief filled Miranda. She'd been so worried all day because she hadn't made any progress toward finding her son, but at least Martin had found an exceptionally good investigator. "I kept him away from anyone of note so he could move freely, posing as Mr. Fenning's pupil."

"That will make locating him harder." Martin sighed. "How is your heart?"

"I'm fine now, Martin, truly better."

"You were not fine when I called on you today." He studied her face. "I assumed you would be out and about, scouring London for the boy, but when I saw you earlier I can understand why you were not. Have you sent for a physician?"

"I appreciate your concern, but I don't believe I'm so bad as that. Returning has been a little more complicated than I'd anticipated, but I'm doing my best to rest whenever I can. I haven't told Kit yet about my heart, but if he will not give me a minute's peace, I will have to." She smiled sadly. "Taverham insists on following me about and has barely left my side for even one hour today."

"He's attentive?"

"Yes." Miranda sighed. "Much as he was before our marriage."

"He's smitten."

"He's a man. Being one, you must know what he wants from me most of all."

"Anyone can see the pull between you is stronger than ever." Martin chuckled softly. "Your husband is scowling again."

"He's always scowling. Likely he has no other face."

Martin stifled a laugh. "Now, now. You're just peevish because Lady Brighthurst is here and staring at him so often."

"Of course I am. What woman wants to see her husband's

dearest love batting her eyelashes at him at every turn?" She shivered. "I keep telling myself not to care, but my stomach is turned by every obvious display."

"Miranda," Martin began as he inched closer. "Have you by chance noticed where Taverham's attention has been all night?"

She shrugged, avoiding looking across the room to catch him and his lover together. She could not take much more before sickening. "I hardly care."

"He's watching you, and only you, my lady. I've seen such a look on each one of my friends faces right before a marriage was announced. No one else can keep Taverham's attention long enough to hold a conversation with him. Daventry made a jest about his distraction earlier tonight and almost had his head taken off, saying something about not needing a week. He's watching me too by the way, but it's not a friendly look I'm receiving. Quite the opposite. He asked me what our connection really was earlier today. I would have to say he's worried."

"What worries can he possibly have?"

"Perhaps worried is an incorrect term. I have an idea what he's about, but let's see what he has to say for himself." Martin grinned. "He's coming this way now."

Miranda jerked her head up in time to see Kit stop before them. He and Martin shook hands in a somewhat abrupt manner. When Martin stepped back, Miranda saw from the corner of her eye that he was flexing his fingers as if Taverham's grip had hurt him. Kit's arm curled around her back, drawing her close to his side.

Having Kit touch her in public was a new experience, one she wasn't sure how to interpret. In any other man she might think it a sign of great affection, a glimpse into the heart of a man in love. With Kit, a man who loved another, it just confused her even more.

"Lord Louth," Kit murmured with just the slightest touch of reserve.

"Good to see you and Miranda again and clearly enjoying the season's entertainments once more," Martin said. "Lady Huntley is beside herself with glee at her triumph of having you both attend and look so content together."

Kit brought Miranda's hand up to his lips and kissed her

knuckles softly, an altogether possessive gesture that added to Miranda's surprise. "Yes, it's good to have her back where she belongs."

"Good, good. I am delighted you feel that way." Martin beamed. "Now, on another matter. I was thinking about your suggestion to take an interest in my cousin Whitney by inviting her to dinner. Were you serious about it? In the hours since I've seen you both, I've come to feel that forcing her out to converse with others might be in her best interest. Would you be amenable to helping me introduce her to suitable gentlemen? I cannot do it myself because of our pact, you see."

"You want our help to trick her." Miranda scowled. "That is a despicable deception, Martin."

"Perhaps," he conceded, looking only a little shamefaced. "But the alternative is giving in to her request to travel abroad. I cannot let her go alone, not in these uncertain times. While I enjoy and encourage her art, I'm not keen to follow her around the world so she may paint new vistas. Perhaps if she were to find a man with an interest in art too, they could travel together and I wouldn't have to worry so much."

Kit's brow creased in thought and then his expression hardened. "Why would you not like to leave London? You are not married and nothing holds you here."

Martin's face darkened. His jaw clenched tightly. Miranda knew that look well, though she'd rarely seen him lose his temper. Martin did not like to be told what to do either. He straightened his spine and glared. "Unlike *some* who married purely for money, my estates are not so well funded that I can leave them unattended for months at a time while I prowl the countryside chasing a bride who didn't want to return."

Miranda winced to have her history brought up.

"You should keep your nose out of our marriage and get your own," Kit said in a tone that warned he was spoiling for a fight.

Seeing an argument brewing, Miranda stepped between them before either man could say another word that might damage their friendship. Enough had already happened to dim the remaining respect between the two men. She wouldn't provoke more. "I can see your heart is in the right place, Martin. You want Whitney to be happy. If we were to host a dinner, we would surely invite your cousin to join us. If she were to meet a gentleman of similar tastes and possessed of a kind heart too, we would of course encourage the match. But only if it is in her best interest. You know my views on unequal marriages. I will not have her made miserable."

Kit's fingers curled over her shoulders, holding her still. As they pressed deeper, she squirmed a little. Her own experiences with marriage and making rash decisions had cost her so much more than just peace of mind.

She turned her face to Taverham's and caught his gaze. "You're in danger of hurting me."

He jerked his hands back, his face flushing with hot color. "My apologies."

"Of course Martin wishes to care for his estates and live his own life. Everyone wants independence to some degree. He cannot do either if he's compelled to travel away from England." She assessed her husband, noting he looked suitably abashed now. "I've not met Martin's cousin, but you have. What do you think of Whitney's chances on the marriage mart?"

He took a moment to collect himself, and Miranda was pleased when he seemed to consider her question with the proper attention it deserved. "We had an enjoyably long talk about life in Town. She is intelligent, more than passably pretty, though a trifle blunt." Kit glanced at Martin sternly. "I do think she is lonely though. I got the distinct impression her chaperone ignores her and sleeps far too much. You should not neglect her."

Martin's mouth twisted, but then he laughed outright. "I'm getting that impression myself. Well, I suppose I shall slip away from the party early and see if Whitney longs for companionship as badly as you claim. Good night, my lord. Oh, and Lady Taverham, one last thing."

Martin leaned close to her ear and whispered, "As I suspected. Your husband is actually a jealous man. Be careful of goading him beyond reason when you speak with other men. Pleasant dreams, my dear."

He sauntered away, blending into the crowd easily despite his height.

Miranda watched him go and then glanced up into Kit's face. "He's a grown man and is doing his best in regards to Whitney.

How could you speak to your friend like that?"

"Is he my friend, Miranda, or yours?" Taverham's gaze bored into her. "I cannot help but wonder if I have been misled about the two of you when I see how you smile so warmly at him."

"Less misled than I was," she muttered angrily. She couldn't believe Kit was jealous of Martin. The idea that Martin desired her was ridiculous.

She turned away as a sudden light sweat broke out over her skin. The evening was too warm. Her nerves poised on a fine edge of worry and fear for Christopher, and anxiety she had to hide from the man plaguing her with his attentions and groundless suspicions crept back again. She needed to rest alone. Martin had never been more than a friend. All he'd ever been was a shoulder to cry on, and that had never been very often. She would do everything she could to help him see Whitney settled, but truly only if such a situation was in the girl's best interest.

When Miranda presented Kit with their son and Martin delivered the written confirmations he held, her husband would regret his doubts about Lord Louth's interest in her.

Kit grabbed for her arm before she'd gone too far away from him, jerking her back to his side. "Where are you going?"

"To get some air." She fluttered her fan before her face desperately as her temperature soared beyond normal bounds. She could feel her face turning red. "I think a door is somewhere to the right, yes?"

Kit's brow creased in alarm as he stared into her hot face. The next moment, he curled his arm around her back gently to guide her through the crush of people. "I forget you are not used to crowds."

The Huntley's terrace was deserted when they stepped outside, and the cool night brought relief and blessed silence she appreciated. Miranda's ears buzzed for a short time and she sat herself down on the stone bench set close to a wall. Although a lady should not slouch, Miranda leaned against the wall so she could relax even more. Discreetly, she pressed her fingertips through the gap in her glove and tested her pulse. The wild, erratic beating proved her fears correct. She had reached her limits. Too much excitement and she would fall into a swoon. Miranda would prefer not to do that where her husband could watch her collapse.

"What were you talking to Lord Louth about?"

"He told me Viscount Carrington will certainly leave London next week. I should like to go see Agatha soon."

"Hmm, I'll come with you, or perhaps we could invite them to visit us instead. Luncheon?"

Miranda glanced up and saw that Kit didn't look particularly happy at the prospect of spending time with the Carrington's. She couldn't fathom why unless he'd developed a dislike for her cousin or for the company of children. Agatha was a sweetheart. "Are you not fond of children anymore?"

"On the contrary. I quite enjoy Carrington's brood. But for now I think they should come to us. It seems best all round to remain in one place. Together, that is."

He shuffled his feet, betraying to her that he wasn't being entirely truthful with that excuse. Was Martin correct about Kit being jealous, or was it just his usual possessiveness rearing its ugly head? "I do not expect your constant companionship, Kit. I am more than capable of paying calls on my own."

"I know," Kit grudgingly agreed. "But I'd rather be with you than not."

Miranda closed her eyes and willed her heart to slow. She hadn't foreseen Kit wanting to be with her every moment like this. How would she find Christopher with him in the way? She had to convince him she wouldn't run away. "I've no plans to leave London for the time being," she murmured softly.

He exhaled loudly. "I'm glad to hear that. Then we stay in Town as long as you wish and visit the Carrington's as often as you like. I would truly like to come with you if I may."

Something Louth mentioned tweaked her curiosity about Taverham's country estate, Twilit. "Do you not have your own affairs to attend to at home?"

"The estate runs itself now. In your absence I have hired the right people and they know what must be done."

"That must give you an enjoyable amount of free time to partake in your own pleasures."

He sat next to her, close enough that she could feel his warmth along her left side. "I *have* traveled quite a bit these past years, and it is nice not to need to anymore."

Miranda opened her eyes but kept her gaze focused on the view ahead rather than study her husband's face. "Oh, you must have been amply entertained these past years. I imagine a peer could spend an entire year simply traveling from one house party, soiree, country dance, to London and back again without having a spare hour to be bored."

She knew he'd not lived a reclusive life. The papers had been full of his deeds for the past decade. Enough of them to make it clear he'd not lacked for female companionship.

"My life hasn't been one round of parties after another, Miranda, if that's what you're suggesting. I traveled to look for you."

She didn't want to believe him, but it was hard to miss that his voice rang with sincerity. She swallowed the lump forming in her throat before speaking. "Where did you suspect you'd find me?"

"Everywhere I went." He caught her hand in his and toyed with the seam of her glove at her wrist. He pulled her hand onto his thigh and held it tightly.

Miranda's pulse leapt and she wished he'd simply leave her to recover her equilibrium in peace. She tugged her fingers back and folded her hands together in her lap. "Where did you think to find me two years ago? In the summer?"

He frowned. "Two years ago? Wales. I hadn't traveled there yet and spent a month or more visiting old school friends. Where were you then?"

"Staying with a friend in the south by the sea." Kit hadn't stood a chance of stumbling over her. "Before that, I spent most of my years in the north counties. You were chasing shadows."

"That is what I've concluded these past weeks." He teased the outer edge of her thigh with the tips of his fingers. "The hope that you lived was to die the night you returned to me. But you knew that too, didn't you?"

Miranda shrugged. "You should know by now that there is nothing the Marquess of Taverham can do that is not spread about England."

He glanced around them. "So if we made love here in this garden..."

Miranda faced her husband. Surely he wouldn't want such a

scandalous activity written about. "The whole of London would be suitably titillated with the news as they had their morning chocolate."

Kit drew closer. "That's a shame. I've always wanted to make love to you by moonlight."

At that moment, the moon burst from behind a cloud, illuminating them both where they sat. Kit smiled silkily. He leaned close and pressed a gentle kiss to her lips. His tongue darted out once, slicking her lower lip so she gasped. He drew back, still smiling wickedly. His fingers slid over her jaw and he cupped her cheek. The next moment, his customary frown returned. "You are distressed by the excitement of the ball far more than I realized. Your skin is so warm."

"That is my only purpose in remaining out here." Miranda fluttered her fan to cool her face.

He grunted. "We shall have to try for more than a kiss another night then."

Miranda closed her eyes again, certain Taverham would keep his head now and behave. "Do not be so certain you will have your wicked ways with me elsewhere or in more favorable circumstances."

"No?" He chuckled. "I'll have to do my best to convince you to at least try being scandalous just once with me. You might enjoy it. When you've rested enough, we'll go back inside. There are some acquaintances I must reacquaint you with before we return home. People who doubted you even existed. I'd love to make them eat their words, but I'll settle for greeting them coldly instead."

Miranda glanced sideways at her husband. "They whispered that you murdered me?"

For an answer, Kit smirked and shook his finger at her. "Just a little death now and then. Well, almost every night we've been together. Enough to make you sob and shake as I make love to you in our bed and elsewhere. I promise never to be any more danger to you than that."

Chapter Twenty-Two

———◆———

Kit kept a close watch on Miranda as the evening progressed, looking for a sign of increasing warmth toward him but uncertain if he was only seeing what he wanted to see. He was encouraged by their conversation on the terrace more than he dared believe. Opening up to Miranda might set himself up for disappointment, but at least she would hear from his own lips that he didn't live the charmed life she'd suspected on the profits of their marriage. There was something more between them. He'd never teased a woman, hung on her every response, the way he did with Miranda.

Occasionally, Miranda ventured beyond the reach of his arm, and he held his breath until he found her in the crowd once more. She moved smoothly through the guests, offering a friendly if reserved greeting to all, deflecting rudely phrased questions as if she'd been navigating high society all of their marriage. Occasionally, she'd glance his way and smile. Not a particularly convincing smile to him, but one that seemed to satisfy everyone else around them. Her cheeks held a flush of color that concerned him still though. If not for his wish to have her seen by all to be alive and largely content, he would have dragged her back home and to their bed, though she would probably resist his suggestion, that was where she would always belong.

It wasn't so irrational to fear he'd lose her again, but the very idea caused him to shiver until she found her way back to his side. He clung to hope that soon there might be some hint of a change of heart in his favor and he was doing all he could to be agreeable. Hadn't he put her needs first that morning in her bedchamber and the night before in their bed?

He wanted to make love to her so much he ached even now.

When she returned, he slid his hand softly over her back as a footman drew close carrying glasses of champagne. "Would you care for a glass of champagne, my dear?"

The corners of her mouth turned down a little. "No, thank you."

So not even champagne appealed to her tastes now. "Would you care to dance?"

Her frown grew and he caught his breath when she didn't deny him immediately. Was she a word away from being agreeable at last? Would she accept his invitation so he might continue to woo her?

He watched her face while she thought over his request but soon grew aware that someone tapped on his shoulder insistently. *Not now.* Not when Miranda might just say yes to him. Her gaze slipped to his shoulder and she scowled. Eventually he had to turn to see who dared interrupt them at such an important moment.

"There you are, Kit," Emily exclaimed as she smiled up at him. Her hand settled on his sleeve. "I was afraid you'd forgotten your promise."

"My promise," Kit queried quickly without a clue as to the promise he'd made. "Certainly not."

Emily glanced sideways toward the dance floor as the guests lined up to take their places in the sets that were forming. "This is our dance."

Damn. He hadn't remembered precisely what set he'd claimed. He closed his eyes and groaned silently. He wanted to dance with Miranda. Their interlude on the terrace had robbed him of precious time and now he was promised to Emily. What to do? People were already watching them and he did not want to hurt either lady's feelings.

Wincing inwardly, he glanced quickly at Miranda, noting as

he did so she seemed farther away. "Would you excuse me, my dear?"

Her eyes met his and the pain in them shook him to the core. The iris had darkened to black, any friendliness he'd imagined and hoped for between them was gone. "Naturally not," she said firmly. "Do not let me stand in your way ever again either."

She took two paces backward, spun about, and walked away—spine straight, stiff, and clearly angry that he'd asked her to dance but couldn't.

He wanted to run after her and apologize, but Emily was tugging him toward the dance floor where the set was about to start. What a mess he'd made of tonight. He should have worried more for offending Miranda than Emily. This was not the way to convince her to stay with him forever.

Kit watched Miranda until she reached his mother. The pair regarded each other warily like a pair of cats meeting for the first time, then his mother spoke and Miranda remained to converse with her.

Emily tugged on his sleeve. "We will miss a place."

"Yes, of course." They faced each other when the music commenced and he quickly fell into the required steps of a quadrille. From the corner of his eye, he kept a watch over his wife in case she made to disappear again. Although he had her promise not to leave London, he was still anxious enough to be wary.

Because of his distraction, Kit missed a change of direction and crashed into another dancer. "Oh, excuse me."

"Might help if you were paying attention to your partner instead of mooning after your wife," Lord Acton hissed. "For God's sake man, get a hold of yourself."

Kit quickly readjusted his focus to Emily and tried not to think of Miranda. It worked for a time, but his attention continued to stray to the sidelines where he found her all alone. His mother had abandoned her and Miranda wandered the perimeter, nodding to some but keeping herself apart from the gathering at large. As she passed certain groups, the ladies in them whispered furiously behind fans, their gazes darted to the dance floor where he twirled about with Emily.

Miranda never glanced his way or acknowledged those

whispers, but he could guess what they were saying and he feared it would be cruel. He gritted his teeth in frustration, knowing that when the dance ended he'd have to rush to Miranda and remain with her all night to dispel any ridiculous rumors.

As soon as the music stopped and he could reasonably make his escape, he bowed to Emily. "Thank you for the dance."

"I do love dancing with you," she said, overlooking the fact he'd not been at his best during the set. She smiled at him warmly. "Would you stay a moment?"

He searched the crowd where he'd last seen Miranda and discovered her in conversation with Lord Applebee, a former guardian of the Taverham estates, a man Kit had always been at odds with during his first years as marquess and then hadn't spoken to since the year after Miranda had run away. The pair appeared deep in conversation.

Kit didn't trust Applebee not to make things worse between them. "I must return to my wife. Excuse me."

The pair didn't notice his approach, so Kit heard part of their exchange before blundering in.

Applebee frowned a moment, then his expression changed to one of astonishment. "He still doesn't know?"

Miranda shook her head. "Not yet."

Applebee breathed deeply, his fingers splaying over his chest. "Why didn't you come to me first then?"

"I've not had a chance, and it's become even more complicated now."

"Well. Well, this is not at all what we agreed, but I can see you might have good reasons for your silence. I'll consult the others immediately. I would have moved heaven and earth to help you if I'd known my dear girl."

Kit smoothly joined their conversation, placing his arm about Miranda's waist. "We don't need your kind of help anymore."

Miranda gasped. "Kit, please."

Applebee scowled. "I see you're still abandoning your wife in favor of friends. What a shame you've never truly appreciated the remarkable woman you married."

"I did not abandon her. But as you know, a gentleman does not renege on his promise to dance with a lady when given some time in advance." Kit held out his arm for Miranda to take.

"Your involvement in my life ended some time ago, Applebee. I do not need to account for my actions anymore, except to my wife."

Applebee shook his head. "You reap what you sow. Don't turn your back on someone who can make all your problems disappear."

"Please," Miranda whispered as she stared at Lord Applebee. "We had an agreement, which I honored."

His eyes softened somewhat. "What evidence is there of that now? I will make enquiries immediately myself. We'll dine together—say, Friday—and discuss what else can be done to recover your keepsake. I must inform Lords Sorenson and Watts tonight."

He nodded decisively and moved off before Kit could say a word against the idea of dining together. He didn't need old grievances aired.

He glanced down at his wife and saw her troubled expression firmly back in place. "Miranda, is everything really all right?"

Her gaze jerked up to his. "Yes, of course it is."

"What was the keepsake you lost?"

"A small thing but very precious." She fanned her face. "Could we talk about it another time? People are staring at us."

Given that her face had pinked to a bright shade, he nodded. But still he ran his finger over the crest of her cheek, alarmed again at how distressed she'd become by a simple conversation with Applebee. "Did you want my former guardians coming to dine with us on Friday? I can always delay them."

She shook her head quickly. "They are coming regardless of what you say to them I'm afraid."

Kit couldn't ever remember Miranda being afraid of anything or anyone, but she trembled now. He brushed his hand softly over her back again. "Dance with me?"

She stiffened away. "Not a chance."

He followed her but didn't touch her this time. "I'm sorry if you were made uneasy by my dancing with Emily. I had promised her a set before your return to London and could not decline so late in the night. That would have been rude."

"And we wouldn't want *her* feelings hurt," Miranda muttered with an angry toss of her head.

The gesture puzzled him. She acted as if she didn't care about him every other time, so why be bothered by a harmless dance? Unless she *did* care and didn't want him to know it now. Buoyed by the idea of Miranda being even a little jealous, even over Emily who meant nothing to him, he leaned close to her ear. "But yours were, and I need to make it up to you."

She glanced at him again, her expression regretful. "That doesn't seem likely. You will hardly promise not to dance with her again."

"I can, but only if I have my preferred partner to take her place in my arms. You." He tipped her face to his and couldn't help but be concerned that her color was so high, even the tips of her ears appeared red. "I think we've been here long enough."

Miranda's shoulders slumped instantly and her face slid from his grip. "As you wish."

He pursed his lips at her relieved tone. Had dancing with Emily really bothered her that much? Surely she knew he'd not want Emily, given how determined he was to fit Miranda back into his life. He was trying so hard to win her over if only she'd let him succeed. "Let's find Mother and inform her of our decision to return home. Without her, if possible."

Miranda gripped his arm tightly as they said their good-byes to their hosts and acquaintances, as if she drew strength from his presence. Kit's worries doubled. Miranda had proved she didn't need him in the past. Why hold him so tightly now? There was something going on with her, and it wasn't just the desire she tried to hide from him.

Although he doubted she'd like it, he would not rest until she explained herself properly and tonight. When the carriage drew up to take them home, he helped her inside, pulled her straight into his arms, and spent the duration of their journey alternatively kissing her lips and nibbling her neck. He was wild for her well before they were halfway home. By the time the carriage drew to a halt before their town house, he was certain she understood he wanted her more than anything else in the world.

Chapter Twenty-Three

————◆————

On legs that had turned weak from the excitement the night had brought, Miranda stumbled into her bedchamber and headed for the flask of the potion that kept her heart beating at a normal pace. Behind her, she could hear Kit's heavy tread as he followed, pausing to speak with Addison about the dowager's later return and wishing him a good night.

Miranda needed a moment or four to recover her equilibrium. Her body was on fire from Kit's unending attentions, her heart galloping one moment, then not steadily the next.

Hands shaking uncontrollably as she grasped the bottle and sherry glass and slumped into a chair set beside her dresser, she attempted to get as much liquid into the small glass as possible.

"What the devil are you drinking?"

"Never granted a moment's peace," Miranda muttered as she carefully lifted the glass to her lips. She quickly swallowed the contents, then washed the brew down with a swift sip of water, wishing such measures were not necessary. "Applebee calls it a cure for a broken heart," she told him when he repeated his question.

Kit snatched up the flask and took a deep sniff. He gagged and coughed uncontrollably. He stared at her in shock. "Do you wish for death?"

"Hardly." She set the glass aside with a shudder and took the flask away from him to stopper it and contain the scent. "Keep me or kill me, but don't ask me to explain what's in it. All I know is it does me a world of good, very quickly if I'm lucky."

She leaned back in her seat and closed her eyes, focusing on her breathing and waiting for her heart rate to calm down. While she focused on herself, Kit crashed around her room, opened a window, and then she heard the brisk snap of fabric and felt the air stir across her skin.

Her chair shifted and creaked as Kit's presence penetrated her senses. When she opened her eyes reluctantly, he was leaning over her, arms braced on each arm.

His concern was all too apparent. "Why?"

"I told you, it's a remedy for my broken heart." She saw he did not understand, but she appreciated that he was concerned enough to ask for details. She sighed heavily at the need to explain. She didn't understand enough herself but believed everything her physician had claimed because after his treatment she'd felt so much better.

Feeling a bit steadier already, she pushed him back with one hand to his chest and stood to rinse the glass clean with water before setting it back on the mantel with the flask. "My mother died young; I never understood the cause until recent years. Long after we married, in fact. My heart beats at an erratic pace when I exert myself overmuch or when I become too agitated, as I must have done tonight. I must rest often and heed the warning signs before collapse."

He drew closer, his eyes wide. He cupped her face gently, thumbs sliding over her cheeks in a delicate caress. "Is that the real reason you wanted escape to the terrace and refused to dance with me? You feared you were becoming ill. I thought perhaps it was something else I'd done that had displeased you."

"Mostly that." The reason she wouldn't dance with Kit was because she would never compete with Emily for his time and attention, but he didn't need to know how much that relationship still upset her. Everyone had whispered about their dance and how tragic their affection was as she'd strolled by on her own, abandoned again in favor of the one Kit truly loved. Why humiliate herself?

Confiding to Lord Applebee about Christopher was the last

straw, causing unrelieved worry to return to prey on her mind. Pretending to be anything but content had been beyond her abilities in the end.

"Applebee has a similar weakness in his heart," Kit murmured, although Miranda knew all about that lord's many ailments. "He was always complaining about the need to be idle and regrets he could never marry because of it."

Kit's guardian had sent her the right doctors and a long list of instructions, insisting she take better care of herself. Avoidance of difficult situations, such as returning to her husband, was what she'd intended to do all along. She could have remained very calm indeed if Kit hadn't planned to declare her dead.

Kit's fingers lifted and skimmed her hair back from her face. "What can I do to make you comfortable?"

"Go to bed. I will be recovered by morning."

His fingers twined with hers and tightened. "Come to my room and sleep beside me."

She dipped her chin, knowing there really was no choice if she wished for a restful night's sleep. Kit might not have noticed the absence of her mattress from her four-poster bed yet, but Miranda could see the gaping space left after its removal.

The dowager must want a grandson very badly to play this game of forcing her into his bed for yet another night. A pity she didn't know the truth but when she did hopefully she would cease her unnecessary machinations. In a way, Miranda wasn't altogether surprised she'd meddle. The dowager marchioness was just as bad as her son when it came to getting her own way. After all, he had to have learned the knack from one of his parents.

She allowed Kit to lead her to his bed. He turned back the comforter and sheets, helped her from her gown. She stood naked before him while his eyes skimmed her body, but then he shook his head and found her nightgown to put on. Once she was clothed in it, he bore her down to the mattress, then all but trapped her in his bedding, tucking the comforter so tightly around her that she could not move an inch in the vast bed, as if she were a child.

When he joined her after turning down the lamps, he wasn't quite on his side of the great bed when he faced her. When he tried to capture her hand and discovered she'd been cut off, he chuckled softly and loosened the bedding at last. He found her fingers and brought them to his lips for a soft kiss. "I needed to know this, Miranda."

"I believed the ailment under better control until tonight. You made a very bad match in me." She squeezed his hand. "I'm sorry."

"Have I ever said I regretted marrying you?"

"But it is true just the same."

He rose above her, eyes hard as stones as he looked into her face. The next instant he kissed her brow, her cheek, the tip of her nose. A sweet gesture that once she would have believed meant something far more caused her heart to ache for what might have been.

"Sleep now," he ordered. "We'll talk tomorrow and over the days to come about what the doctors have told you and what we must do. No more secrets from now on. All right?"

That would be difficult to agree to until she found her son, but she nodded anyway.

He leaned close, pressed one final kiss to her temple, and then collapsed on his pillow.

Miranda didn't want to argue with him now when he was being so nice and she was beginning to feel better. When her heart raced, she feared each beat might be the last it made, so she said nothing and twined her fingers tightly with his, pretending for the night that she could be loved by him, though she doubted he would like her enough to worry for her health after Christopher came into his life.

"Miranda," he whispered. "I'm to go riding in Hyde Park tomorrow morning with friends, and while I'd like nothing more than for you to join us, I don't think that's wise given what I know of your health now. I'll do my best not to wake you. Promise me you'll rest as long as you can."

It would be so easy to believe he cared, but she did have to go out herself to look for Christopher. "I'll try."

He kissed her palm and let her go but remained close by her side as her eyes drifted shut. The sound of his steady breathing was the last thing she heard till morning.

Chapter Twenty-Four

———•———

Mornings hadn't always been Kit's favorite time of day. In the past he'd woken to an empty bed, and a day empty save for the business of appearing busy. He'd much rather be in bed with Miranda now, watching her sleep so peacefully as if their problems didn't exist and her heartbeat was as strong as his. It had taken all of his resolve not to wake her this morning just to check she was feeling better. Worrying for her was nothing new, but now he had a specific ailment rather than the vague idea of losing her as the world swallowed her up.

A troubled heart did not bode well for their life together though. What he knew of the complaint was very little. He remembered Lord Applebee's face, alternatively pale and red, depending on the state of his health. Keeping to a sedate life had seemed to ease his complaints.

A quiet life was easier lived in the country than in Town. Knowing what he did now, he wasn't sure why Miranda hadn't jumped at the chance to return to the quieter pace of Twilit Hill when first suggested. Perhaps he would never understand what drove her.

Miranda's possible mortality was not an issue he wanted to face yet, although he'd always been afraid to discover she'd died somewhere. There was so much he'd wanted to share with her and now might find that chance taken away. Every day would have to count as if it were their last together. He would spoil her as no woman had been before. He drew back on the reins. "Time to go back, Acton," he shouted to his companion as Acton's gray mare pulled away and Kit's chestnut slowed.

Acton hauled his mount around rather carelessly and trotted back to where Kit had slowed to a walking pace. "We've hardly begun."

"I have some business to take care of."

"Does your wife demand your undivided attention now?"

"Miranda was asleep when I left."

Acton smirked. "So ride farther with me. She'll be none the wiser."

Kit shook his head as he turned his horse toward the park entrance and home. Acton didn't understand what it meant to Kit to be married and able to see his wife at last. He wanted to be with her more than anything. Miranda would hardly care if he was late, he expected, but it mattered very much to him. "Continue without me and I will see you later."

After a few yards, Acton's horse drew level. His friend's face wore a bitter expression. "I guess this is how it will be now she's returned. Your friends will come a poor second the moment she so much as snaps her dainty fingers."

"You're being ridiculous."

"Am I? I don't think so." Acton scowled. "I waited for you to join me in the card room last night, except I understand your wife demanded to go home early instead. Emily was especially upset and had to be jollied into any sort of good spirits."

Kit sighed. "Miranda makes no demands of me in public. She never would. It's me that is eager to see her."

A low chuckle left Acton. "So the rumors are true then."

"What rumors?"

Acton seemed to consider his words a moment. "By all accounts your wife is a demon in the bedchamber."

Kit wrenched the reins of his horse, stopping him dead in the middle of the path and blocking Acton's way. "Who the hell said that about my wife?"

Acton appeared startled and jerked on the reins so his horse stopped, dancing in place. His face paled. "Surely you've heard the worst by now."

Kit gripped the reins tight, overcome by fury. "No one has ever mentioned seeing her before," he growled.

"Well, they are saying it now. It's not good."

"Tell me."

Acton considered it a long while, then shook his head. "Wives have affairs all the time and no one thinks twice about it. I'm on your side."

Kit's temper, barely in check, soared. "I want to know what they say about my wife."

Acton rubbed his jaw and leaned forward. "Everyone is talking about her appetites. Gobbles a man up and makes him beg for more. You were better off without her."

"I want a name for the source of that rumor."

Acton's face fell. "She really has blinded you, hasn't she, even when you have Emily to distract you. It's not one man talking about her, but many. I don't think it's in your best interest to know those names. They'll just deny the rumor to you, and you're bound to look a jealous fool."

Acton moved off, shaking his head.

Kit kicked his mount forward. "Acton," he growled.

Acton turned in his saddle, his expression distressed. "Yes, I think you were right to head back home and set your mind at ease. Keep close watch over her. Who knows what the lady could be up to with so much time on her hands?"

Acton kicked his horse into a trot and changed direction, leaving Kit free to head directly home. But he kept his mount still and swore. Damn it all, he would be jealous of anyone his wife so much as looked at twice. He'd already considered at length what he'd do to Louth should they be involved. He retained a niggling doubt about them, a suspicion that had burrowed deep in his mind and refused to be quieted despite reassurances.

It was just a rumor and not necessarily a fact. The same as the rumor about himself and Emily, which was certainly malicious speculation and should not be believed. Miranda could not engage in so many affairs if her heart was truly fragile. He did not believe she lied about the state of her health.

Suppressing his suspicions, though, took work, and he walked his horse through the park instead of galloping. He and Miranda were mending their relationship a bit at a time. He would not risk it by making an unsubstantiated accusation until he had proof she'd been unfaithful to him.

On his way through the park, he stumbled upon Lord Carrington with his large brood of children running around him. Seeing the family together in so happy a group made him wish his marriage was vastly different than what it was now—barely held together. He'd always wanted a large family instead of continuing the Taverham tradition of such a lonely childhood as he'd endured. Miranda had seemed interested in the same, although she didn't want to talk about having offspring now.

Since he was overdue in paying the promised call to the Carrington's, he drew to a stop and swung down from the saddle. The chestnut was trained not to wander or start at sudden noises, so he let the reins dangle on the ground and walked to join them. He would invite them to visit Miranda today and maybe that would make her happy. "Carrington."

The man glanced up from his conversation with the youngest child and smiled broadly. "Well met, my friend. How did Miranda enjoy the party last night?"

"Very well, although I'm not certain she was at ease in the crowd, and we left early to spare her the discomfort of greeting so many people." He smiled ruefully. He'd probably caused her considerable distress. "I'm sorry we have not called on you yet."

Carrington held up his hands. "I quite understand. I am sure there are many who wish to make her acquaintance again. Agatha would likely be cross if she hadn't seen her for herself already, but she hoped to call on Miranda today if she will be at home. I think Agatha's finally over the shock of having her cousin return."

"I wish I were so lucky."

Carrington tipped his head to the side to distance them from the children. "I take it the happy couple still has a way to go before they can be called such a thing?"

"Miranda is different."

"How so?"

Kit removed his hat and raked his fingers through his hair. "The things I thought I knew about her seem entirely wrong. It's as if she's a complete stranger to me."

"Marriage takes some adjustment. Give it time, or are you reconsidering a divorce? There are many in society who would understand she doesn't suit anymore."

Kit met Carrington's gaze and the other man looked away quickly. Had he heard rumors of Miranda and her lovers too? "I dislike the idea of a divorce immensely. I won't give up on her just because she's become a greater challenge."

Carrington nodded. "I'm glad to hear you have so strong a view. May we call on you then? Today. Agatha has it in her head to introduce all the children at once but perhaps that is too many if she has had a difficult night before. The youngest three have been remarkably well behaved of late. I'll convince her those three will be enough to begin with and they can convey their thanks for the gifts she sent yesterday. The children have talked of nothing else."

Kit glanced over at the children where they stood about his horse. He should have considered a similar thing, surprise gifts for the struggling family, but truthfully until he'd watched Miranda pick and choose gifts for them all, he wouldn't have done well at it. She'd seemed to understand intuitively what was most likely wanted.

All but Simon were fixated on patting the chestnut's nose, and Kit smiled at him. A remarkable boy. Simon never caused the slightest trouble for Carrington. That in itself was impressive for an orphan.

The boy left the others to come closer. His expression was keen. "Did you find your wife?"

"I did."

"Is she well now?"

Kit frowned, startled that the boy knew his wife had been ill when he'd only learned about it last night. "As well as can be expected."

The boy frowned fiercely. "You did not bring her to see us."

Kit squirmed at the child's surprisingly hostile accusation. "My apologies. We will be home today and I think Carrington here is going to bring some of the younger children to see her."

Simon stared at Carrington. Simon was the eldest boy. "You are making me stay in Berkley Square?"

Carrington attempted to ruffle his hair, but the child stepped back out of reach. "We are overwhelming in great numbers, and the marquess thought his wife might not like that. You can see her another day. Perhaps next week if we are all still in London then."

"I see." The boy's eyes lowered.

Moved by the boy's disappointment, Kit placed his hand on the boy's shoulder and leaned down to look into his face, which was difficult to do since the boy seemed long overdue to have his hair trimmed. Kit could barely see his eyes behind his fringe of hair. "I'm on my way home now and will tell her myself that you were keen to see her."

The boy bit his lip, eyes darting left and right, anywhere but at him. "She's at your town house now."

"She is. When I left to go riding this morning she was still asleep in my bed. I hope she'll still be there when I get back as she was very weary after last night."

The boy nodded again and stepped back, apparently satisfied with his promise. Kit watched him after he left them, puzzled by his obvious disappointment before and behavior now. Simon surveyed the park in swift glances, almost as if he were studying who was around him. Tension gripped Kit. What was the child about? He returned to the other children, leaned down to speak to little Mabel, who hung on his every word. Kit sighed and dismissed his anxiety as inconsequential as the boy straightened.

As Carrington began to ask if Miranda might not be too tired to have visitors at all, the boy met his gaze and grinned.

Kit's heart stopped at that expression.

The next moment, Simon bolted for the entrance of Hyde Park, running in the direction of Mayfair as if he were being chased by the very devil.

Chapter Twenty-Five

———◆———

There was one thing to be said for the life of a peer in that doing nothing and resting seemed rather easy to manage. Miranda sat forward as April plumped cushions behind her back and urged her to lie against them. "Is that better, my lady?"

"They were fine to begin with, you know. I'd like to get up if you don't mind."

April, who had been showing more promise each day until today's fussing, ignored her soft reproach and turned for the breakfast tray. "His lordship said I have to make you happy, and you needed another pillow behind your back to be comfortable. If I were a lady, I'd stay there for hours."

April's brow furrowed as she lifted the heavy tray, tiptoed across the chamber, and gently deposited it over Miranda's lap. When she let go, her sigh of relief was loud.

"Hours in bed make me very cross." Miranda chuckled softly. "I am not made of glass."

"Yes, but his lordship said I had to take care of you and wanted you to rest until he comes back."

"I don't believe he meant I couldn't get up at all. Who knows how long he'll be?" Another hour yet she hoped. Long enough for April to tire of fussing and allow her to dress. Then Miranda could slip out and begin her search. A walk in the square seemed to be a good start. Miranda picked up a corner of toast and buttered it while April crept about the room straightening things. Miranda frowned. "April, where have you gotten the idea that you need to tread so quietly? Surely I never told you to do that."

April fidgeted. "The dowager marchioness' maid said I had to learn to be quiet or expect to be sent to work in the kitchens."

"The dowager marchioness' maid has no idea what I expect from you. I don't believe I have even seen her. Go on as you have, dear girl, and if you do something I do not like then I will assuredly suggest a change, but you will hear it from my own lips and not the dowager's servant."

April bit her lip, but the tension seemed to ooze from her limbs. She sighed. "If you say so."

"I do indeed." Miranda stretched out her hand. "Now, where is today's paper?"

"I'm sorry. Mr. Addison wouldn't give it to me. He said the master of the house always reads it first before anyone, then the dowager receives it."

"Even when he's out he gets his way," Miranda muttered under her breath. Reading the papers on the day they were published rather than a week later was an advantage she enjoyed when in Town. "I'll make arrangements for Landry to secure my own copy from tomorrow onward. You will ask him for it rather than Addison."

"Mr. Addison won't like that. Landry's not popular as it is."

Miranda leaned back. "Landry is popular with the person who employs him. Addison's opinion is no more valuable than the air he spoke with."

April giggled and then hurried into the other room where Miranda's clothing and possessions were stored.

Miranda finished her toast, dusted off her fingers, and considered the rest of the feast set before her. Unfortunately, her appetite had waned already. She had so much to do today, and nothing was more important than finding her son.

Miranda finished the last of her tea, calling for April to take the unwieldy tray from her lap.

A loud bang sounded through the house, and Miranda frowned at the rare noise. Usually the servants were so quiet as to be unheard, except perhaps for April and Landry when they were close, but that noise couldn't be one of them. She detested creeping servants surprising her when she suddenly noticed them at her elbow. Her heart couldn't take the strain of enduring such behavior all day and every day.

A man shouted *stop* at the top of his lungs beyond her bedroom door and Miranda flinched.

She quickly handed her breakfast tray to April. Likely no one yelled at Twilit House unless it was the marquess, and he never sounded as panicked as that voice had been. As she rose to an upright position, the door to her bedroom was flung wide.

Christopher grinned at her. "Mama."

Miranda shrieked and flung herself across the bed as Christopher raced across the room and into her arms. Her son had finally found his way home to her. Miranda drew him against her tightly and rocked him from side to side wildly. She'd believe this moment a dream except he smelled of horses and sweat and the boy she loved with all her heart. "My boy. My darling little man. Where have you been?"

Christopher tightened his grip around her neck and clung. "Waiting for you. I was so afraid you'd never get better."

"Nothing could keep me away from you." Miranda drew his head back, brushed his long hair away from his face, and kissed his forehead soundly. "I'd never dessert you. I love you so much."

Miranda pulled him toward the bed and waited till he sat down, ignoring how April stared and listened to every word. "Come back later," Miranda told her swiftly.

When April disappeared into the next room, Miranda ran her hands over her son's head, brushed his soft cheeks, and stared into his pale green eyes. "You've grown so much since I saw you last."

Christopher laughed. "And you're still in your nightgown. Are you sick still?"

Miranda nodded. "It comes and goes. Finding you missing from Mr. Fenning's care did nothing for my peace of mind."

Christopher dipped his head. "We said we would only return together."

She brushed his long hair back from his eyes and lifted his chin so she could stare at him. She couldn't recall him ever wanting to grow it so long before and hoped he wasn't overly attached to it. She smiled at him warmly, heart filling, bursting with love for him. She drew him closer to her side and wrapped an arm about his shoulders. "I know what I said, but dear God, where have you been? I've been so afraid I'd lost you. You look like a street urchin, except you are somewhat cleaner."

"No one looks twice at an urchin." He scrunched up his face. "I went to the orphanage cousin Agatha and Grandfather supported. I've lived with Agatha for the past year since she married Lord Carrington."

Miranda gasped. "But I was there, in that house, not two days ago."

"And I was here speaking to *him*. I came at once. I saw your name mentioned in the paper and everyone was talking of you that morning. We missed each other."

Miranda hugged Christopher close against her again as she thought over her previous conversations with Martin. "Agatha never mentioned your name among her children."

"I chose another name. I'm Simon to everyone else."

"Oh." That explained quite a lot about how he could be with Agatha and still be so well hidden. But… she rubbed her forehead at how complicated matters would be now. "Agatha will be upset with you over the deception. With us both probably. Did you tell her who you really were?"

"Not once, though I did consider it when she cuddled me when I was sad. When I missed you the most she was the nearest thing to having your arms about me." Christopher shrugged. "I like her, but she'll understand she cannot keep me."

"I hope so." Miranda drew her son close and rocked him in her arms. "I missed you, my dearest love. We have all the time in the world to be together now."

Chapter Twenty-Six

Kit froze outside the door to his bedchamber as Miranda's shocking words carried into the hall. He'd followed Simon's dangerous run all through Mayfair on horseback since Carrington was burdened with his children and too slow to follow the surprisingly fast child as he tore through the busy streets on foot. He was puzzled that the boy had come here of all places. The front door had been wide open and he followed the voices of those lingering in the halls.

Yet the moment he'd realized Miranda was entertaining a man in his bedchamber a fury unlike anything he'd felt before consumed him, and he didn't care one whit for Carrington's runaway son nor where he'd gone.

Around him, a half dozen upper servants had gathered, trying now to look busy polishing the bannisters and dusting paintings instead of eavesdropping on the scene inside.

Miranda hadn't even done him the courtesy of closing the door so the servants wouldn't hear every word she spoke to the one she truly loved.

How dare she flaunt her affairs so brazenly beneath his own roof as if he were nothing? As if their marriage didn't matter. As if she could do whatever she wanted. Well, he'd not stand for it.

He shooed the servants away with an impatient flick of his hands, astonished to find some in tears, others dazzled by the conversation taking place inside the room.

He crept closer, determined to find out who it was that claimed his wife's heart. He wouldn't let her know how badly she'd hurt him, but he would insist she leave immediately. He'd throw her out onto the street if she didn't go willingly.

Just outside the doorway, he paused to draw a steadying breath before he took three more steps to cross the threshold.

His wife lifted her face away from the little man she held tightly against her breast. Kit gaped at her. This was whom she loved?

"Kit," she said, a smile brightening her entire face regardless that her deception had been discovered.

The man in her arms twisted around and Kit found himself face to face with Carrington's child, Simon. Kit blew out a breath as relief slammed into him. Miranda was not meeting a lover. He'd been utterly mistaken. "You gave us all a scare, young man. Your father will be furious with you for the fright you just gave him."

He glanced between the pair when they said nothing to that but continued to touch each other as if it was the most normal thing in the world. He glared at Simon. "What the devil are you doing on my bed, boy?"

Simon licked his lips, a nervous gesture Carrington needed to cure him of and soon if he ever wanted to win at cards one day, and gained his feet. The boy circled the bed bravely, set his hands behind his back, and stood at attention. "I was greeting my mother properly."

Kit rocked back on his heels, swung his gaze to his wife. Miranda only looked at the boy Simon, a smile of such love and devotion on her face that he couldn't mistake her feelings were strong for the child. He blinked in astonishment. When he turned his attention back to Simon, he was still there, chin lifted, eyes defiant.

The boy smiled softly. "Hello, Father. I apologize for interrupting your ride in the park."

Kit's breath seized. His ears roared with nameless sound, then his heart shuddered, pounding painfully against his ribs. He stared at the boy he knew as Carrington's, a fatherless, motherless boy these past two years that he knew of. He shook his head repeatedly.

Miranda slipped from the bed still in her nightgown and joined Simon, her hands closing over the boy's shoulders tenderly. She grinned at him, brushed her fingers across his forehead to move his hair aside from his eyes. "I take it you two are already well acquainted."

Simon glanced up at her. "We met last year after Great-grandfather Birkenstock died. He said very nice things about him and has always been kind to me."

Miranda curled her arm about the boy and whispered in his ear. "Everyone is kind to you."

The child smiled so delightedly that Kit found it painful to look upon. "You had a son."

She nodded, her expression open and the happiest he'd seen since their wedding breakfast ten years ago. "I delivered your heir, as you predicted I would. Now you have everything you ever wanted from me. I hope you can learn to love him as I do."

Kit shook his head again to clear the fog from his mind. He must be dreaming. He must have misheard her and there was another explanation. He couldn't be the boy's father, or Miranda a mother. She would have told him long before this. He would have known they had a child. She should never have kept such a secret from him.

Simon turned to look up at her, jiggling in place as excitement gripped him. "Father was riding Ares again in Hyde Park. Have you seen him? He's smashing."

Miranda kissed the top of Simon's head and chuckled. "No, but I've heard he spent a pretty penny to purchase him last year, so he must be a worthy mount."

Her eyes met Kit's briefly and a flicker of puzzlement appeared.

Kit shook his head and she sighed.

Simon turned back to Kit, his expression excited. "A groom at the Duke of Staines' stables tried to teach me to ride a bit when we were in the country, but I'm not very good yet. When I'm grown a bit more may I ride Ares? Will you teach me to be as graceful on horseback as you? Father? I say. Are you all right?"

Kit staggered back several paces, bumping heavily into a chair and sinking into it. He stayed exactly where he was and watched in shock as the scene before him unfolded. The pair continued to chatter as if fatherhood wasn't supposed to surprise him. Well, he was *very* surprised. If he had a son, he would have taught him to ride his horse long before this. They would have spent hours in the saddle together riding over Twilit Hill, the estate the boy would inherit, and would never have been an afterthought left to a servant to teach.

As he listened to Miranda and Simon make plans to spend the day together, the roaring sound grew louder again.

Miranda had lied to him. Why would she have kept the news of their son a secret? There was no reason except to cause him pain. She knew he'd hoped for an heir. They had talked about his need for a son on the eve of their marriage, well before her disappearance and several times since her return too. They had discussed plans for their children's education and upbringing. He'd always planned ahead. Yet he'd never expected this.

The boy was his heir if they spoke truthfully. He'd had a son for ten years. Or had he?

He narrowed his gaze on Miranda as she laughed softly. She had not told him of the child for a reason. It was clear that she was fond of the boy. Too fond. No Marchioness of Taverham had ever displayed such affection for their offspring. Kit's own mother had never embraced him as Miranda was now doing with Simon.

She did love him. The boy had her heart.

But that did not make Kit a father.

He narrowed his gaze on Simon, looking for proof of parentage. The boy didn't look much like either of them in his opinion. Sandy-brown hair, unremarkable, pale green eyes hidden behind hair grown too long. Intelligent, but that did not mean much. He could be anyone's child.

Miranda smiled and his blood ran cold. She must be enjoying her joke at his expense. She intended to foist another man's child on him to steal the Taverham estates for herself and the offspring of one of her many lovers, just to hurt him.

He shot to his feet, straightened his waistcoat, and smoothed his hair before he addressed the pair. "If you'll excuse me, I believe I need to speak to my solicitor."

Simon froze, facing him quickly. "Why, Father?"

"Do not speak to me, boy."

Simon flinched, drawing close to Miranda for comfort. As before, her arms curled about his chest protectively as she sought to comfort him in the face of Kit's anger. The glance she speared him with was filled with disappointment. "You must do what you think is right for you, of course, husband, but you are making a mistake."

The knife in his chest turned. Husband? Father? He'd been neither. He'd never had a fair chance to be anything he should. If he'd truly had a child, there was nothing he would not do to make them feel wanted, valued. He'd vowed never to ignore his children the way his parents had done to him.

He strode from the room, past servants who gawked at the scene they'd just witnessed, past his mother on the stairs, who demanded an explanation for the ruckus he couldn't speak of, and crashed headlong into Viscount Carrington and his weeping children in the entrance hall. When asked about Simon, he could only gesture to the staircase behind him. He was too furious for words.

He'd been made a fool.

He locked himself inside his study, drew out pen and paper, and drafted an urgent letter to his solicitor explaining everything he knew about Miranda. There was no choice now but to suffer the embarrassment of divorce. A very public and messy divorce that would reveal his wife's infidelity.

When he was done, he sat back in his chair and discovered his face was wet with the first tears he'd cried in his adult life.

Chapter Twenty-Seven

He didn't believe. Miranda swallowed back the unexpectedly painful hurt and hugged Christopher against her one more time. "Are you hungry, darling?"

"No. Why does Father need a solicitor?"

To annul their marriage most likely. Or at least attempt to begin divorce proceedings. When Lord Louth came with her letters, and Kit's guardians confirmed the contents as legitimate testimony on Friday, he'd be hard-pressed to win that particular battle. The cost to his reputation would be too high.

"Never mind about that for now," she told her son, wishing not to worry him. She held Christopher at arm's length and drank in the wonder of seeing him again. "Let me have a proper look at you. I think you've grown at least three inches in height since we were together last, and that hair has to go or I'll forever be pushing it back from your face. Anyone would think you've been utterly abandoned if we leave it that way."

A throat cleared behind her. A feminine sound. Old and impatient too.

Miranda turned slowly and curtsied to Kit's mother.

Christopher bowed. "A pleasure to see you again, Grandmother."

She lifted her quizzing glass to her eye and looked her grandson over with a sniff, leaning heavily on a walking stick. "You are mistaken, young man. I would never have a grandson who thundered about the town house as you just did. Why, you're positively wild. I will not stand for it happening again."

"I was in a hurry, and Addison was in my way. I will apologize to him of course when Mother gives me leave to go." Christopher bravely took a pace forward and smiled at the dowager. "You'll get used to my ways eventually. I'm really quite charming, or so Cousin Agatha claims."

"Charming, and possessed of a slick tongue of the kind my son employs on occasion when he wants his way with a minimum of fuss." The dowager put her quizzing glass away. "The pleasure is all mine. Welcome home at last, Christopher Reed."

Miranda rocked back on her heels in shock. "You knew."

Kit's mother glanced at her, annoyance twisting her expression. "Do not mistake my knowing as approval of your selfishness." She glanced over Christopher again, her eyes narrowing. "I learned you'd delivered a child, a healthy boy, quite by accident. Luckily the midwife who attended you had a weak, grasping character and could be persuaded to confess her part in the deception. But she did not know who fathered him, and since you stayed in hiding I said nothing of it to my son."

Her sharp appraisal reminded Miranda that someone had tried to hurt her son. She pushed Christopher behind her. "I won't allow you to hurt him."

The dowager's gaze darted between Miranda and Christopher. She leaned forward. "Don't be ridiculous. I have waited an eternity for my son's child to arrive. Why ever would I hurt him?"

Miranda considered that. It was true that she and the dowager had never warmed to each other, but did that make the woman a danger to Christopher? She didn't know but intended to find out. She watched the old woman's face closely as she began to speak. "Someone certainly tried to hurt him. Someone that knew about Christopher and had his tutor's home set alight while my son was still inside it. He is lucky to be alive."

The dowager shut her eyes briefly, her fingers shifting restlessly on the handle of her cane. "I would not hurt him. I swear I would not. If I'd known where he was, I would have abducted him instead and ensured the succession was never in danger to begin with. The boy belongs to his father."

Despite the threat of abduction in the dowager's words, Miranda was inclined to believe she spoke truthfully. A little of her tension eased and she loosened her grip on Christopher. She glanced down at him quickly.

He nodded. "She wasn't the lady who came that day."

Miranda stared into his eyes. "Did you see who it was, sweetheart?"

"Yes." He glanced at the dowager. "Grandmother never rides and the pale lady was young and sat a horse very well. I would know her anywhere."

Miranda pulled Christopher hard against her. She kissed the top of his head repeatedly and rocked him to and fro. "She won't ever come close to you again. I swear it on my life."

"I know." He smiled and Miranda ruffled his hair. Christopher was safe now. She'd die before she'd allow him placed in danger again.

The dowager cleared her throat again. "Now I see this impudent fellow in the right setting, at your side, I understand a little of why he wasn't with you on your return. Your cousin's orphaned ward indeed. I thought my son had more honor than this."

She moved to sit in a chair, an unexpected groan passing her lips as she did so.

Christopher rushed to her side. "Is your leg paining you today, Grandmother?"

"Never you mind my leg or trying to charm me. I suggest you follow your father's footsteps and prevent that letter from being sent to his solicitor. The contents might cast aspersions on your inheritance claim. He'll never listen to me about acting rashly. He didn't listen to my warnings when he married your mother either, and this misunderstanding is as much his fault as hers. Use your charm on him and the butler to get the letter back."

Christopher hurried to Miranda and kissed her cheek. "I know where they will be."

Miranda held out her hands, frightened momentarily to have Christopher out of her sight again so soon. "Are you sure you want to face your father alone?"

He nodded but bit his lip. "Can Landry come with me?"

Miranda nodded swiftly. "Keep him with you at all times. I trust *him*."

"Get the letter first, boy," the dowager interrupted. "Addison still listens to me. Have him deliver the letter into my hands rather than yours if he protests giving it up."

"Yes, Grandmother." Christopher strode out, spoke to Landry briefly at the door, and then disappeared from her sight with her servant trailing after him. Miranda ached to follow.

The dowager met her gaze. "We knew little more beyond the midwife's confirmation of his existence."

Miranda frowned. "We? You and Kit questioned the midwife? I thought he seemed so surprised, but I never could read his intentions properly."

"My sons shock is understandable." The dowager frowned. "Emily and I acquired the information together, and we didn't tell him. She has been looking into your disappearance discreetly for many years as a way to give my son the peace he needed to set your marriage aside."

"Then it was Lady Brighthurst who found Christopher." Miranda clenched her teeth. Anger bubbled up inside her so strongly she couldn't breathe. Had the woman tried to erase Christopher from existence so Kit, once he'd given in and had Miranda declared dead, would be free to marry her without any further obstacles? "She must have found my boy two years ago and never told you."

Miranda glanced across the room at her mother-in-law and saw only confusion in her old eyes. "She would have told me," the woman whispered softly in a shocked voice. "She knew how badly I wanted a grandson. If not for you and the money, Kit would have married her long ago. She's the daughter I always wanted."

"So he kept her as a mistress instead. That must have been quite the insult." Miranda shook her head. "No wonder she tried to kill my son. We have always been in her way."

The dowager's spine stiffened. "My son is an honorable man. I would know if my son kept a mistress and certainly he would never dishonor our Emily with such a vulgar suggestion. Their love is pure."

"Please don't insult my intelligence. I saw them together on my wedding day. They were intimately involved then, and still are." Miranda paced the room. She had to keep Christopher and Emily apart. But how could she do that when Kit would never believe her? She faced the dowager. "Would you prefer Emily as Kit's wife even if she had tried to rob your grandson of his life?"

"Well," the dowager said. But then said nothing more and looked down at her hands a long time. After a time, her head rose slowly. "I cannot countenance such measures being taken for any reason."

"Then we are stuck with each other."

The dowager grimaced. "Yes, I can see we may very well be."

Miranda stared at the dowager. "You know I don't care about the title or the money. I never did. I just want my son to be happy and safe. To grow into a strong and honorable man in possession of a kind heart."

"We are in agreement." The dowager stood slowly, leaning heavily on her cane. "The Taverhams have ever been stubborn."

"I am aware."

"They possess not the slightest trace of patience."

"Don't I know it," Miranda said, failing to keep the bitterness from her voice.

"You robbed my son of his chance to know his child and heir these past years. When society learns you not only left him but bore him a son you then hid, he will be made a laughingstock. Speculation will rise again as to why you left."

"That is between myself and Kit." Miranda grimaced. "Christopher's life had been planned down to the last detail long before I was even sure I carried him."

"But that is what Taverhams do. They plan ahead for every eventuality." The dowager huffed. "You may be the first Taverham bride who made their husband wait for anything. I never managed such a feat despite my attempts with his father, but perhaps you will have some small success. The boy has remarkable potential, but don't push his father's limits too far or you will live to regret it."

Miranda bit her lip. Perhaps she already did regret surprising Kit in this manner. His face had been one of shock and then anger. She'd expected him to demand an explanation, an apology even, but all he'd done was stare at Christopher as if he were in a nightmare.

The old woman took her leave without a word, her steps slow as she used the cane for support. Christopher must be correct that the old woman was in pain. Miranda would not have guessed, but as she'd avoided the woman since her return as much as was possible, she wasn't surprised to have missed the signs. Their conversation today was the warmest they'd ever shared, and that was not saying very much.

How strange to find her son so well acquainted with the people she'd warned him to avoid. Now she had to be certain he kept away from his father's true love.

Eager to discover what was transpiring below, Miranda rushed into the other room where April still lingered so she could help Miranda dress for the day. She ignored the girl's speculative gaze. Likely she'd listened to Miranda and the dowager's conversation. Miranda had no time to issue warnings or denials. She had to protect her son.

When she emerged from her room, she gasped to discover Lord Carrington pacing outside her doorway, arms folded across his chest and two children lolling on the carpet. Another two were rushing up and down the impressive stairs of Twilit House and having a grand time being children. Behavior Miranda wholeheartedly approved of.

He inclined his head. "Lady Taverham at last."

"Cousin." She curtsied low to him, offering her respect and gratitude as if he were of higher rank to a marchioness and not merely a viscount. "Thank you for keeping Christopher safe."

"Christopher? Oh, you mean Simon. I see. I see." He swallowed. "So it's all true. I couldn't help but overhear your conversation with the dowager."

Miranda winced, moving closer to him. "I am so relieved that you and Agatha had him all along. I must admit I feared for his life when I discovered he ran away from his tutor and learned of the troubling events prior to that."

Carrington shook his head, much the same as Kit had done earlier. "I had no idea who he was."

"I am so sorry he deceived you, but surely you can understand he was driven by fear for his life." She drew in a shuddering breath. "But he says he found his way to Agatha, and I must thank you and my cousin for your kind and generous hearts in taking him into your home after the orphanage was forced to close. A terrible business that. I read about it in the papers last year but never suspected he could be involved. I will scold Christopher for the deception later and the worry and hurt I'm sure he's caused you both."

Carrington held up his hand. "Are you saying he chose to be an orphan on purpose?"

Miranda nodded. "So he tells me. He is likely with his father now if you wish to speak with him. I have had barely half an hour with him to discover what else he's done since leaving his tutor."

Carrington glanced down the staircase. "I intend to as well."

She smiled warmly at him. "Cousin, I must ask one more thing of you. Please help Christopher. He must convince Kit to listen to him about the danger or they will both lose each other."

"Simon—Christopher—has always been wary of strangers, more so than any other child of ours. I guess he did have a reason. I will certainly try to convince Taverham to keep a close eye on the boy."

Carrington glanced about him. His children were playing and oblivious to the troubles going on around them.

"Any help would be appreciated, and soon." Miranda winced. "I am sure my husband would rather not see me at the moment, so forgive me if I don't accompany you. Your children may stay with me while you speak to Kit. I promise you I will watch over your children as closely as you have my son. I owe you so much more than that, but it is the least I can do for the time being."

"Thank you."

When Carrington moved away, Miranda gestured for April to join her in the hall and then sent her down to the kitchen for lemonade and ginger biscuits. Then, because Miranda had never been a proper marchioness even one day of her life, she settled beside the youngest child on the carpeted rug and started to tell her the story of the lost prince. A story she'd created so Christopher would know where he came from and never forget who his real family was.

Chapter Twenty-Eight

———— ◆ ————

"I swear I did not know anything about his true identity," Carrington pleaded, eyes darting to the doorway behind him. "He never said a word to me."

Beyond the door to Kit's study, Miranda's boy peeked at Kit cautiously around the thick doorframe but did not come any closer. A wise decision given his current mood. The letter was on its way to his solicitor, requesting an urgent meeting to discuss grounds for divorce. There was nothing now to do but wait for a reply and their appointment time being set. Until then, Kit neither wanted to see his wife or her son ever again. And that bloody servant lurking in the boy's shadow could get the hell out of his house too.

Yet the child would not run back to Miranda. He hovered at the door, glancing Kit's way with pleading eyes that would make a lesser man reconsider his decision. Pleading would do no good. It wasn't possible to have a son of that age and not know about it. "Oh, I believe you. You've been entirely taken in by their scheme, as I was by her."

He had to expedite the removal of his wife and her child from his home today before they were seen and people began to talk about this scandal. He didn't particularly care where they went as long as he didn't have to lay eyes on her devious, lying face ever again. He gritted his teeth, struggling to keep a growl of anger inside at how he'd been played the fool once more. To think he'd actually begun to suspect he might have loved Miranda once upon a time. Now such a feeling was out of the question.

Simon peeked at Kit again and then looked to Carrington, eyes pleading. "I told you my mother would come for me. I always knew my father's name and my future."

The idea that this child had been convinced he would inherit Kit's title when he didn't deserve it was not amusing. He raised his eyes to the roof for help from above but found no comfort there. Keeping a civil tongue in his head would be up to him. He'd explain the facts and leave Carrington to soothe the child later. "You don't know truth from fiction, Simon," Kit argued hotly.

"My name is Christopher. Christopher Everett Reed."

Kit struggled not to react that the boy claimed to possess his first name and the name of his best friend. Miranda had planned her revenge well.

He glanced at the boy. Didn't he deserve the unvarnished truth? Kit couldn't allow him to remain in ignorance another day. "Your mother misled you about a great many things. She has swanned about London without a care in the world for the last week. She forgot all about you. You will never inherit my title or lands. You could be anyone for all I know. How do I know she even gave birth to you?"

"Grandmother knew."

Carrington gasped. "What?"

Christopher lifted his chin stubbornly. "She's been looking for me. *She* believes Mama."

"Poppycock. My mother is too sensible to fall for any flimflam nonsense your mother could concoct."

"My mother hasn't spoken an untrue word to you." The boy stepped into the doorway, hands fisted at his sides. As if he would fight a grown man to protect her honor. "It's not her fault she couldn't find me so we could come home together."

Kit set his hands on his hips, irritated he'd started a conversation with the boy about his mother. Miranda had deceived him so completely that he'd concluded she'd never once been honest with him. "Then whose fault is it?"

"Mine, sir. I was afraid." He took another pace forward. "Mother was ill, too ill to take care of me, and placed me in the care of someone she trusted."

Kit scoffed at that. "Really?"

"Yes, sir. She didn't want to, but was convinced to send me away to be tutored while she recovered by the sea. I was very afraid for her. She was very sick, her lips turned blue so often, and I'd get upset. They said I was making her worse with my crying, and I had to be a brave boy and let her rest."

Kit, caught up in the boy's misery, held his breath. Clearly that part might be true. A child so young couldn't pretend such strong emotions. "Go on," he whispered.

"There was nothing I could do but keep my promise to study hard and stay with Mr. Fenning until she sent for me. She was ill for a very long time."

"Where is your tutor now? Why were you at that blasted orphanage? If she loves you so much, how could she have let you spend one day thinking you belonged there?" Kit's chest heaved. He had visited orphanages in the past. He wouldn't leave his worst enemy's child in one if there were another choice.

The boy swallowed. "My teacher wasn't a strong man, and people came to frighten him. He was all I had, but when he set the fire and his house burned down I couldn't stay with him any longer."

Kit gripped the arms of his chair, struggling not to show concern over the incident. Incredible as it was, he could almost believe it.

Carrington caught his eye. "Miranda and your mother spoke of this. They want the boy protected."

Kit leaned forward. "Your tutor set fire to his own home? Why?"

The boy frowned. "I don't think he wanted to, but they put a pistol to his head and he had no choice but to toss the candle in."

Kit shuddered. "You were inside?"

The boy nodded quickly. "I always watched for Mama's coming and my window was open because it was a hot night. They said bad things to Mr. Fenning, and I ran for the woods to get away. After the fire we came to London."

Kit glanced at Carrington. He didn't know whether or not the man believed this fanciful tale, but Kit certainly had doubts, "Who on earth would want to harm a child? Miranda has no enemies."

"So you chose to become an orphan?" Carrington interjected. "Why not come to your father for protection since I gather you knew who he was all along?"

"He would never have believed me. He doesn't even now. I would never have gotten past Addison to even speak to him. I almost didn't get past him today." Simon inhaled a sharp breath and glanced down at his hands. "I saw Aggie and the orphanage children leave St. George's church one day. I thought she was Mama for a moment until I saw her hair. One of the children said her name clearly, so I followed her and discovered who she was."

Carrington frowned, holding one hand out to the boy. "Agatha said naught about your true identity either. I take it you kept her in the dark too. How could you know she wouldn't turn you away?"

Christopher remained behind the chair. "I didn't, sir. I took a risk that she could learn to care for me. Mama said she had the sweetest disposition of anyone in London. She was my only hope to find my way back to Mother. I didn't want the mean people to find me first. I didn't trust Fenning to protect me anymore."

"Makes a strange sort of sense." Carrington smiled tightly.

"Leaving one last question." Kit leaned forward on the desk, his stomach in knots. "How can I believe you are my son?"

Christopher circled the chair. "Am I not born within your marriage and therefore your heir?"

Kit's eyes widened slightly that a boy of his age knew about the legalities of inheritance. But then with Lord Carrington taking in the orphans, it was likely a topic he'd heard much of in the last year. "Legally, yes. But you don't resemble me in the slightest."

The boy glanced down. "I cannot help the face I was given. Aggie says God designs us as he sees fit and likes variety. Not every child can be as beautiful or handsome as their parents— some must wear a plain face and crooked teeth."

Christopher surprised him then by holding out both hands. They trembled slightly but remained outstretched. "My father has the right to punish me for any trouble I've caused, and I accept that I've been very dishonest."

Kit swallowed as his throat tightened. He could never raise a hand to a child. "I will not strike you, boy. Your mother will deal with you as she sees fit."

The boy's breath shuddered from his mouth and his hands dropped like stones. "Mama does not hurt me either. She'd rather send me to the kitchens to scrub pots."

Kit stared. Miranda had a unique way of punishing the child. One he'd never heard employed before by someone of her rank. Surely the boy was jesting? "And what else does your mother do to you?"

The boy's eyes finally rose to meet Kit's. "She reads parts of *Tom Jones* to me because you liked it best, tells me about my family, tucks me in at night as I go to bed so I won't have bad dreams. She drinks tea while I eat breakfast and makes me wash everywhere."

Christopher's face scrunched up on the last comment about washing, but every other punishment he seemed happy to endure. Kit had not expected the boy to have had such a warm upbringing with Miranda. Those few facts made him even more curious. "And who else takes care of you?"

"No one. There's never been many servants in Mama's employ, at least not before she became ill. Mr. Landry did most anything that required strength greater than Mama's or outside, or to do with her carriage."

Before he could ask where Miranda might have obtained the funds to possess a carriage to care for there was a sharp tap at the door. When Kit glanced across the room he spotted Lord Louth poised at the door. Kit scowled. "What are you doing here?"

"Interrupting in time to prevent you from making an ass of yourself." His gaze shifted to the boy. "Simon? Or is it Christopher?"

The boy smiled. "It is Christopher, my lord."

"Thank God for that." He let out shaky breath then wagged his finger. "Crafty little devil, hiding in plain sight all this time with not a word to me about your real name. I would never have guessed you were Miranda's son by the look of you, but then I never did like the noise you all made en masse and never looked closely. I had no reason to when you were supposed to be somewhere else. You've given us all quite the fright." He smiled softly at the boy and stretched forward his hand to shake. "A pleasure to make your acquaintance again. You've grown quite a bit since our last meeting. You were no taller than my knee the last time, I think. Now, run along to your mother and let her know I'm here. She'll be anxious about that."

Christopher turned to Kit. "May I go, Father?"

Kit wasn't the boy's father to say yea or nay to him, but he nodded slowly. He'd enough information for now.

When the boy was gone, Miranda's servant following close behind, Kit stood, hands curling into fists. "You knew about him?"

"Wait." He dug into his pocket and extracted three envelopes. "I had hoped to have more witnesses than us but..." He passed them over. "With compliments of Lords Applebee, Sorenson, and Watts. I trust you recall the names of your former guardians. These letters were placed in my safekeeping some time ago."

"What do they want now?"

"Read them and see," Louth advised cryptically.

Kit opened the first, sinking down into his chair as he read Watts' words. As soon as he'd finished the first, he ripped the second one open, then the third. By the end he was both enraged and mortified. "They knew about Miranda's son too. How dare they meddle in my life? Those bastards."

"There's an ill-fitting description if ever there was one." Louth moved to stand beside the chair Simon had hidden behind.

Kit glared at him. "Do you know what these claim?"

"The boy is your son. Make no mistake it is the absolute truth."

"Truth?" Kit swallowed to sweeten his mouth. "I have heard nothing but fanciful tales all day and my patience has reached its limits. Why are you involved with my wife? Are you her lover?"

Louth's cheeks pinked. "Never. She's been faithful to you."

"And yet you have become a great influence on her life. She trusts you. Confides in you. What else can I think when there is such a great intimacy between you?"

Louth stiffened. "Believe me, I wasn't an entirely willing holder of those letters nor her secrets."

"Yet you said nothing."

Louth sighed deeply. "I gave my word to Miranda not to interfere even if I thought her barking mad to avoid you. The last few days I've had men scouring London on Miranda's behalf, praying I was not too late to protect *your* son."

Kit folded his arms across his chest. Louth's loyalty to Miranda was something he'd realized for himself, but the depth of their connection he had not. "You should have told me. About everything and from the start."

"And betray her trust as you did?" Louth scowled. "Have her hate me so much her heart would falter when she thought of me too?"

"I am not responsible for Miranda's ill-beating heart. It is merely an illness and wholly unconnected to me." He shook his head. "I've yet to hear just reason for Miranda's flight from our marriage. I've no idea what imaginary wrongs I inflicted on her. I'm the wounded party here. She left me. She gave birth to a child without telling me. It is me that should be heartbroken."

Louth's eyes narrowed. "But how could you be heartbroken if you never loved her?"

Kit struggled for a response to that, remembering his earlier tears with some discomfort. He couldn't account for them and was glad any trace had vanished.

Undeterred by his silence, Louth drew closer, eyes boring into his. "How could you ever be so destroyed by the one you loved that remaining or going back sent you into spasms of fury? She ran away with nothing to support herself with. Only the clothes on her back. Believe me, I have argued with her for many years about returning, and it did no good. I gave her money enough to keep a roof over her head, clothes on her back, and tutors for the child so he would be prepared for when her heart softened and they returned to you."

Louth glared for a moment before continuing. "But I've seen her at her worst over you. Shrieking mad over a report of you in the scandal sheets. Don't think she hasn't had good cause to be jealous."

Kit blinked. "Jealous?"

Louth came round the desk. Stopped right before him, chest heaving, his fingers curling into a fist. "You cared nothing for her feelings. You never deserved her. She gave you everything and you showed her that her gifts, the dowry you needed, her body, her love, meant less to you than nothing."

"How would you know what I supposedly did to her?"

"I was there. I saw you making love to another woman on your very wedding day. Have you no shame? Why wouldn't she have cause to hate you for that betrayal?"

Kit shook his head at the ridiculous suggestion. "I did nothing of the sort."

Louth's eyebrow rose. "The rose garden, at dusk, in the arms of a woman who claimed to be a friend to Miranda."

Kit frowned and then his memory came flooding back. "You saw that?"

"Oh, I saw the pair of you cavorting in the garden so intimately it made me ashamed to call you a friend all these years." He shook his head. "And so did Miranda, Lord Applebee, too, and several others. They saw you abandon your wife, your vows, on the very day you married her. That is why she couldn't stand to be near you. That is why she ran off into the night with nothing. You shattered her heart."

Kit shook his head, heart racing at the idea of how that forgotten event might have appeared to Miranda, to anyone else. "It wasn't what you thought."

A muscle in Louth's jaw tightened as if he were on the verge of causing Kit bodily harm for denying it still.

Carrington stepped close to Louth and placed a restraining hand on the man's arm. "This isn't our business, Louth. Let it go."

"I'll keep silent no longer." Louth shook his head stubbornly. "A grappling pair of dogs had more grace that night. I saw clearly enough to know your hands were on the woman's breasts and your mouth against hers."

Kit swallowed in shock. That was more than he remembered had happened. But he was only half-guilty. Louth must have had an incomplete view of that encounter to think that he'd ever want to seduce another woman. He pushed Louth back with the tip of one finger to increase the distance between them. He would not fight a friend over a mistake such as this. "And then? Did you see how it ended?" He couldn't have, as Kit hadn't made love to anyone that night. Miranda most likely hadn't either seen the end either, or she wouldn't have run off believing he'd betrayed her.

Louth said nothing.

"You did not see me break my vows that night," Kit stressed. "Because I didn't."

"No, but…" Louth frowned. "It was clear what happened next. You had Miranda's hand in marriage; her dowry would save your estate. You barely spoke to her after the ceremony and then you ran off to rut with that other woman."

"Partially true. I had to leave the estate discreetly and I did not speak to Miranda again that day. The rest is a lie."

Kit scrubbed a hand over his face. He'd been found guilty without a proper hearing—accused and condemned for merely being a good friend.

He squinted at Louth. "You took Miranda away from me for no good reason."

"I took nothing. I found her wandering the road a mile from Twilit Hill, still clad in the gown she'd worn for the wedding the day before. My carriage almost ran her down. When I stopped, she was so distraught, so unable to speak clearly for her tears that I intended to put her in my carriage and take her back to her father rather than to you. But Lord Applebee came along then and once he'd seen what you'd done to that proud woman, he placed her in his carriage and swore she'd never need to go back to you ever again. It took me a month to discover her whereabouts again."

Kit grimaced at the scene described. Applebee hadn't looked at him in a friendly way since the wedding, and Louth's recounting explained a great deal about how Miranda had disappeared so completely from the district. His guardian had intervened. If they had just let him explain, he might have had a chance to fix his marriage. He could have saved them years of estrangement.

He would have known he had a son long before today.

He had a son. He had his heir.

He had everything he'd ever wanted, except for a wife who believed in him.

He sat down with a groan, thinking of his letter on its way to his solicitor. He'd been very clear in his wishes and reasons for seeking a divorce. The solicitor would know precisely how he felt about Miranda, his doubts about Christopher's parentage, and why he was now eager for an end to his marriage. "It's too late to prevent a scandal now," he whispered in shock. "I've already sent word to my solicitor to begin divorce proceedings."

Louth reached into his inner pocket again and removed a letter he then tossed on the desk. Kit squinted at the handwriting and recognized his own on the letter Kit had ordered sent to his solicitor. The one he had just regretted writing. Relief filled him. "How did you get this?"

"It seems your mother intervened with Addison in the nick of time and had the post delayed. Of course, you can still claim the boy isn't yours and send it along, but if your mother agrees the boy is her grandchild, why can you not?" Louth frowned. "Don't ruin Christopher's life just to hurt Miranda by pretending you're not his father. Miranda wanted your child. She just couldn't bear to live with you believing you love someone else."

With that parting remark, Louth turned on his heel and left. After a few attempts to speak and failing to find the words, Carrington followed suit, quietly shutting the door behind him so Kit would remain undisturbed.

Unfortunately, Kit was already very disturbed. For the first time in his life he didn't know what to do. He placed his hands over his head and curled forward. What the devil was he supposed to do with a son, or a wife, when he hardly dared believe he knew either well enough to ever trust?

Chapter Twenty-Nine

Miranda rapped on the study door and entered when she heard Kit's gruff invitation. She had never been in this room before and had needed Addison to guide her here when he'd delivered the summons an hour ago, shortly after she'd dined with her son alone in her bedchamber. She stepped into the room, heart thumping wildly.

Kit glanced up quickly and waved her to a chair. "Sit."

Miranda drew closer and perched on the edge of a chair, aware that Kit was boring holes into her head with his hard stare. He'd locked himself in here since Lord Carrington and Lord Louth's departure and she'd not heard a word from him since, not even to kick her out onto the street as she was sure he planned to do soon.

Her trunks were packed in readiness for that moment.

He shuffled the papers on his desk, laying out three stacks very precisely. She gave them a cursory glance. "You wanted to see me?"

His finger tapped the closest paper. "Tell me what happened that night."

She would not tell him of her heart breaking as she'd run from Twilit Hill, away from the betrayal she'd witnessed. "I don't recall."

"I want to know about the night you gave birth to my son."

Miranda's heart lurched, and she clutched the seat as a wave of relief swept her. Kit had claimed their son. She took a moment to collect herself and Kit said nothing more. She thought back to that night and what she remembered of it. "I'd been in labor since the morning before. Sorenson had brought a midwife to attend me, and the housekeeper had experience too, so I was in as good a hands as anywhere."

"Who else was there?"

"A few servants and your other two guardians." She raised her head. "They wouldn't leave."

She glanced down again when Kit's jaw clenched tightly. "Around six of the second day, the midwife was getting anxious, and Applebee came in to see what the delay was. I remember they argued about him being in the birthing chamber. It wasn't done, you see, and the midwife was shocked and rude to him. I was so tired by then and just wanted it to be over and hold our child in my arms. Applebee took over and he remained for the birth. He held my hand."

"Sorenson's recounting is much more lurid than your clipped retelling. He was afraid for you."

She glanced up at her husband. "I don't remember that. As soon as I held Christopher in my arms, I forgot all about the pain or the worry. The midwife said that's common."

Kit grunted and drew another letter toward him. He peered at the sheet. "Applebee writes, *She screamed in agony.*"

"Lord Applebee, though a dear man in most circumstances, thinks stubbing his toe is akin to being murdered." She smiled fondly at the lord's grumblings. "The pain was nothing unwanted and easily recovered from."

"And the names chosen for my son. Whose idea was that?"

"Yours. You told me once what names you'd prefer for your son. You were so sure about many things." She rubbed her hands over her thighs as her palms grew slick. Her heart was racing and she couldn't stop it. "Your guardians would have had Christopher named after each of them. I was very sure that would displease you."

"Immensely." He grunted again and stacked each sheet atop the other. He left a paper on the desk, a fourth she hadn't noticed. There was a long list of sentences scrawled on the sheet.

"Since I apparently have a son and heir, things will proceed a great deal differently than I once envisioned our future might be. You deprived me of him for the first years of his life, and I cannot forgive you for that. As such, I will expect now to make the decisions for Christopher's upbringing. Given what he's claimed about being almost burned to death in a fire, deliberately lit or vividly imagined, you'll understand my desire to protect him from any evil influence no matter where I find it. I trust you've no objections. Carrington will send over the boy's things tomorrow from Berkley Square, and those children will visit Christopher here once a week for as long as they are in town."

Miranda swallowed the hard lump in her throat and focused on her hands and keeping her disappointment from showing. It was exactly as she'd expected Kit to do even if she hadn't run away from their wedding. He'd decide Christopher's life without consulting her about anything. That he'd rule their son's friendships and discard those that brought little chance of social advancement stung. She hoped the lesson's she'd taught Christopher about respecting the feelings of others lasted in the years to come.

She nodded slowly. She had no illusions she'd see much of the boy now. He belonged to Twilit Hill and those concerns took precedence over a mere mother's wishes.

"Good." Kit's chair creaked as he shifted. "You may go."

"I'll have Addison summon a hack if you've no objection."

Kit stood quickly, rounded the desk, and caught her arm. "The most strenuous objection. You are not leaving my house ever again, Miranda."

She stared at him in horror and jerked her arm free. "You cannot keep me prisoner."

"I don't have to. My heir will reside under my roof. If you want a chance to see him, you'd better grow accustomed to staying here."

Miranda opened her mouth to protest but when she looked upon her husband's face, truly took in his wild, disheveled appearance, she thought better of speaking out. He'd claimed her son as his heir, intended to watch over him. In the end, that was all Miranda wanted. She could bear living with Kit and his anger as long as her son was happy here and safe.

Although she wanted to run from the room, from her

husband and his disapproval, she left the room with all the dignity she possessed and headed for the staircase. Behind her, the study door slammed shut and she jumped at the noise. Kit was indeed furious if he'd succumbed to the childishness of slamming doors.

She passed Addison in the hall, who watched her without speaking as she made her way to the staircase. At the top, she heard her mother-in-law speaking and Christopher's piping voice in reply. Miranda turned toward the sound.

"This will be your room for the night," the dowager told Christopher as she led him into a near-deserted portion of the town house well away from Miranda's bedchamber. She stopped at the door and stared around the barren room, wishing there was a way to brighten the space.

The room was so far away from her own that she feared Christopher wouldn't feel safe at night. Her heart ached for him. He would be very lonely with only the company of servants to comfort him if he should have bad dreams or be afraid.

At that moment, Peter Landry hurried in, juggling an arm full of objects. Coals for the fire, water to wash. A towel draped over his shoulder. Miranda caught the fabric and folded it neatly just to give herself something to do. "Lord Carrington will deliver your things tomorrow, my love."

Christopher glanced around, a frown forming on his face. "I've not spent a night alone in a long time. It's quiet here."

Miranda dug her hand in her pocket. "I know and that's why..." She held her hand out to her son with a smile. He grinned when he saw her gift and twisted it so his baby rattle made the familiar sound. Christopher had asked her to keep it when he'd gone away to study with Fenning.

"Why are you giving him an infant's toy at his age?" the dowager asked, her lips turned down in dismay.

"It's mine." Christopher held it beneath her nose and shook it till it twinkled again. "See the pattern. Lord Sorenson says the scene is of Twilit Hill."

The dowager huffed but she did take a peek at the plaything. "Be that as it may, I'd prefer not to have so much noise about Twilit House just to amuse you."

Christopher giggled at her suggestion and carefully placed the object on his windowsill. "There, now I really am at home."

Another footman appeared with a tray and set it on a table. "Thank you, Goode," Christopher said as he hurried across and lifted the lids from his evening meal.

When the footman was gone, Miranda sat across from her son and served him. "How do you possibly know that servant's name already? I've not even seen him."

"Addison told me about the new man the last time I came. He's told me ever so much about life here and about my grandmother." Her son peeked across the room to the dowager with a smile.

The old woman huffed again. "Well, good night, young man. Do not wake me in the morning with all your wild comings and goings."

Christopher ran to her, kissed her wrinkled cheek, and ran back to the table again. "I'll try not to."

When the dowager's shuffling steps couldn't be heard anymore, Miranda glanced at her son curiously. "What do you think you're doing?"

Christopher shrugged. "She's lonely."

"I see." Christopher must see a great deal more than Miranda did of her mother-in-law. Loneliness was the last emotion she'd expect.

Christopher destroyed his dinner in a few short minutes, then yawned widely. "Can I go to bed now?"

"Now?" She looked at him in alarm. "It's barely seven o'clock."

He smiled sleepily and climbed into bed, then looked around him with a satisfied expression on his face. "I'm home now. I want to hurry up and sleep in my own bed for the first time ever."

Miranda smothered a laugh and went to him, grinning. Christopher had always looked for the brightest moment in a long day. "Yes, you are."

She leaned down and pressed a kiss to his forehead, then tucked the bedding firmly around his little body. Her heart ached still that she might have lost him. She would take a long time to recover from the fears of the past few days.

He wriggled his arms free and looped them about her neck.

"You're home too, you know."

"Yes, my love."

But home wasn't the warm place it was for Christopher. This place never would be hers, and she would always be the interloper. Miranda trudged back to her bedchamber and summoned April to help her undress for the night. When she was ready for bed in her primmest nightgown, she dismissed the girl so she could be alone once more with her thoughts. She drank the vile potion to calm her heart and, like Christopher, she climbed into bed ridiculously early, forgoing her supper. She was simply too upset to eat anything.

Chapter Thirty

"So what do you think?" Kit prompted at Christopher's continued silence. The boy had been staring too long and the proprietor was beginning to fidget.

"May I pick one up if I am careful?"

"Of course, young master." The proprietor of Gable and Son's Silversmiths beamed as he lifted the lid on his display case. Inside, a dozen small pewter soldiers lay at rest on a black velvet tray. Craftsman's work and not inexpensive to boot. Kit was impressed that the boy asked permission first.

Christopher gently lifted one, turned it around in his nimble fingers as he studied it, then just as carefully placed it back. He grinned at Mr. Gable. "They're smashing."

Kit's son said *smashing* quite a bit. He hid another grin, overcome with pride that his child was polite, inquisitive, and knew exactly when praise was needed. Kit assessed his new plan once more. A list of activities that grew longer by the minute. "We will need infantry, cavalry, and artillery if you have them to take today."

Mr. Gable gaped in astonishment, an expression Kit had seen more often than not over the past three days, which he'd spent spoiling his son during their daily excursions around the great city. Kit had made a list of all the birthdays, holidays, and treats he should have spoiled the child with in the first years of his life. Material possessions were easy to come by in London.

Recovering the time lost was not.

They'd spent every moment together from sunrise to sunset, and Kit had even sat with him last night, long after he'd fallen asleep, just so he could say with certainty that his son twitched in his sleep before growing still again. Kit's mother thought him mad, but Kit had been denied so much of Christopher that he'd promised himself he wouldn't miss another moment. If only their days were longer.

He glanced at his pocket watch, noticing the hour was growing late. Tonight he planned nothing more special than to watch Christopher eat his evening meal. Tomorrow they would dine with his guardians, and he would deal with them once and for all. He just didn't know what he needed to say to them. His anger had cooled, replaced by disappointment in Miranda and in himself.

She should have known his nature, but if he'd never told her his feelings or understood them enough himself, then he could see how she might not realize his attachment for Emily only went so far. The mistake had cost them their marriage and happiness.

Kit settled the bill and when it was apparent that packing the soldiers would take time, he arranged for delivery, his mind half on the task.

"Father?"

Kit smiled down at Christopher, and lifted one brow. "Yes, son?"

"Are we going home soon?"

He nodded, signing his name on the bill with an enthusiastic flourish of the pen. He couldn't deny that having a son made him happy. Christopher's existence made his life complete. "Once our business is concluded."

Christopher worried his lip and when they left, Kit noticed his son hurried to the carriage ahead of him and didn't delay climbing inside as he occasionally did when he saw something else of interest.

When Kit joined him, he couldn't help but notice the boy appeared anxious still. "Is something the matter?"

"I missed her today."

Kit looked down at his hands as his stomach tied in knots.

He'd monopolized the child, kept him apart from Miranda with their many outings and expeditions. Miranda remained at home, content as far as he knew, seeing Christopher in the mornings and late in the evenings. But since the day Christopher had burst into his life, he'd avoided his wife and even his friends, preferring to get to know his son instead. He didn't know how Miranda's heart fared and he was quite frankly afraid to ask.

But he could not put that off forever. They were married and forever bound to each other through Christopher. He had demanded she had to live with him if she wanted to see their son. He couldn't ignore her existence. "We'll be home soon."

The boy smiled broadly, face pressed to the glass the whole way home. When the carriage stopped, he bolted from the carriage to reach her, running almost as fast as he'd managed when he'd left Hyde Park that day. He quickly disappeared inside and Kit followed, laughing as he went.

Addison hid a smile as he took Kit's hat and gloves. The butler had quickly learned to step aside when Christopher was in a hurry. "You have correspondence on your desk, my lord."

"Anything else I should know about?"

"Lady Taverham left, about an hour after your departure today."

Kit's stomach dropped to his toes; his hands grew icy cold as he glanced upstairs in shock. Miranda couldn't leave. He loved her.

He set his hand to his stomach, utterly shocked by that discovery.

He'd always loved her.

He swallowed the lump in his throat. Despite everything that had gone wrong, the mistakes they'd both made, he did love Miranda. He loved her so desperately that he'd follow her anywhere she went. He grabbed his hat and gloves again. "Call the carriage back. Did she say where she was going?"

Addison frowned. "She went home, my lord. At least that is what she said to me, but it is a day earlier than planned. I'm sorry if that wasn't what you wished for."

Kit couldn't understand why she'd leave without at least saying good-bye to their son. He'd be distressed. He might cry, and Kit wasn't sure how to comfort him. "Miranda should have stayed here with us."

Addison's eyes widened in shock. "Forgive me. I meant to say the Dowager Marchioness Taverham departed this morning, bound for Twilit Hill. The dowager left a note for you in your study."

Kit stumbled back a step as relief slammed into him. Miranda was still here. The woman he loved. The woman he wasn't even sure he could live with, let alone without. He couldn't believe how even that complication filled him with joy. But did they have a chance to make this marriage work?

He left Addison and retreated to his study, conscious that he was more relieved Miranda remained in his life than he expected to be. His desk was piled high with correspondence, likely invitations for parties and balls and opportunities for people to gawk at them some more. Kit ignored them all and picked up his mother's note. Short and tersely worded, she bid him good-bye and good luck in his marriage and then bluntly suggested she'd like another grandchild. Preferably a granddaughter next.

He sat down quickly. Could Miranda even safely deliver a child with her troubled heart?

Kit pursed his lips. He'd wanted to hold his children in his arms while they slept and did those things small humans did. He'd wanted to see Christopher that way, but since he was ten now that would prove impossible. The only way that could happen was for Miranda to have another child with him.

He didn't know whether she'd ever agree to that. He glanced at the letter again and noticed a last line he'd overlooked reading. *Emily knew about Christopher before Miranda returned.*

Kit swore. How could Emily know about his son and not tell him? He had certainly never confided in Emily or even Acton that his relationship with Miranda had been profoundly intimate before they married. Why would Emily say nothing of the matter? He'd thought they were friends. The best of friends.

All he'd ever wanted was his family—a wife and child to love him and make his lonely life complete. He'd thought Emily was on his side these past years. He could barely believe she'd keep him in the dark about a son, even if his mother had sworn her to secrecy. She could have—his pulse raced—she *might* have set the fire that had almost killed his son. The moment he thought it, he feared it to be true.

He left his study at a run, sprinting up the stairs to reach his child. He listened for Christopher or Miranda's voice on their floor and only relaxed when he heard their soft laughter. He stopped in the hall a moment and caught his breath. As irrational as his fears might be, he couldn't shake the idea that Christopher needed him desperately, even here.

He followed the sound of their voices and found them in Miranda's bedchamber, curled up on her settee, heads together and talking softly. They looked so happy, and guilt ate at him that he'd denied them so much time this past week.

Christopher was telling her all his news, a jumbled-up accounting of one of the best days of his life. He smiled at the scene, heart aching with regret for what might have been, but also with hope at what could be if they worked at their marriage together instead of against it.

They were both fine and safe. They would stay that way too for as long as he lived.

When Miranda noticed him loitering at the door, she straightened quickly as if she were afraid to be scolded and set a distance between herself and their son. Her behavior gave him pause. Why did she have to be so lovely and yet so completely unfathomable? He strolled in uninvited. "Mother left?"

"Yes. She said her good-byes to me at nine and should be well on her way to Twilit Hill by now."

Kit drew closer, noticing Miranda's face was very pale today despite her elegant appearance. The family jewels to match her ring encircled her delicious neck. Her hair was simply styled. The low-cut bodice of her gown made his mouth water.

He wondered why she'd dressed so formally, but he appreciated the view. "I trust the arrangements for tomorrow's dinner with my guardians will go smoothly without her?"

"Tomorrow?" She glanced at her gown in dismay. "Your mother said they were coming tonight. I should have known any help from her was simply to make me look foolish."

Kit groaned. "It was tonight, but I persuaded them that a delay of a day was preferred. Mother must have forgotten there was a change of plans."

Miranda nodded slowly, avoiding his eyes still and settling

back in her chair with a defeated air. "Your mother forgets nothing. This is simply her revenge."

"Not much of a revenge when I'm reminded of how beautiful you are."

Miranda stiffened and glanced at their son quickly.

Christopher caught his mother's hands. "See, Mama. You are beautiful. May I go now?"

Miranda bit her lip, her gaze darting in Kit's direction. "You must ask your father, my darling."

Kit frowned at her words. "Of course you can go if your mother says so. I wouldn't mind a few moments alone with Mama actually."

Christopher kissed his mother's cheek, hugged her tight, and skipped from the room, looking for all the world the happiest boy that ever lived. Miranda did not lift her head to watch him go or look in Kit's direction once, even when the doors crashed shut so loudly they both jumped.

The silence progressed until Kit couldn't bear it. "Have you been resting?"

"Yes."

"Do you need anything?"

She shook her head quickly. "No, nothing."

Kit paced the room, aware that Miranda seemed very uncomfortable around him. He glanced away, troubled by the new tension between them. He had not yelled at her after accepting Christopher was his. He had controlled his temper because of fear for her ill-beating heart. He had given her no reason to be afraid of him, yet her behavior was that of one who expected trouble.

Dear God, he wished he could fix them, make her love him as he loved her. He tore his gaze away from her and searched for a reason to stay near. One that didn't involve peeling her from that gown and kissing every inch of her skin.

On her mantel was stacked a large amount of correspondence. He flicked up the first to see who wrote to Miranda, discovering a letter from Lady Ettington had not been opened and another from Lady Hallam in the same unread condition. "You have letters here."

"Yes."

Kit shuffled through the rest of the pile, noticing all had been ignored. "Why haven't you opened them?"

Miranda's shoulders rose and fell slowly as she breathed deeply. "There seemed little point renewing acquaintances with people I will never see."

"Why won't you see them?"

She turned her face away. "You've always been very clear about what you want, and you made my position clear the other day. If I want to see my son, I must stay beneath your roof. No point in opening invitations if that's the case."

Kit jerked at the bleakness of her voice. "You may see our friends."

"They are your friends."

"I didn't mean it that way." Kit crossed the room and sat on a stool at her feet. Miranda looked everywhere but him, and frustrated, he touched her face to turn her gaze in his direction. Her gray eyes were weary and sad, and he leaned forward to kiss her.

She jerked away. "There's no need to pretend you desire me."

He smiled softly. "Never once have I had to pretend about that."

Miranda swallowed. "Even so, I'd prefer you did not. You've got what you want now. Leave me in peace."

"I don't have everything I want. I want everything I don't have yet, and that includes you."

Miranda started forward and her face blushed to a bright shade. She buried her face in her hands and sobbed. "I can't do this. You don't want me. You don't need me. You have your heir. Don't pretend anymore. I thought I could bear the silence, but no more. Please."

"You mean everything to me." He ran his fingers over her skin lightly as she sobbed again. "Let me in. Don't push me away Miranda."

He wanted to lift her worries from her shoulders. Her belief his affections lay elsewhere only made things worse. How had he ever botched his marriage so completely?

He pressed a kiss to her hair, cupping her bent head gently. Even without her glorious eyes revealing her pain, he felt it in the way she held herself. She expected him to hurt her again. She didn't know his anger over Christopher had already begun to fade, replaced by the joy of his astonishing existence. Her agitation was clear in the way she worried at her wedding ring. Now that he had the son and heir he'd longed for, she expected the worst from him. "Let me have a chance to love you."

She cried in earnest then, and Kit pulled her onto his lap, holding her as she shook with astonishing force, as if she hadn't cried in a very long time. Great gasping sobs that broke his heart, too. It took a long time for her to grow quiet, and when she did, Kit simply held her tightly against his chest. He kissed her brow and stood, taking her with him.

He carried her to bed and gently laid her down.

Chapter Thirty-One

Miranda stared at her husband—uncertainty keeping her silent.

She had no idea yet what he planned to do about their marriage, their life together, but forcing her into bed didn't bode well. She couldn't bear any more days of being ignored so thoroughly. Being kept to the side while her son began his new life was breaking her heart.

Miranda blinked back tears and squeezed her eyes shut. She'd asked for this and yet could not deny that the end of her short, ill-fated marriage made her sad. She squeezed her eyes shut as regret filled her with pain. She was sorry. More sorry than Kit would ever believe her to be. He'd be a good father to Christopher. She saw that now. He could take her place in their son's affections all too easily. Neither one would miss her if she slipped away.

Her bed dipped and she started, opening her eyes once more. Kit moved into view, his expressive face serious and yet dear to her.

He moved closer, a tight smile playing around his lips. He leaned over her, bracing one arm on each side of her body so she could barely move to escape him. He met her gaze directly. "Miranda, I want you to listen very carefully because I won't ever repeat this. I want to tell you about my lovers and you are going to listen to the truth about me."

Miranda gasped as tears slipped over her cheeks. Kit was too cruel, but she would listen and find comfort that her decisions ten years ago were justified. She jerked upright and scuttled away from him, pressing her spine against the headboard. She would hear about Lady Brighthurst, and tomorrow she would leave Kit for good.

Regardless of her distress he began to speak. "The first lover I ever had was a maid in our house. I was very young, only fourteen at the time, and when my parents found out, I was punished, sent away from the estate I loved and forced to live with Lord Sorenson in Kent."

The carved-timber headboard dug into her skull and she winced at the pain, a welcome distraction from his words.

Kit shifted, dragging an additional pillow toward her and tucked it behind her head. He smiled again. "Lord Sorenson had less puritanical views on pleasure than my parents. Instead of punishing me for my wicked ways, he encouraged them. While my parents believed I was studying and suffering, I was also being tutored in the sensual arts by a very resourceful courtesan. She taught me everything I knew about pleasure. Enough so I lost that distracting urge to seduce any woman I met and grew in confidence."

Miranda had wondered where he'd learned those wicked tricks. She'd enjoyed them, but in the back of her mind she had wondered how many lovers he'd taken before her. Now she knew the beginning.

"We parted on good terms and I returned to Twilit—wiser, satisfied, and more aware of what I needed in my life for it to be successful." He sighed and moved closer, his touch ghosting over her thigh. "When I went home, I discovered Twilit was floundering. My father had burned through my mother's dowry so completely that we were in danger of having to sell everything not nailed down. He died, from embarrassment I suspect, and I inherited the debts, but with the burden of three guardians breathing down my neck and criticizing every single decision I made. It was never easy. They did not particularly like my plan to marry young to save the estate from disaster, but in the end they knew I had little choice and gave grudging agreement, providing they approved the lady."

Miranda couldn't keep her astonishment hidden. "They chose

me?"

"No, I chose you." He brushed her leg with his thumb and her legs trembled. "The year I met you, there were two other potential brides my guardians were very keen on. Lady Verona Marshall, and our friend Virginia, Lady Hallam now. Both had excellent dowries and connections."

Bitterness crept through her being. And envy. Those two ladies were very beautiful. "You should have married one of them."

Kit leaned forward and touched her face, fingers sliding across her lips to shush her. "I chose you because I was attracted to you from the moment we met. Just you. Not your dowry, though that did sway my guardians to agree to the swift wedding I wanted. And I wanted to marry you quickly because the idea of waking up beside you, making love, and hearing you laugh with me, was the sweetest life I could ever have imagined possible."

Miranda's heartbeat quickened. "Would you have married me if I was poor?"

He drew back, his expression pained. "That is an unfair question. If you were poor I doubt we would have ever met."

True. Kit moved in the best circles, and it was only by chance they'd attended the same ball. Her fortune had made her invitation inevitable, something she regretted and cherished too. Without that invitation she would not have met Kit and never have had Christopher to love. "You say nothing of your current lover."

Kit sighed, then met her gaze and held it. "The last lover I had was three years ago—a country girl new to town who reminded me enough of you that I could set aside my pride and pay for her passions. We met at a time when I despaired of seeing you again. You'd been missing for seven years and I could have petitioned for my freedom then."

Kit cleared his throat, then said, "Doris was practical, though desperate to improve herself. I taught her the trade of a courtesan, how to entice and tease. She changed her name and I set her up as my mistress for a while in London. But it couldn't last. She knew I could not love her."

Miranda's throat tightened. "Do you love anyone?"

"I do," he whispered. "Louth tells me you had good reason to leave."

"I did."

"You were both wrong." He shifted suddenly, moving to sit directly over her legs, pinning her in place. He smiled softly. "Listen very carefully, for I do not like to speak ill of my friends. I want to talk now of Emily."

Miranda's heart broke again and she squirmed to be free of him. She couldn't dislodge him and he held her hands to the bed so she couldn't struggle more. "You don't have to explain."

"Emily had too much to drink on our wedding day. I took her outside, away from prying eyes, for some air so she would not embarrass herself and her family. She was my friend, and I wanted to protect her from causing a scandal. *She* kissed me. I don't know what she was thinking that night, but I remember her being upset and unusually bold. I promise you we were, and have only ever been, friends. She was unlike herself, and fearing for her reputation and her husband's wrath should he have learned of her behavior, I spirited her away from the gathering, but not to seduce her. I took her home, placed her in the care of Acton's housekeeper, and returned as soon as I could. Events after that delayed me from seeking you out until the next day. You must have been very far away by then."

She ceased struggling and he released her hands.

"I've not thought about that kiss until Louth mentioned you'd both seen it." He sighed heavily. "I don't find Emily the least bit attractive, although she is a fine woman. The only woman I've truly wanted was you. Ten years ago I was too young to make that clear to you. I'm sorry."

"A clever explanation. You forget that I have other sources for my intelligence."

He frowned and drew back. "Such as?"

"Your guardians explained how determined you were to keep her in your life. They said you'd never give her up."

"I remember a conversation I had with them about Emily and about running wild with Acton. They were always lecturing me about something and most often I tuned out their words. They said as a married man I should spend more time at home. I told them to sod off most days." Kit shifted off the bed immediately, freeing her. "Damn them. They twisted my words and hurt you."

"They made the situation very plain to me that you would always have a mistress. It was always Emily this and Emily that. Who do you think really cares for the roses that adorned our wedding breakfast tables? We may be married, but it was her wedding, not mine."

Miranda swallowed her bitterness. "I wish I had seen what everyone else knew before we went to your estate. She loves you and she had your mother's approval. Something I doubt I ever will possess. It was a pity she'd not the funds to save you then."

"The lack of funds wouldn't have mattered if I had truly loved her." His shoulders sagged. "I don't love Emily. I've never felt for her one tenth of what I feel for you."

Miranda shook her head. "You needed money desperately. That was all anyone could talk about. The afternoon of our marriage, but even in the earlier weeks before, there were so many hints about the lack of love between us. I could dismiss it as simple teasing since you were always in my bed, but not after I saw the two of you together in the rose garden. I was such a blind fool. I let you into my bed and ensured my own ruin."

Kit stared.

Miranda shrugged. "So my only purpose was to give you money and an heir. You had his life, Christopher's life, planned down to the smallest detail even before I was sure I carried him. You didn't care for my opinion."

Kit shifted toward her, his hands falling gently on her arms to soothe her. "I'm so sorry. When my father died, I had the world upon my shoulders and when I met you I couldn't believe my luck. I doubt I could have kept out of your bed if I tried. Those hours alone with you were so soothing, but it was selfish of me. I never meant to make you believe your money and our child was all I wanted. I was so young and blind to everything but the passion we shared then. I wanted so much to have you to myself, and in order to keep what we had private, I talked too much about what I wanted and failed to listen to you. Instead I put my friends first and made that day into the worst instead of the best one of our lives."

Miranda hugged her chest tightly as the pain she'd tried in vain to snuff or to hide burst free. "They've hated me since the moment we met. I still see their disapproval now I'm back, and suggestions that I'm an interloper in your life have already begun. Acton will never accept me and nor will your Emily."

Kit was silent at her accusation that his friends did not really like her. Silent and still as he likely pondered how to pretend it wasn't so. But Miranda did know they were waiting for Kit to give up on being a married man. Waiting in the hope they didn't have to share the marquess' attention with anyone.

"I grew up an only child, you know. Raised by servants at Twilit Hill. My parents had no interest in me or each other. Acton and Emily were my only childhood companions. They included me in their games and intrigues and became the siblings I never had." Kit bit his lip. "You may be right about their feelings being against you. The pair never let anyone else join us in fun now I think on it closer. I never saw it so clearly until your return, but during your absence Acton has been the most insistent I should have the marriage annulled. He even went as far as to claim you've had lovers recently. Lots of lovers."

He jumped from the bed and paced before the fire. Miranda drank in what might be her last unguarded view of her husband. He was beautiful and she loved him with all her heart. Miranda lowered her face to the bed. She loved him, and despite all her insistence that she didn't care one whit about him, she always would. She cared what he thought of those rumors. "What do you think?"

He stopped suddenly, head bowed.

"Because really, that is the only opinion I care about, Kit. Do you believe I was unfaithful to you?"

"No."

Miranda leaned forward, curious about the certainty in his tone. "And why is that?"

He drew closer. "Several reasons. Our son being one. I understand you took the extraordinary step of raising him with little help from servants until your illness, and he loves you more than I ever cared for my own parents at that age. To have lived the life you were rumored to be living, to have been so wanton, you'd never have hidden it from him. What son could respect a mother who behaved in such a manner?"

He continued to pace.

"Your return to my bed is another good reason. Despite our

arguments on the subject of an heir, you could have said no and I would never have forced you. No one fights so hard with someone they care nothing for unless their heart is deeply involved.

"But the most obvious reason has no proof, no discernable sign to back it up. You, Miranda Reed, meant every word of your marriage vows. That's why you left me as you did. Heartbroken and embarrassed, convinced I'd used you so badly when you saw what you were told you'd see. I want to thank you for our son. He is the most amazing child I've ever met, and I thought that the moment he boldly sidled up to me one day and introduced himself as Simon."

Relief filled Miranda. She wiped the tears from her face and waited. "So, what now?"

"Tomorrow I meet with my solicitor to discuss the succession and Christopher's inheritance. I will also deal with Lord Acton and Emily. You are my wife. I have a family. You and our son are more important to me than they will ever understand, but they will hear my feelings very plainly tomorrow. We will see what happens after that. They should have befriended you for my sake, yet all they did was drive you away. I should tell you now that Mother left a note for me before she departed and confessed that Emily knew about Christopher. I want to see what she has to say to that accusation with my own eyes."

"And if it was Emily that found Christopher and tried to hurt him?"

Kit's face grew troubled. "I don't know what I'd do yet. But if it is true, I will make sure both he and you are always safe. Is that an acceptable answer for you for the moment?"

"It is."

He took a deep breath and Miranda held hers. "If they cannot make you feel welcome, I'd rather not see them again. I have lost ten years with you thanks to a foolish misunderstanding. I'll not lose another day if I can help it."

Tears fell down Miranda's cheeks unchecked, and she feebly brushed them away. His support was all she could ask for. It was more than she'd ever expected to have.

He touched her hair softly while she composed herself again, shifting the long strands that had fallen from her bun back behind her ears. "My Miranda," he whispered. "How I have missed you. I am so sorry your heart was broken."

She caught his hand, astonished by the warmth and regret in his voice. She held it against her cheek and he drew closer. Wordlessly, she encouraged him into her bed to lie down at her side.

He pulled her into his arms almost immediately and held her tightly against his broad chest. "Do you believe me? About Emily?"

Miranda pressed her ear over his heart, counting the measured beats and finding comfort in the sound. She turned her face up to his. "Yes," she said simply. She believed him about Emily most of all. She had not seen the end of that encounter, only pieces, and had perhaps drawn the most logical but wrong conclusion about the depths of their relationship. Her age and inexperience at the time they married had made her easily manipulated, her faith in Kit tested and broken by the fear of being wanted only for her dowry.

Miranda smiled tentatively.

He kissed her gently, a soft brush of his lips across hers. The kiss deepened as Kit's hands roved over her gown. She had not forgotten the joy she found under his hands, how even when uncertain of everything else she knew desire such as this wasn't to be taken lightly. It was precious and only found with him.

He drew away slightly. "I shouldn't muss you. I don't want to ruin your gown when you've gone to so much trouble."

Could she risk her heart once more and give him the chance he begged for? Miranda set her hand to her fluttering stomach and laughed softly. "It's just a gown. Easily laundered to look fine again."

His fingers swept over her thigh and her gown rose higher. Miranda didn't mind being rid of it. It was beautiful to lie naked with Kit and feel like the most desirable woman in the world. Only he made her feel that way.

Once she was stripped down to her corset and shift, he settled his hips between her spread thighs but seemed only interested in soft kisses. That wasn't enough for Miranda, so she pushed him onto his back and straddled him. "I recall you liked this position once."

"My memory is very good, too." He threw her over again and caught her wrists, pushing them high over her head. "I remember you were just starting to enjoy this position very enthusiastically."

Flames licked up Miranda's spine as his hips wedged between her spread thighs. "This could become a problem."

"How so?"

"We can't do everything at once."

His smile grew wicked as he reached for the placket of his trousers before rearing up to his knees and struggling out of his garments. "We'll have to learn to compromise and share the decision-making in everything."

Miranda watched him unveil his body, aware she was growing wet and restless. Between them, his cock was as full as she'd ever seen it, tempting her to reach out and touch, reminding her of how good it had felt to be loved by him. The muscles in his arms and chest shifted, forcing her to jerk her gaze up to his face. Maybe this time he could be on top. Just for tonight of course. "I'm willing."

"I was hoping you might be." His length pressed hot against her and his arms bracketed her body tightly. He kept his weight off her, and the next moment he was there between her legs, begging entry to her body. Miranda looped one leg over his hip, opening herself to his invasion. He entered slowly: firm, hot, and wonderfully filling.

Miranda wrapped her legs about his waist as he buried himself, his groan against her neck when he settled against her signaling his complete satisfaction.

For Miranda it was as if she'd come home.

She kissed him deeply, twined her arms about his neck, and clung to him as they became one, straining toward their mutual happiness.

His pace quickened and Miranda's body throbbed as she matched his passion. Very soon she would come, and she wouldn't need anything more than this. Kit suddenly rotated his hips in a slow circle and Miranda stiffened.

She sobbed as she came, dragging her nails down Kit's back as her sex clenched around him tightly. Kit slammed hard into her, his shout muffled against her throat. Miranda tightened her legs around his hips to hold him while he shook and gasped.

It was a long time before they drew apart. Kit lifted his head first. "How is your heart?"

Miranda lifted her hand to his hot face and smoothed her fingers over his rough, whiskered cheeks. "It beats for you."

Kit kissed her hard, then rolled till she lay sprawled over him. His fingers trailed down her back softly, soothing Miranda's heart in a way her potions never could. The past ten years had been terribly lonely. Remembering what she'd lost, given up, and had a chance to claim again made her smile. She kissed his chest, twisting her head a little more to flick her tongue over his nipple.

He groaned. "Miranda, do you remember what I said about claiming kisses for each day of our marriage?"

"Hmm." She kissed his skin wherever she could reach easily.

His fingers tangled in her hair and he caught her eye. "I should warn you now that I've reconsidered my position on kisses."

Miranda frowned. "Oh?"

"Kisses are all very good and exciting, but I think the bar should be set much higher. We should make love as often as we can. In every position and place that appeals to us. We have ten years of pleasure to catch up on, and I must say I am looking forward to beginning again." To show his intent, he flexed his hips, proving himself well on the way to being hard once more.

Miranda laughed softly and raked her nails down the sides of his chest the way he'd once liked. "You've made a plan already."

Kit grunted and rolled her onto her back once more. He buried his face in the crook of her neck and licked and nipped at her skin until she was gasping. "One tries to make the most of every opportunity when one is in love."

Miranda stilled as Kit rose over her.

"I love *you*, Miranda Reed, so very deeply, and yet I never understood the true reason I waited for you all this time. Don't say anything in return, I don't expect it after all we've been through, but I wanted you to know that you have me. You've always had me."

Miranda bit her lip as tears filled her eyes. She had desperately hoped to know how he felt about her when they married, but she didn't know how to respond to him now. There was so much to talk about and set straight, and their relationship was fragile still. She was afraid to say the words and risk greater disappointment later. Giving in to desire was easy, but she'd never recover from losing him again.

She cuddled against Kit instead, and when he disappeared beneath the sheets to make good on his promised amended plan, she couldn't think of much else but him and the wicked flick of his tongue against her sensitive flesh.

Chapter Thirty-Two

———— ♦ ————

Kit rolled Miranda under him and lightly nibbled her neck. The room was filled with the light of a new day and Miranda was warm and unbelievably inviting. "I could get used to this," he whispered.

Despite making love four times during the night, he was hard as stone again this morning. He flexed his hips against her leg so she would notice that desire filled his mind and smiled as her hand shifted to grasp his length.

"So I see."

"I've always missed you in the morning. I'm looking forward to always starting our days together."

She released him suddenly. The tiny lines around her eyes deepened in amusement as she cupped his face, smiling. "Kit, I don't think our morning will go quite the way you hoped today."

"Oh? Why not?"

"Good morning, sleepyheads."

Christopher's piping voice cut through Kit's skull, and he threw himself off Miranda to sit bolt upright in bed. He glanced around in panic.

Christopher grinned at him from the foot of the bed. "I thought you'd never wake up."

"I was ah…" Kit glanced at the space beside him in the bed. Gods, he'd almost been caught making love to Miranda by their son. Miranda stifled a laugh, and then she shifted to sit up in bed, pushing pillows behind her back, drawing the sheets high up her chest over her nightgown. "Good morning to you, too."

When had Miranda had time to slip on her nightgown, and why hadn't she warned him sooner that the boy was in the room? He glanced down in horror and then jerked the sheet higher over his lap to cover his cooling ardor. The one thing he hadn't expected was ever being caught in a state of undress by his own son. Was any man prepared for that shock when his passions were high?

Christopher glanced toward the door, frowning. "You have callers. Addison wasn't sure what to do."

Kit blinked sleep from his eyes. "Why the devil not?"

"It's Lord Acton and Lady Brighthurst. Acton was going to come up, but Addison managed to delay him. But then he wasn't sure whether to disturb you, so I decided to come in and find out what kept you." Christopher stared at the door, his expression growing puzzled.

Kit glanced at Miranda and saw her expression change to wariness. "At least I don't have to send for them to clear things up," he reassured her quickly.

Miranda worried at her ring and he caught her hand tightly in his.

He winked at Christopher. "Have Addison say we will be down in half an hour. Have him also send in a tea tray for Lady Brighthurst and an ale for Lord Acton."

Christopher walked to the door, spoke to someone just out of sight, and then said quite grumpily, "It's perfectly normal. Lord and Lady Carrington always wake up in the same bed together and it takes ages to get them out in the mornings too."

Miranda stifled a laugh. Kit grinned at her, thinking he quite liked the way their son viewed a normal married couple's morning rituals. He could never remember his own parents sharing the same bed, but he'd never wanted the sort of marriage they had anyway. He'd happily start his own traditions with Miranda.

Christopher disappeared, and Kit could hear him berating someone outside the door for not doing as he asked. When he returned, he carried a teacup and saucer very carefully across the room toward Miranda. The door was slowly closed behind him. "You have silly servants, Papa. Anyone would think you were shocking them by still being in bed at this hour."

Papa? Kit couldn't keep the grin off his face. Until today he'd been only Father and had occasionally felt like his son was speaking to a stranger. He much preferred the informality of papa. He made to stand and then remembered he had nothing on beneath the sheet. Christopher handed the cup to his mother and sighed with relief. "Nothing spilled."

Miranda winked at him and took a sip. "Thank you, darling."

Kit fidgeted, unsure of how to escape the room without revealing his privates. "I should get dressed."

"Pierce is already waiting," Christopher told him.

Kit looked around, hoping to find a garment, any garment, that he might cover himself with. Where had he tossed their clothes last night? There was nothing but a pillow close by, or the sheet covering Miranda. He couldn't exactly take the sheet out from around her. "I see you're running the house well in my stead."

"Yes, sir. Mama told me that you'd expect me to take charge."

He smiled because it was true, yet he didn't want his son to miss playing at being a child too much. "Ask Pierce for a robe and bring it to me."

When Christopher left, Miranda began to laugh, so hard he feared she'd spill her tea. "That expression on your face was priceless."

Kit laughed too. "That was one thing I'd never planned for."

"You cannot plan for every eventuality. Children are unpredictable but very simple. They always turn up when you don't want them to interrupt."

Kit smiled and leaned across the bed. "Then I'll remember to lock the door before we go to bed each night so we are not interrupted."

Her smile slipped a little. "Don't keep him at an arm's length. I couldn't bear not to see him in the mornings."

Kit kissed her softly. "Some mornings he will have to wait a bit, especially when we want each other as much as we clearly do. We're newly wed, after all."

Her expression turned shy. "I suppose we are."

He drew back reluctantly. "We will see them together," he said, thinking of Acton and Emily waiting downstairs.

"All right. Then you should go so April can assist me. She won't come in while you're here."

Kit kissed her cheek and then slid out of bed. Christopher hadn't returned and Pierce had seen him without clothing many times. Since he usually slept nude, Christopher would have to expect that on some mornings his papa didn't look at all proper when leaving his mother's bed.

He dressed quickly and then loitered near the adjoining doorway to Miranda's room while she finished having her hair dressed. He talked quietly to Christopher about everything and nothing at all. Every now and then, he caught Christopher smiling for no reason, watching them both with a transparent joy. Kit leaned forward and for the first time in his life, he kissed his son's head.

Christopher wrapped his arms around his waist and squeezed him tightly. "Is this all right?" His query was hesitant.

Kit hugged him back. "It will always be all right with me."

They went down together, his arm about Miranda's waist as they descended the stairs, Christopher holding his hand.

Lord Acton and Emily had been shown to the library, and Miranda paused a moment, her gaze wary as she looked up at him. "I love you too," she said softly and then strode forward without the aid of his support.

Kit trailed after, his joy in the day soaring to incredible heights at her confession. Miranda loved him? Christopher squeezed his hand. "Everything will be all right now, Papa, won't it?"

Kit smiled. "It certainly will be."

"I say what's all this nonsense about you having a son?" Acton was on his feet in an instant, ignoring Miranda's greeting to come peer into Christopher's face.

Christopher smiled at Lord Acton, but his grip on Kit's hand tightened in the face of so much intense scrutiny.

Kit led Christopher around Acton and sat him down beside Miranda on a long leather chaise facing Emily. He sat beside his son. "Do sit down, Acton."

Acton resumed his seat, his gaze boring into Christopher

with suspicion. Christopher moved closer to Kit, but stared at the pair across from them. He put his arm about Christopher's shoulders and squeezed. "Christopher, this is Lord Acton and Lady Brighthurst if you've not been introduced before. They are our nearest neighbor to Twilit Hill. Lord Acton's property abuts the southern border and you will see a great deal of them in the coming years, I expect."

Christopher nodded. "I know who they are. A pleasure to make your acquaintance, Lord Acton."

Kit glanced down when Christopher failed to offer a greeting to Emily. The boy stared at her, his lips pressed tightly together as he trembled.

Miranda caught Christopher's other hand. "What is it darling?"

"That's the lady," he whispered.

"I'm here, darling," Miranda exclaimed shuffling closer to their child.

The boy clutched Kit's hand very tightly.

Acton frowned. "What's going on? Is he simple?"

"I am not," Christopher hissed.

Miranda scowled at him. "Surely you can understand that my son might be afraid of someone who wish him harm."

Acton's countenance changed to one of barely concealed hostility. "Madam, you insult me."

She leaned forward, intense and angry. "Then explain why he's afraid."

"He's no reason to be afraid of me." Acton glared at Kit. "What is this nonsense? Are you sure the boy is yours?"

Kit watched his friends with dismay. "He's mine, but I'd dearly like to know what's going on myself."

"I'm not afraid of *him*," Christopher whispered to Kit. "She wanted the fire lit."

Kit froze. "The fire that almost killed you?"

Christopher pressed closer as Emily smiled, saying, "Come now. What a fanciful suggestion. Why, I've never seen the boy before this very moment."

"But you knew about him," Kit interrupted. "Mother confirmed that before she left."

Emily wrinkled her nose. "Perhaps I did."

"And you said nothing to me. Why is that?"

"I had my reasons." She tossed her head. "The child could have been anyone's."

Christopher squirmed in his seat, drawing Kit's attention immediately.

"Go and find Landry now," Kit told the boy. Christopher should be spared the rest of this conversation. He'd been frightened enough and Kit had learned all he needed to know. Emily was not on Kit's side. She was selfishly on her own. When his son was safely out of the way, Kit glared at Emily. "He is my son."

Acton sat forward, his posture hostile and unconvinced. "So she says."

Acton did not even deign to look Miranda's way when he spoke and Kit's temper soared to new levels. He cast a glance at Emily's face and saw her nodding to her brother in complete agreement. When she glared daggers at Miranda, Kit placed Miranda's hand in his. "For the last time, Christopher is our son, conceived before we married."

Emily looked down at her hands. "You know what they say about her. She's utterly wanton. She's misleading you all over again."

He hadn't counted on their stubbornness. He'd thought they would take his word at face value without question. "But I suspected Miranda was with child when we married."

Emily fidgeted. "We should have known she'd seduce you. Of course you would have married her because of that."

"I offered for Miranda because she was what I wanted. It was me climbing into her bed before we married, not the other way round. I wanted her so badly. I wanted our child very badly. Christopher will inherit Twilit Hill from me one day, and I will never let him out of my sight again. Believe me, if anyone tries to hurt him again, they will live to regret it. I will bring the full weight of my influence to bear to punish the culprit and anyone else that conspires against us."

Emily's face turned a furious shade of red. "You're throwing away your life."

"My life was always to ensure his future. Enough of this. I cannot believe we are even having this discussion. Will you also doubt the words of Applebee, Sorenson, and Watts? They've all written to support the boy's claim. Even my mother has accepted her grandson with less fuss than you pair have managed today."

At that, Emily glanced away and seemed to shrink in place.

Acton sat forward. "Then it's all true."

"You owe my wife an apology," he told Acton without any hesitation.

Emily stiffened and said nothing, and Kit accepted that she might never offer one or accept that his heart had been committed to Miranda long ago.

Acton frowned. "I'll not. She should not have left you as she did and made you look a fool. You could have married for love, and all you got was this mess."

Kit leaned forward. "I did marry for love, Acton. I chose Miranda for the feelings she stirred in me even if I didn't understand what I felt. Her dowry was important, but there were other women with similar fortunes that I didn't look at again once I met her."

Acton's eyes widened and then he glanced at his sister. "But I thought…" He swallowed. "I thought you loved Emily but couldn't marry her because her dowry was insufficient for your needs. She cried for weeks and only grudgingly agreed with me that she had no choice but to wed Brighthurst since you could not offer for her."

Kit shook his head sadly. "You've been misled and saw what you were told to see. As misled as Miranda was when a certain person's words and another's behavior convinced her that was the case too. That was why Miranda left me. She thought I loved another when I never did. I love her so much that I couldn't forget her. I couldn't move past the hope that she'd come back to me one day. You know that."

Acton's jaw clenched as he stared hard at his sister. "It seems I was misinformed on quite a few occasions then."

He was tense and silent for a long time and then he faced Miranda, his brow furrowed with deep lines. "You have my deepest regret, my lady, for the discomfort and suffering I must have caused with my words today and in the past. There is no excuse I can offer that will ever make up for my mistake. Congratulations on the birth of your son. I wish you and

Taverham all the happiness that's been denied you these years."

When Miranda nodded, Acton glanced at his sister, eyes hard and unforgiving. "Lady Brighthurst, since you have nothing to say against the accusations leveled at you, I can only believe you guilty. We should take our leave as I'm sure the family has much to do together without us getting in the way. Unless, of course, Lord Taverham wishes to call for the magistrate to investigate the threats against his son."

Kit looked to Miranda for her decision.

She shook her head quickly. "Please, just keep her away from us."

Emily was slow to stand and Acton jerked her to her feet. "Little fool," he hissed and hurried her for the door. "You don't know how fortunate you are Lady Taverham is a forgiving sort."

Emily cried out to Kit, but he wasn't going to pretend everything could be all right again. She had kept the truth about his son from him and, even worse, might have tried to harm Christopher. He could not forgive that and turned his face away so he didn't have to see her leave.

"Lord Acton," Miranda called before the siblings crossed the threshold. "My husband will still expect to see *you*. Hyde Park is where you usually meet while in London, yes?"

Acton stopped, his eyes widening in surprise at her question. "Yes, most days."

She nodded. "I'm sure you don't need me to organize your amusements. I'm not one for riding, so I'll happily leave you two gentlemen to your own devices there."

"Thank you." Acton swayed, appearing amazed by Miranda's olive branch, but then shook his head and dragged his sister from the house so fast she scrambled to remain upright.

When the door was closed, Kit turned to Miranda. "It was not necessary to be so kind to him."

"I think Acton was deceived by his sister, too, as to who loved whom." She folded her hands in her lap. "Besides, I don't ride and I am sure when Christopher wakes you as the sun rises each day, you will want to escape the house to ride together."

"Emily always could convince Acton she told the truth even when as a girl she was fibbing. But that doesn't excuse him for being unkind to you." Kit swept Miranda onto his lap. He curled his arms about her hips tightly. "Now, where were we this morning?"

She leaned into him, head settling against his. "You were going to make love to me."

He kissed her cheek and sighed as Miranda's warm arms wrapped around his shoulders tightly. "For all the days that remain of our lives. I promise you'll never get away from me again."

Epilogue

———◆———

Sunshine after weeks of rain at Twilit Hill made the perfect accompaniment for a family outing. Across the field, Chris was chasing butterflies with Lord Carrington's children following along like devoted puppies hard at his heels. Around them their guests chatted gaily, lapping up the sunshine and each other's company. There had been so much merriment during their first house party that even his mother was pleased by the event.

More than one couple had strolled away from the group with sly looks for each other, which Kit knew to be anticipation. There were many married couples visiting Twilit Hill this year and he was pleased. So many of his friends had married for love, and it seemed to him to be a sensible decision for all involved.

He kept a close watch over his son as he always did, noting how happy he appeared with his rough-and-tumble friends. Kit glanced across the blanket to where his wife sat, jiggling someone's baby on her lap and crooning to the squirming infant. Her health had improved considerably since leaving London, and he no longer worried for her quite so much. "Is he going too far away do you think?"

Miranda squinted across the field at their son. "You worry too much. He will go far enough to tire them so they sleep soundly tonight during the ball."

Kit grunted. They'd planned the ball together to celebrate Chris' birthday most of all, and also for their own enjoyment.

They'd spent weeks planning it together, and he was pleased that despite the occasional silly argument, Miranda seemed at last happy to be his wife and partner in all things. He checked Chris' location again.

So far, their son seemed to be enjoying himself with his friends, though Kit was never certain he did enough to make up for their lost years. "Should he stay up with us tonight beyond eight do you think?"

Miranda cooed at the child she held once more and then passed him back to his doting mother. "Eight will be late enough. He's not too interested in dancing yet. The children will have their own amusements for the final hours before bed."

Kit frowned as Miranda picked up a piece of cheese, popped it in her mouth, and then licked her fingers clean. "Should one of us stay with him?"

Miranda shook her head and smiled at him as if she was in danger of laughing outright. She patted his hand. "He will be fine without you for a little while, my love. Children don't always want us around. They like to have their own time too. It gives them a chance to have their own secrets as we have ours."

She reached out for a slice of cucumber and took a bite, savoring the taste.

"I suppose you are correct." Kit turned back to watch his son. Truly he couldn't get enough of watching him run about their home and was considering making yet another adjustment to his education schedule. The boy didn't really need to be gone all but a few weeks a year in order to learn Latin properly. Maybe he could stay away from school another year altogether. He turned to Miranda to suggest it but found her eating again.

He glanced down without speaking but kept a close eye on her behavior. She really was hungry today, and when he considered it, she had seemed to be that way all week. The three closest plates to where she sat were empty, so she had to stretch for a piece of cake. Her second helping if he was not mistaken.

Suddenly he recalled that there *had* been a time when Miranda had seemed to have a larger appetite than normal. His mother had actually pulled him aside and complained of it before they'd married. It was that discussion that had made him so hopeful that Miranda could be pregnant.

His face ached with the urge to shout out his suspicions to all around him.

Since he'd missed the pregnancy and Chris' birth, Kit had begun to listen discreetly whenever a woman discussed the rigors of motherhood to find out what he might have missed. Some claimed their appetites increased, some went away entirely, and others were dreadfully sick morning, noon, and night. There seemed no pattern to a pregnancy that he could see, other than slight changes in appetite.

Something Miranda seemed to have done recently. She followed up the cake with a slice of pork and he gasped. If she could eat a food she'd thoroughly detested not one month ago, then something had definitely changed with her.

Yet when it came to Miranda, he'd learned never to assume anything without at least talking about his theories first. He shifted closer to his wife. "Miranda, darling, how are you feeling today?"

She smiled at him fondly, the little creases around her eyes crinkling with warmth and love and desire. "I am well, as you see."

Her gaze returned to the picnic spread before them and he caught her hand gently before she could snag another bite to eat. He brought her to her feet with a laugh. "Walk with me for a moment?"

She nodded and they strolled away from the guests. Kit slipped his arm around her back and she leaned against him with a sigh. "The party is going well. Your mother is even behaving herself and seems happy to leave me to manage things at last."

"That's good to know. I spoke to Acton this morning as Chris and I rode the boundary. He's sent his sister to live in a house he owns in Bath so we don't have to worry about seeing her even by chance. I did as you asked too and made sure he knew he was invited for dinner tomorrow night as well as tonight's ball. He's graciously accepted both. I wasn't sure he'd want to come."

"I am glad. He seems keen to make amends if the birthday gift he sent Christopher is any indication." She shook her head. "I cannot believe he sent a horse."

"Acton never does anything halfway. The animal is well trained for an inexperienced rider to manage. I think he wanted to prove to you that he remains our friend despite his sister's lies. I didn't have the heart not to accept. Chris seemed so very keen on the animal." He stopped beneath a shady tree and caught both her hands in his. As he looked down into her face, all the love he'd known in his life built and built. "Do you remember before we married that I suspected you were carrying our child?"

Her gaze narrowed but then she smiled at the memory. "I remember you were so certain about everything. You were proved right in the end, weren't you?"

"I'm not worried about who was right or not, now." He tightened his grip on her hands. "We have been intimate more times than I can count, but do you realize you have not turned me away from your bed since your return."

She blinked slowly, then her eyes widened a touch. "I haven't needed to, have I?"

"No. Miranda, I wonder if we are having another babe."

She took a step backward and Kit followed, irrational panic filling him that she might run away at the very idea. Yet the only sound she made was soft and unformed. She shook her head. "I'm sure there's an explanation."

He'd discreetly queried her doctor about the risks of a pregnancy some months ago and had been assured that there was no way to tell how her heart would bear the strain. He'd been advised to keep her calm and rested and content. He would always do his best to make that happen, but a second child would be a blessing and he couldn't help but be hopeful. He grinned. "You just ate pork and licked your fingers afterward."

Her brow creased. "But it turns my stomach. I haven't been able to eat it since before Christopher was born."

"Perhaps it is a sign."

She looked up at him and then a choked laugh left her. "Oh dear, that does explain how sentimental I've been feeling. They say women do any number of irrational things when they are with child. I cried a great deal last time, but I thought it over losing you."

"Just don't leave me again." He drew her into his arms and gently brushed his fingers over her belly. "I don't want to miss a moment with you for this little one."

She covered his hand with hers and held it in place on her

stomach, a soft smile playing on her lips. "Do not get ahead of yourself. We will wait and see what the physician has to say."

Kit pulled her against him and held her tightly. "I cannot wait. I want another child with you. One I can hold in my arms the moment they take their first breath. I want sleepless nights and mornings of laugher like we have now with Chris. I want it all and so many times over."

She laughed. "Wait till the babe wakes you just as you finally fall asleep for the third morning in a row."

"I won't mind. Well, maybe not at first, I suppose, but I will get used to the necessary changes quickly." He glanced down at her, wicked thoughts filling him. "I love you so much I've not words to say how happy you make me. So until we are sure, I think you should prepare yourself to be so coddled and so loved that you become in danger of growing sick of me."

"I would not, could not, ever be that. Besides, I am already so coddled and loved that I fear you will grow tired of me." She winced. "I do not have the best temper when my girth is as round as a barrel and I cannot get out of a chair without assistance."

Since no one could see them from this distance, he slipped his hand along her body and cupped her breast. "Come inside and I'll play at being your physician. I know my way around a lady in need of reassurance that she could never be more desirable than she is now or even when as *round as a barrel* as you put it."

"Any excuse to lure me back to bed." She laughed softly with no ill feeling. "What about our guests? They will wonder where we've gone."

He groaned as her hip brushed against his groin as she looked behind them to their scattered guests, teasing his cock with the lightest of touches.

"They can entertain themselves for a few minutes," he assured her.

"A few minutes?" She laughed, full of warmth and wicked excitement at the idea of a short romp, which had never been their way.

"You're absolutely right. What was I thinking?" Plans enough formed to fill quite a bit more time than minutes. "I'll need at least an hour for a proper examination, maybe two. There's no sense in rushing love, is there?"

She smiled so brightly his heart skipped a beat as hers sometimes still did.

"No, my darling," Miranda whispered as she looped her arms around his neck. "You simply cannot hurry love. Not when it's a love like ours."

An Improper Proposal

Chapter One

Iris Hedley was not afraid of the world, although a series of unfortunate events had taken away everything that had once been comforting in it. At one and twenty years of age, she should have been settled into marriage like so many of her former friends, rather than left on the shelf and a secret visitor to the Marshalsea Prison for indebted gentlemen.

"Come and eat, Father," she urged gently as she polished Alexander Hedley's spoon so it gleamed as brightly as the poor dented thing could manage then placed it beside the smuggled repast she'd served up to him. Oh, how there were times when the memory of her former happy home life caused a lump to form in her throat, and made her miss what had been lost in recent years.

Unfortunately, as had become his habit, her father did not budge from his slump on the edge of his cot in the room he shared with two other men in the musty barracks. He'd once been a fine man, wealthy, possessed of great wit and intelligence, courted by those in society who valued such things highly. Now he stared off into space quite often, absorbed in his own thoughts and lost in his memories of the past. The change had begun prior to his imprisonment and she feared for him. Her father had not taken his confinement well, but she supposed few independent gentlemen did. He was not in his right mind. He hadn't been himself in a long time.

"Father?"

He grumbled, "Goose again?"

Cold goose breast and turnip soup was a luxury in this place, but Iris didn't dare remind him of his situation. She was grateful Lady Heathcote's cook set aside this meal every day, but she was always aware she spent someone else's coin to care for her father. Pointing out that fact only added to his distress. "Yes, Papa. Come and sit down now so I might share it with you."

As hoped, her father brightened at the news she would share the meal with him and perched on the stool beside the makeshift table. She handed him the spoon so he could start on his soup. "I cannot stay long today. Lady Heathcote has given me a list of errands to run on her behalf before tonight's entertainment."

Her father stared at the spoon a moment then snatched up the bowl of cooled soup and drank from it directly. He shuddered, wiped his mouth with the napkin and then glanced sidelong at her plate, where a single slice of goose rested. "Lady Heathcote has servants to do errands," he grumbled. "And you should be resting so you are prepared for the evening."

"I don't mind helping her. Running errands to the dressmaker gives me something to do with my days, and in a small way makes up for the burden of providing me with food and lodgings. I am indebted to her." Esme, a popular widow of independent fortune, had taken her in before her father had fled the country and his debts. She didn't like to imagine what would have happened to her without Esme.

At first, her father had remained on the continent to assess his true situation, leaving Iris in Esme's temporary care with a promise to return soon. While away, the scale of his losses must have preyed on his mind and he'd returned much sooner than expected, only to surrender himself to his debtors. He'd entered the Marshalsea willingly, although few knew that small detail, and she planned to keep it that way. The tally of losses had steadily risen against him until Iris had feared he might never be free. Esme insisted they conceal his location for the sake of her reputation, but it was difficult to allow others to believe her father had abandoned her for a life abroad.

"A woman should have a home of her own, a child to bounce on her knee and a respectable situation." Her father sighed and looked about them mournfully. "This is not the life I wanted for you."

What he'd wanted was for Iris to marry a viscount, have a home in the heart of Mayfair, and a dozen grandchildren perched on his lap as he sipped whiskey in a library. Unfortunately, a life of that nature would be forever denied them both. Her father was ruined good and proper and Iris, despite all Esme had done, had fallen victim to greedy, unscrupulous men.

She hugged him close. "We will win through Papa, never doubt it."

Despite her words, Iris did find it hard to remain optimistic, especially here in this dreary place. Perhaps it was better that her father often could not remember he was entirely at fault for the decisions he'd made that had brought him to this damp and undesirable place.

As her father finished his meal, she began to repack her basket and then prepare herself to face the turnkey. "The turnkey asked for the name of your governess this morning. I think he wishes his daughter had half your grace."

"He's only being polite, papa." The turnkey's real interest was blackmail. He did have a daughter, almost of an age to marry, but Iris was due to hand over funds to him to ensure her father was taken care of in her absence. More of Esme's funds. Iris bit her lip as worry filled her. Esme did too much already and an alternative source of funds to pay for her father's upkeep had to be found. One day soon, she must attempt to repay Esme for her many kindnesses.

Unfortunately, there were few honorable choices for a woman who needed to improve her life. Marriage, of course, was the preferred option for a young woman to elevate herself in society. Snaring well-to-do and titled gentlemen had been the ultimate goal for her friends. With her substantial dowry, Iris had her pick of anyone and had chosen a young man with a modest title of viscount because she'd liked him best of all her suitors. Lord Grindlewood had not been a wealthy man and her dowry would have assured them a comfortable life.

However, before they could be wed, her father had lost his fortune, including her dowry. Iris had felt honor bound to release Lord Grindlewood from their engagement.

Her chances of a second match had perished with her dowry and that left her with only unpalatable choices.

"I intend to speak to Fitzhugh on the way out to ask after his wife and daughters," she lied. "They've not been in the best of health of late."

"If you must single him out for conversation be sure to have a care for your reputation and stand in the open at a respectable distance," her father warned unnecessarily. "I don't want anyone to misconstrue your interest in his family as an attempt to curry pecuniary dispensation on my behalf."

Through her daily visits to the Marshalsea, a hoard of

scandalous options for lining ones pockets had presented themselves. Thievery was rife around the Marshalsea and she'd learned to carry little of value in her hands. Prostitutes parading their wares in the yard in the hope of customers were impossible to ignore, and while she'd deflected any untoward advances since her father's fall and retained her innocence, such a final profession might be the only means of securing a large regular income. Men were said to pay their mistresses handsomely if they were kept well satisfied. Fitzhugh had already expressed an interest in bedding her.

She shuddered and pressed her gloves to her cold cheeks. "I will keep our conversation as brief as possible," she assured him. She would never give herself to Fitzhugh but she might have no choice but to become a mistress to someone else. "I must be going."

Her father stared out the tiny window of the barracks room with no idea of her inner turmoil; no idea Iris was contemplating a life beyond good society in the demimonde, wherever a mistress plied her trade. His already battered pride would never bear the disappointment, so she would tell him nothing until she had settled her mind on the subject.

He caught her arm as she stood. "You will be careful out there."

"Of course, Father." Truth to tell, it was more dangerous in the Marshalsea for a woman in her situation. The turnkey, Mr. Fitzhugh, liked to remind her not to give herself airs above anyone else. Thieves, even thieves' accomplices, had to adhere to the pecking order. She was at the very bottom of the hierarchy and utterly expendable. The turnkey took his cut but the real wealth went elsewhere. Fitzhugh's solicitous behavior and kind inquiries masked his real intent, as he never failed to remind her who was really in charge of her life.

She kissed the top of her father's gray head. "I am always careful."

He stood too and placed her hand on his arm. He led her down the rickety wooden staircase to the courtyard as if they were arriving at a ball. On the way to the main gate, he nodded to fellow captives but kept a distance from them. Mr. Fitzhugh, surrounded by other prisoners, lounged against the gate following their progress with hooded eyes. He swung his keys, a tactic to remind everyone he was in charge. She hated him but didn't dare show how much. As she drew closer, she buried her loathing. If not for her father's need, she would tell him exactly what she thought of him and his so-called friends.

However, the men worth befriending in the Marshalsea, the most influential, were the turnkey, and those on the prisoner committee. Iris didn't dare slight them, no matter how dark or dangerous her thoughts became toward them. She smiled instead at them all, never singling out one over the other for attention. "Good morning, gentlemen."

Thankfully, the men gathered around Fitzhugh murmured a greeting in response but continued their own conversation and did not impede their progress.

At the gate, her father stopped. "I'll be thinking of you," he whispered, casting an anxious eye at the gate and back at the prison yard.

Mr. Fitzhugh strolled toward her father and placed a restraining hand on his shoulder. Her father was not allowed to leave the Marshalsea until his debts were paid in full. Iris, as a visitor, was free to come and go between the hours of eight in the morning and ten in the evening as often as she liked. Father would be drawn away, likely back to the room he slept in.

She hugged her father quickly. "I will be back before you know it."

Fitzhugh smiled, as a cat would when it hungered for a bowl of cream. "You're looking remarkably pretty today, Miss Hedley."

Go away! "Thank you. How is your wife faring of late?"

"Much improved." He strolled to the gate and held the latch, his ring of keys clanking against his thigh. "Does it look like rain today, Miss Hedley?"

A chill swept her at the question. "It won't rain."

"And the rest of the weather report?"

She glanced at her father anxiously, who stood a short distance back from the gate with his hands clasped together. "Lord Hazelton's library on Conduit Street tonight. Behind the portrait of his children," she whispered. "The safe is there."

She swallowed the lump clogging her throat. Being an accessory to robbery didn't make her a lady or honorable. One more reason to hate her life. Lord Hazelton had recently purchased a seed-pearl necklace and matching amethyst brooch for his beautiful young wife, and the flattered woman hadn't been able to stop talking about it to everyone she met. She had set herself up to be robbed by revealing where it was kept to a room full of gossipy women and gentlemen several times. There was no way Iris could be a sole suspect, so she felt safe enough to pass this intelligence along.

The turnkey smiled. "Mr. Talbot will see you at eleven. Do not forget what's at stake."

My father's life. She shuddered. "How could I?"

He shrugged and when a knock sounded on the gate, he managed to stand between her and freedom to open it. Although she tried her best, she could not get past him without rudely shoving the visitors aside. Many considered visiting the Marshalsea as a lark, unless you had family trapped here. Fitzhugh tipped his hat to them. "Talbot said to tell you he will dance with you tonight."

"I will not agree to that." She looked for the comfort of her father but he'd already turned away for the company of other men, leaving her alone with this scoundrel.

"Were you about to tell your sweet old pa about your arrangements? I wouldn't do it if I were you. He'll froth at the mouth and start biting the balustrade. Should by rights send him where he belongs." He mimicked a shooting star and then slapped his thigh. "Straight to the madhouse for him if I had my way. You should be grateful a man like Talbot thinks to spare him."

She'd be grateful when they both dropped dead. "Leave my father alone."

"Then do your job." The turnkey opened the gate, so slowly she wanted to scream in frustration. When she could squeeze through, she marched away from the prison, furious but afraid. Iris lived in fear that her father would be sent to Bedlam if she did not do what Talbot demanded. No one ever left a madhouse.

She squared her shoulders and set off for Lady Heathcote's home, Fitzhugh's threats following her into the better part of London despite her best efforts to forget. She had to find a way out of this mess, and soon.

About Heather Boyd

Determined to escape the Aussie sun on a scorching camping holiday, Heather picked up a pen and notebook from a corner store and started writing her very first novel—Chills. Years later, she is the author of over thirty sexy regency historical romances. Addicted to all things tech (never again will Heather write a novel longhand) and fascinated by English society of the early 1800's, Heather spends her days getting her characters in and out of trouble and into bed together (if they make it that far). She lives on the edge of beautiful Lake Macquarie, Australia with her trio of mischievous rogues (husband and two sons) along with one rescued cat whose only interest in her career is that it provides him with food on demand and a new puppy that is proving a big distraction.

You can find details of her work and writing at
www.Heather-Boyd.com

www.ingramcontent.com/pod-product-compliance
Lightning Source LLC
Chambersburg PA
CBHW032128180726
48284CB00002B/700